169020

S

ABRAHAM LINCOLN IN COURT & CAMPAIGN

A Novel
By
Warren Bull

Abraham Lincoln in Court & Campaign
By Warren Bull
Copyright 2016 by Warren Bull

Bull, Warren.
Abraham Lincoln in Court & Campaign

Historical Fiction

ISBN 0-99-845460-5
ISBN 978-0-9984546-0-3

To my family and friends

Author's note: This is a revision of *Abraham Lincoln: Death in the Moonlight.* The language of the time of the Lincoln-Douglas debates includes terminology referring to African-Americans that would be extremely offensive if it were used today. I included the language in this novel because it is historically accurate.

CHAPTER ONE

November 9, 1857
Mason County, Illinois

Hannah Armstrong leaned over the bed and blinked away tears as she stared at her motionless husband. His eyes were closed, and he was not breathing.

"Breathe," she demanded.

For a long moment nothing happened. Then, with a shudder and groan, Jack Armstrong's body convulsed. Jack took a labored breath. Hannah spied a small spot of soap at the side of his mouth. She picked up a wet cloth from the clay basin nearby and dabbed at the spot. Armstrong's eyelids fluttered and opened. His eyes focused on Hannah's careworn face. She pushed locks of her grey hair back under the edges of her kerchief.

"Did you shave me?" he rasped.

She nodded. It was hard to keep her composure.

"Good. Thank you. I've been shaved and shriven. I'm getting ready to meet Jesus." His eyes started to close. He forced them open. "Still, I'm not quite ready, not with Duff facing a hangman's noose. Abraham Lincoln is our best hope."

He closed his eyes and rested. Even under the pile of finely stitched quilts, he shivered. Sweat plastered his grizzled brown hair to his scalp.

His eyes opened again. "Dying ain't bad. So far," he whispered. "I've felt worse than this a score of times. I'm sorry to be leaving you, my love, but except for the mess Duff is in, I've made my peace with the world. I'm going to a better place. And thanks mostly to you, I've had a life I would not trade with any king or president. But Duff's murder trial troubles my mind."

Hannah sat rigidly in the chair beside the bed. Tears filled her eyes as she studied her husband's face.

"I don't know if Mr. Lincoln would even remember simple people like us, Jack. He's an important man now — a railroad lawyer and all. They write about him in the newspaper. Folks say he's going to run against Senator Douglas."

Jack took a deep breath. "He won't forget when I had my hands on him. I'll warrant no man ever gripped him harder."

"He argues before the highest courts in the land," she added. "He may not want to remember his days as a farmhand."

"I'm sure he hasn't forgotten your many kindnesses toward him," said Jack.

"Even if he remembers, how would we pay for his services? He must charge a king's ransom these days." As Hannah spoke, she dabbed the cloth around Jack's chin.

A cough rattled through Jack's chest and he closed his eyes again. "You could borrow against the property. You know the boys would never allow you to lose the farm." His voice was thick with phlegm.

"I don't know if Mr. Lincoln has the time to spare. He must be terribly busy."

Jack let out a theatrical moan.

"Surely you wouldn't deny a dying man his last request," he teased, opening his eyes and winking at his wife.

"Why do I put up with you?" she asked in mock exasperation. "All right, I will ask the man. That's all I can promise."

"Thank you. That eases my mind considerably. I trust Mr. Lincoln will take care of the rest."

Hannah stroked her husband's face. Tears dripped from her cheeks.

Jack Armstrong slipped into sleep and never woke up.

CHAPTER TWO

June 16, 1858
Springfield, Illinois: The Hall of the House of Representatives

Abraham Lincoln towered over the crowd in the hallway of the statehouse. Nearby, Samuel Anthony and two men with notebooks were pushing their way through the throng.

"Abraham Lincoln. Mr. Lincoln!"

Lincoln turned toward the sound of the person calling his name. He looked gaunt and awkward in his ill-fitting black suit. His face was an assemblage of sharp angles, and his brow protruded over weary gray eyes.

"Mr. Lincoln, it's good to see you again," Anthony said, holding out his hand. A heavy-set man in his forties, Anthony's florid complexion revealed his fondness for alcohol, and his body sagged beneath his wrinkled, ash-mussed suit. "I'd like to introduce you to two gentlemen of the press who have traveled far to listen to your speech."

Lincoln smiled as he and Anthony shook hands.

Anthony straightened his shoulders and turned toward the dapper, pale-complected man on his left. "Meet Thaddeus Chapel, a journalist for the Richmond Enquirer, which you no doubt know has expressed strong support for the extension of slavery. Mr. Chapel just arrived this morning from Virginia."

Lincoln extended his hand toward Chapel and spoke, "Virginia — state of presidents, land of George Washington, Thomas Jefferson and other giants in liberty."

Chapel's hand nearly disappeared in Lincoln's as the men shook hands.

"Pleased to meet you, Mr. Lincoln," said Chapel. "As a challenger unknown outside Illinois, do you really think you can beat the distinguished senator with his national reputation?"

"Fortunately for me, I only have to worry about his reputation with the voters within Illinois."

Anthony caught Lincoln's glance and nodded to the young blond man on his right. "And this is August Dietrich, who scribes

3

for the Dutch readers of the Penn Statesman. His publisher calls for the immediate abolition of slavery."

Dietrich was a solid man whose blue coat and white shirt were too tight for his frame. He thrust forward his hand. "Mr. Lincoln," he said.

"You hail from Pennsylvania," said Lincoln, gripping Dietrich's hand and shaking it. "The great Benjamin Franklin and many other patriots lived there. I very much enjoyed my visit there some years ago."

"What would you like to say to those who demand an immediate end to slavery?" Dietrich asked, his accent markedly German.

Lincoln was quick to reply, "I would say that they should act with reason and seek to use the means established by the fathers of our nation to change the laws of the Constitution. I would also say that, personally, I have found that making demands of another person does little in the way of persuading him toward my point of view."

"May I ask a follow-up question?" asked Chapel. "What part of Senator Douglas's reputation in Illinois leads you to believe you may defeat him in the canvass?"

Lincoln gave him a thoughtful look. "You know, of course, that Judge Douglas was the man who destroyed the old agreement about where slavery could and could not flourish. In the Kansas Territory where the future of slavery was uncertain, both the Border Ruffians supporting slavery and the Jayhawkers opposing it ravaged settlers as they sought to force their will on the residents. While Judge Douglas did not intend to initiate violence and bloodshed, he certainly lit the torch that set the prairie on fire."

Lincoln paused. "I hope you gentlemen will not judge all of us in Illinois by my sartorial appearance and the elegance of Mr. Anthony. Some men of the West are actually civilized, a claim I do not make about myself or my friend, the distinguished editor of the Springfield Clarion."

Anthony chuckled. "These gentlemen are looking forward to hearing your acceptance speech," he said.

"Don't expect too much," warned Lincoln. "Please excuse me. I must prepare." He turned and walked through the crowd.

Anthony smiled. "Working with Mr. Lincoln, I was able to learn the entire text of his speech word for word. I'm having the Clarion presses print up a special edition about the Republican convention. It includes his acceptance speech. It also has the names of all of the delegates and a bit of information about each one. The edition will come out in time for the delegates to have a copy to take home with them. Mr. Lincoln worked hard on his speech. This way he will have it come out exactly as he wrote it."

"And you will have a stream of ready customers who otherwise might not buy the paper at all," said Chapel.

"Spoken like a newspaperman," answered Anthony.

In the packed hall the crowd chanted, "Lin-coln! Lin-coln! Lin-coln!" Men stood and cheered, swaying and clapping and passing around bottles of whiskey as they jockeyed for a position where they could see.

The hall reeked of tobacco, whiskey and the sweat of too many men in too small a space. Desks and chairs had been haphazardly pushed to the long walls on either side of the hall. Scattered among them were spittoons, snuffboxes, pens and bottles of India ink. Papers spilled from the desks. The double doors at the back of the room hung wide open in the vain hope of attracting a breeze. Curious people crowded around doors and windows.

Standing in the stifling air around the speaker's stand, Lincoln felt sweat roll down the back of his neck. It soaked his starched white linen collar and glued his shirt to his back. The noise of the crowd rang in his ears.

He patted his vest pocket and felt the paper, folded neatly in thirds, with the words of the resolution the Republican convention had passed unanimously earlier in the day: "Resolved, that Abraham Lincoln is the first and only choice of the Republicans of Illinois for the United States Senate as successor of Stephen A. Douglas."

When the noise lessened, Lincoln stepped forward and began to speak, sending his high-pitched voice to the furthest corners of the hall.

"Mr. President and gentlemen of the convention, if we could first know where we are, and whither we are tending, we could then judge what to do and how to do it. A house divided against itself cannot stand. I believe this government cannot endure permanently half slave and half free. I do not expect the Union to be dissolved — I do not expect the house to fall — but I do expect it will cease to be divided. It will become all one thing or all the other. Either the opponents of slavery will arrest the further spread of it and place it where the public mind shall rest in the belief that it is in the course of ultimate extinction, or its advocates will push it forward till it shall become alike, lawful in all the states, old as well as new — North as well as South."

"Damn, I wish he had not said that," Anthony grumbled, grinding a short cigar between his teeth.

"It sounds like a challenge to us Southerners," said Chapel.

"Nonsense," answered Dietrich. "It is another milk-and-water statement — the ultimate extinction of slavery; the Union can not endure permanently. Mr. Lincoln's no Abolitionist, for all his fine talk."

"Lincoln has managed to challenge slavery supporters without satisfying the real Abolitionists," said Anthony. "I told him he would please nobody but himself. But he would have it that way."

Anthony shook his head. "He's one hell of a lawyer. I don't know anyone else who could have done what he did earlier this year in the Duff Armstrong murder trial. You gentlemen might want to keep him in mind if you are ever caught dead to rights and expected to hang." He looked at the two reporters skeptically, like a horse trader evaluating a Mexican plug. "Of course, this is not for publication and I know you fellow gentlemen of the press will not quote me on what I am about to say. I count on your discretion and your solemn word."

Chapel and Dietrich nodded and leaned forward.

"Sometimes Mr. Lincoln acts like he has some special mission in life. He will not listen to common sense but insists on having things his particular way. I don't know who he thinks he is. I wonder what Judge Douglas will make of Mr. Lincoln's speech."

"The judge won't need our advice on what to say in answer to those remarks," Chapel answered, looking around the hall and then scribbling a note.

"Senator Douglas wouldn't listen to me, anyway," said Dietrich. "My paper will not support him. He has done well with Democrats in the South, though."

"I cannot say what my editors will do," said Chapel, looking directly at his colleague. "They are curious about Senator Douglas since he is obviously the leading presidential candidate for the Democracy, if he can get past his Republican state challenger, Mr. Lincoln. He may prove acceptable, or he may not."

Anthony sighed. "I first saw Mr. Lincoln back in the early days when we were both Whigs opposing the Democracy, who were the majority party. I complained then that surely the party could do better than to put up a ragged beanstalk. Then he started to speak, and I decided that we had done well. There is something about that man." He glanced around the hall. "There are reporters here from all over. Mr. Lincoln versus the great Senator Douglas attracts the attention of the entire country. Deep issues are at stake."

"What does Mr. Lincoln say about his opponent?" Dietrich asked Anthony.

"Mr. Lincoln reminds us that the Nebraska Bill, authored by Judge Douglas, allowed the Border Ruffians to use violence to hang a fraudulent constitution around the neck of the Kansas Territory. I could not agree with him more."

"You cannot blame that on Senator Douglas," snapped Chapel. "He didn't support the fraud of the Lecompton Constitution of Kansas."

"The stench of Southern slavery proponents flooding the state and intimidating anti-slavery residents by violence and threats of death offended him and every other man who believes in democracy," said Anthony. "Judge Douglas faced down the president, a member of his own party. I'll give him that. He and a handful of the Democracy voted with all the members of the Republican Party to reject the fraud. Given a chance for a real election, Kansans voted slavery down."

"Violence was also the coin of the Abolitionists," answered Chapel. His look was searing. "Reverend Henry Ward Beecher and other Abolitionists sent Sharps rifles to anyone who would oppose slavery. They labeled the crates 'religious materials.' Called the rifles 'Beecher Bibles.' Abolitionists organized parties of men from other states to go to Kansas and vote as if they were citizens there."

"True," admitted Anthony. "John Brown and a few other Abolitionists are like madmen. They made Kansas bleed as much as anyone else. Maybe more, but Judge Douglas opened the ball."

Dietrich pointed at Lincoln. "I think he's about to discuss what the Supreme Court ruled in the Dred Scott case."

Lincoln surveyed the men in the hall. He seemed to be talking to each man individually.

"No Negro slave, imported as such from Africa, and no descendant of such slave can ever be a citizen of any state. Neither Congress nor a territorial legislature can exclude slavery from any United States territory. Whether holding a Negro in actual slavery in a free state makes him free the United States Supreme Court will not decide but will leave to be decided by the courts of any slave state the Negro may be forced into by the master.

"We have another nice little niche, which we may ere long see filled with another Supreme Court decision declaring the Constitution of the United States does not permit a state to exclude slavery. We shall lie down pleasantly dreaming that the people of Missouri are on the verge of making their state free, and we shall awake to the reality instead that the Supreme Court has made Illinois a slave state."

Someone in the audience booed.

"Slavery has been attacked," Chapel said to his colleagues. "Southerners, both slave owners and not, have been threatened. Abolitionists from the North denounce us in terms formerly reserved for Satan. They encourage slave revolt, despite the risk. Already rivers of blood have rolled through the land. They break the laws to harbor slave fugitives. We have to grow in new territory, else non-slave states swamp us."

Anthony and Chapel turned to face each other. Each man was breathing heavily.

Dietrich stepped between the men and asked, "Mr. Chapel, please help me understand. At one time, Southern slaveholders headed the movement to end slavery. George Washington freed his slaves in his will. Thomas Jefferson proposed abolishing slavery, in one way or another, a dozen times. When did that movement end?"

Chapel looked at Dietrich directly.

"It suffered a mortal wound in 1829 when David Walker, a northern Abolitionist, published a pamphlet calling for bloody revolt by the slaves," said Chapel. "It died in 1831 along with the slaughtered innocent women and children when Nat Turner and other slaves rampaged across the land."

"Then in 1837 John C. Calhoun made the amazing claim that slavery is a positive good for Negroes as well as whites," said Anthony. "Mr. Calhoun also sponsored the resolution to disallow all discussion of slavery in the Senate. Is it not strange that such a beneficial institution cannot stand the light of examination and discussion?"

The three men fell silent, moved by the distance in thinking between Chapel and the other two. In the silence, Lincoln's voice could be heard.

"Two years ago the Republicans of the nation mustered over 1,300,000 strong. We did this under the single instance of resistance to a common danger, with every external circumstance against us. Of strange, discordant and even hostile elements, we gathered from the four winds and formed and fought the battle, though under the constant hot fire of a disciplined, proud and pampered enemy. Did we brave all then to falter now — now, when that same enemy is wavering, disservered and belligerent? The result is not doubtful. We shall not fail. If we stand firm, we shall not fail. Wise counsels may accelerate or mistakes delay it, but sooner or later victory is sure to come."

The crowd broke into thunderous cheers and applause. Anthony, Chapel and Dietrich stood silent, each man lost in his own thoughts.

CHAPTER THREE

June 16, 1858
Springfield, Illinois: Eighth and Jackson Streets

Shoes and hat in hand, Lincoln pushed open the door to his house and entered quietly. He had taken only a few steps when Mary Todd Lincoln spotted him and rushed toward him. With her chestnut hair, creamy complexion, blue eyes and matronly figure, Mary was a beautiful woman.

"You thought you could slip by me, did you?" she challenged, stopping in front of her husband.

"Not really. I thought I'd see how long it took you to notice that I was home." He smiled. "As I suspected, it did not take long. I like to see you like this, with color in your cheeks and clear eyes."

"Enough of your foolishness," she said, trying not to smile. "Tell me what happened. Don't leave out a thing. Was the speech well received?"

"Well enough, I'd say." Lincoln set his shoes by the door and his hat on a nearby table. "All these years, when all I could do was stand in the audience and hold onto the coats of those in the political fray, I've wondered if I would have another chance. Today's response suggests that you backed the right horse when you settled on me. You still might just end up a United States senator's wife."

"I've always told you to look higher," answered Mary. "You undervalue yourself. Senator will do for a start. I aspire to be the wife of the president."

Lincoln shook his head and smiled. He and Mary entered the front room and sat down.

"I should have listened to you and skipped the state legislature," admitted Lincoln. "I had to resign to run for the Senate. That delayed my preparation for the campaign." He drummed his fingers on the arm of the chair.

"Then a member of the Democracy was elected to your former seat," Mary added. "The legislature always votes along party lines when electing a senator. Your replacement is one certain vote against you. I know you had to do it, but you put a lot of time and effort into preparing for Duff Armstrong's trial when you could have been campaigning. Time is short, and you have much to do. I see this canvass as a very close election, one that Judge Douglas has been laboring at for some time."

"You were right then, Mother, and you are right again. It will be a near thing, I hope. Judge Douglas will certainly reply to my speech tonight."

He pulled off his mismatched socks. Mary grimaced but said nothing.

"I will answer his speech," said Lincoln. "Then it's thrust and parry." He gestured with his socks as if he held a sword.

"That should interest the newspapers and the voters," said Mary. "They like fuss and feathers of two men contending. Perhaps, Father, you could extend that in a debate, or better yet, a series of debates all around the state."

"I wonder if Judge Douglas would accept. He is very much better known than I am, being Senator all these years. He has a national reputation. There are many parts of Illinois where they say, 'Who is this man, Lincoln?' It would not be to his advantage."

"Don't you think he would fear what the papers might say about a refusal?" Mary asked.

"He would find it hard to refuse. I will think on that. Yes. For certain, I will think on it."

CHAPTER FOUR

July 8, 1858
Springfield, Illinois: Lincoln and Herndon Law Office

Billy Herndon — tall and bony, with a bramble of un-combed hair as dark as ink — introduced himself to August Dietrich in the hallway outside the Lincoln and Herndon law office.

"I have the honor to be Mr. Lincoln's junior partner. He is engaged at the moment. If you do not mind waiting, I expect he will be free shortly. If there is anything I can do to assist you while you wait, please let me know."

Dietrich said, "There is one matter you may be able to help me with."

"If I can, sir, I shall."

"I must admit that I do not altogether understand the Supreme Court's Dred Scott decision."

"Nor do I," said Herndon. "Not altogether. I shall endeavor to convey the meat of the matter." He paused for a moment. "The legal odyssey started in 1846. Scott brought suit for his freedom in the Circuit Court of St. Louis County, Missouri. His argument was that years of residence, first in a free state and then in a free territory, made him a free man. He lost his first trial, but a retrial was granted and in 1850 the court declared him a free man."

Dietrich said, "But if he won…"

"It was a momentary victory only. His owner, Mrs. Emerson, appealed to the Missouri Supreme Court. In 1852, by a two-to-one vote, the Supreme Court reversed the decision. Admitting it had, in eight other cases, freed slaves who came under the emancipation laws of other states, the court asserted that previous judgments had been made on the basis of uniformity between states, which was optional."

Dietrich said, "So the various courts said Scott was a slave, then he was free, then he was a slave again."

"Exactly," Herndon said. "It shows what a muddle slavery creates in this country. The United States Supreme Court is usually exceedingly reluctant to review the findings of state supreme courts. However, Mrs. Emerson remarried and became a citizen of Massachusetts. Scott was left in St. Louis under the control of her brother, a citizen of New York. That allowed Scott's attorney to appeal to the federal circuit court in 1853."

"I don't understand," said Dietrich.

"Scott's attorney argued that with three different states involved, the proper venue had to be the federal courts. In another legal quagmire, the federal circuit court ruled that Scott might bring suit, but that he was still a slave."

Dietrich looked puzzled.

"A slave does not have the right to bring suit against his master. Scott's attorney was able to appeal the Missouri Supreme Court decision to the United States Supreme Court. Having reached the United States Supreme Court by a most unlikely trail, the case was finally heard in 1856. Once that court started to trudge through the swamp, the morass only got more confusing. The court had to clarify what questions to decide."

Herndon raised one finger. "First, there was the question of whether or not Scott was a citizen of Missouri. This in order to determine if he had the legal standing to bring suit. Remember, if he was a slave, he was not a citizen and could not bring suit. The federal circuit court ruled that he could bring suit, albeit he was a slave. So the Supreme Court was not being asked to rule on that issue."

Dietrich nodded.

Herndon raised a second finger. "Second, there was the question of whether or not his residence in a free state and a free territory made him a free man. The court had to decide to rule narrowly — is Scott himself free? — or to rule broadly — what are the rights, if any, of slaves as a class of persons? Most broadly, the court could decide to rule on the constitutionality of antislavery laws as a class of laws, although that question too was not being asked."

"What did the court do?"

"The court moved as slowly as an overworked mule," answered Herndon. "It heard and reheard arguments. Despite the agitation and wrangling in the political world, the court stalled its judgment through the election of a new president, James Buchanan, who is pro-slavery. President-elect Buchanan wrote to Justice Catron about the case. Justice Catron and Justice Grier replied."

"Isn't that unseemly and unethical?" demanded Dietrich. "Wasn't the president-elect actively conspiring with Supreme Court justices over a case still being heard?"

"Yes, sir. It was political manipulation of the highest court in the land by the president-elect, a dastardly act scarcely matched in the annals of infamy. Two days. Two days after President Buchanan was inaugurated, the court finally ruled. A coincidence? I think not. All nine judges wrote individual opinions that varied in nearly every particular. Chief Justice Taney, in support of what he said were 'states rights,' opined that Scott was not and could never be a citizen of the United States since he was born a slave, an offspring of slaves. He declared that Negroes were so inferior to whites that they had no rights at all that whites must respect. Taney maintained that the state court would have to decide Scott's status, since Scott was not a citizen of the nation. He argued that Negroes, slave or free, had never been awarded citizenship in any state."

Herndon's voice hardened. "Of course, he had to ignore the five states that had already given free Negroes the rights and privileges of citizenship —including the right to vote. In those states he shattered states rights. Taney fractured logic to insist that, under property considerations, the exclusion of slavery from territories was unconstitutional. It was his answer to one of those questions that had not been asked."

Herndon scowled.

"Six of the judges found that Scott was not a citizen, without agreeing that a free Negro could never be a citizen. Six judges agreed that laws prohibiting slavery from territories were unconstitutional, without agreeing as to why. Grier was the only Northern judge persuaded. McLean and Curtis dissented vigorously. Curtis opined that the ruling should not be binding since it was made in response to a question that had, in fact, not been legitimately asked."

Dietrich noted a change in the timbre of Herndon's voice. "What good were all these divergent opinions? Was there anything uniform that resulted from all of this?"

Herndon shook his head. "Out of this tortured logic came the tyranny of the court. First, Taney invented an entirely new definition of due process. Second, for the first time in the history of the United States, a major act of legislation by the Congress was found to be unconstitutional. Third, for the first time ever, the court limited the power of another branch of government, to whit, Congress. Finally, the reasons for these radical ideas were specious and invalid. So, even if the concepts were appealing, the process by which they were conceived was appalling."

Herndon continued. "When Andrew Jackson was presented with a Supreme Court decision he disagreed with, he said the court had made the ruling and the judges themselves would have to enforce it. He would not. The idea that the old men of the Supreme Court should create law and dictate to the other branches of our government is monstrous."

Herndon paused just as the office door opened a crack. He went to the door and peered in. Then he nodded to someone in the office.

Herndon turned and said to Dietrich, "Mr. Lincoln is free to see you now."

Herndon escorted Dietrich into the office, closing the door behind him.

Dietrich was surprised to see Chapel already seated in a chair facing Lincoln, who sat with his feet propped up on his desk. Lincoln slowly folded his knees and put his feet on the floor.

Lincoln motioned toward an empty chair next to Chapel. Dietrich sat in it.

Lincoln spoke: "Gentlemen, as each of you petitioned to see me on similar matters, and as I have need to be in Chicago tomorrow when Judge Douglas is scheduled to arrive, I thought I would feed two horses from one manger and speak to you together."

Chapel and Dietrich glanced at one another and then looked away.

"I see you are embarrassed, but there is no need. I am something of a public person. If a sufficient number of state legislators from the Republican Party are elected, they will vote for me and I will become the new senator from Illinois. The questions you have are of interest, and I stand willing to answer them, on my own terms. I have read both of your accounts of my speech, and I deem both of them fair. Each emphasized the concerns of the different readers you write for, as you should. This one question has been raised in the past so it does not surprise me that your editors seek to have you ask it again."

Chapel spoke first. "I want to assure you that the description of your physiognomy in the Richmond Enquirer was the addition of my editor. I wrote nothing so crude. I do not believe that a man's appearance should be held either in his favor or in his discredit."

"It wasn't as bad as some I've seen," said Lincoln, smiling. "'Ape,' 'baboon' and 'freak of nature' are much worse than 'human jackknife.' As reporters, you do not need to apologize for investigating into sensitive areas of a man's past. If done openly, with regard for the truth and with even hands on the reins toward each candidate, you may hold yourselves as honorable as any man in any profession."

"Do you ask us to inquire about something from Senator Douglas's past?" asked Chapel.

"Not at all," said Lincoln. "Judge Douglas is a man of probity. His honesty and sense of decency are beyond reproach. I am certain that there is nothing of substance to investigate. I have crossed swords with the man for many years and I know him to be honorable. Our differences have always been about what each of us truly believes would be best for our nation. I would remind you, gentlemen, that it is not he who asked you to question me on this matter. I believe that Judge Douglas would not bring it up. I would not raise questions about his past."

Lincoln exhaled.

"It is surely not surprising that allegations of 'infidelity' from the past have bobbed to the surface again like an old cork. As in the past, however, I state that I believe this question has no proper answer in the political present or future. I will not discuss the character and religion of Jesus Christ on the stump. I do not wish

16

that what I say shall be quoted in the canvass. I have had the unpleasant experience of sharing confidences with reporters who swore to keep silent but then revealed everything. However, if you gentlemen will pledge to keep the information I am about to give you unpublished, I shall depend on your honor. For the satisfaction of yourselves and your editors, I shall respond."

Chapel and Dietrich looked at each other.

"I so swear," said Dietrich gravely.

"On my honor, I will publish none of this," said Chapel, putting his hand on his breast over his heart.

"Then, please, gentlemen, ask away."

Dietrich started hesitantly, barely meeting Lincoln's eyes. "Sir, there are those who say that you do not, or at least did not, believe in God. They call you an infidel. How do you respond?"

"After first responding that I would have more respect for them if they would make their charges in person, I say that I have a simple belief in God. I admit that as a young man I read Volney, Burns and Paine and was attracted to their ideas. The influences that drew me into such doubts were strong ones, those men having the widest culture and the strongest minds of any I had known up to that time. Since then, I have become more aware of the workings of Providence."

"But you do not belong to any church," said Chapel.

"I do not," Lincoln answered without hesitation.

"It is said that you wrote a book as a young man in which you questioned the divinity of Jesus, the infallibility of the Bible, eternal damnation and predestination," said Dietrich. "It is said that a friend of yours threw it into a stove so it would not see the light of day."

"I can deny that," answered Lincoln with a smile.

"You can, sir?" asked Dietrich.

"Yes. I can deny it was a book. It was more of a pamphlet than a book. If you can read old discarded ashes, you can see what it was about. As I recall, I wondered in writing how those who believed in predestination could also believe in hell. Would God punish people endlessly for doing what he required them to do? I also wondered how a loving God would spoil his most beautiful and beloved child and insist on a blood sacrifice before he would forgive man for his fall from grace. Is that a God who you could love and worship? Can either of you explain that to me?"

Chapel and Dietrich glanced at each other but did not respond.

"If the Bible is infallible, how is it that there are two entirely different versions of the creation of man? If Adam and Eve and their children were the only people on earth, who is it that Cain married when he was sent away from his family? Gentlemen, that hardly scratches the surface of Genesis. As to the exact nature of Jesus, can either of you describe that with total accuracy and certainty? Do all denominations agree on such matters?"

"No, sir," said Chapel. Dietrich shook his head.

"Perhaps you have had doubts about some doctrines yourselves. If the Baptists have it correct, are the Methodists in error? If Lutherans have the truth under lock and key, what does that say about the Presbyterians?

"One of my early political opponents, a circuit-riding minister, made similar charges. I replied that I had never denied the truth of the Scriptures or spoken with intentional disrespect of religion or any denomination. In truth, I have great respect for those who find solace and meaning in belonging to a church. I would never attempt to pry a person away from a faith that they embrace and find nourishing. Rather, I envy them their certainty and peace of mind."

"You rent a pew at the First Presbyterian Church but your wife attends a good deal more than you do," said Chapel.

"Guilty as charged," answered Lincoln. "It was ever so with my father and mother, too. What was it like in your family? I have benefited from the counsel of Doctor Smith, the minister of the First Presbyterian Church. He has helped me understand that reasoned thought and the ability to question are two of the many gifts from God. They are clearly not the greatest gifts given, but, humble as they are, they need not be abandoned or scorned in pursuit of faith. I learn from his sermons even as I admit I do not attend them all. It was Doctor Smith who told me about the old Presbyterian who objected to the arrival of a Universalist preacher in town. The old man announced in church, 'There is one among us, preaching the salvation of all men. But brethren, let us hope for better things.'"

Lincoln's laughter and open enjoyment of the joke he told reduced the two younger men to laughter.

"As a young man I was willing to rely on my thinking alone," said Lincoln. "Since then, I have learned that all the thinking and planning a man can do will not change a jot of what happens to him. There are forces that are more powerful than we can imagine at work. As a young child, I lost my mother to milk sickness. My wife lost her mother at a young age. Not so long ago, her grandmother, who was like a mother to her, died. Then her father and our young son, Eddie, perished in short order. I feared that, due to her grief, I would lose her, too. My own father died while I was still estranged from him. It is now too late for us ever to reconcile."

Lincoln sighed. "I urge you to resolve any differences you have within your families. You never know how long you have together. I was proud of my mental capacity as a young man. I thought I could reckon any problem. I now humbly admit that I do not understand the workings of Providence and I do not expect to in this life. I have endeavored to live in such a way that no one could describe my treatment of my fellow man as less than Christian. Even among my political opponents, I believe you will find very few who deny me that. I hope that counts for something."

Lincoln was silent for a moment. His face fell into a look of deep melancholy.

"The days of trouble found me tossed amidst a sea of questionings. The experiences brought with them great strains upon my emotional and mental life. Through all, I groped my way until I found a stronger and higher grasp of thought, one that reached beyond this life with a clearness and satisfaction I had never known before."

Lincoln's expression lightened.

"The Scriptures unfolded before me with a deeper and more logical appeal than anything else I could find to turn to, or ever before had found in them. I do not claim that all my doubts were removed. Since that time, my doubts have not been swept away. Probably it is to be my lot in life to go on in a twilight feeling and reasoning my way through life, as questioning and doubting as Thomas. But in my poor maimed withered way, I bear with me as I go on a seeking spirit of desire for faith like the man in the Bible, who in his need exclaimed: 'Help thou my unbelief.'

"I doubt the possibility or propriety of settling the religion of Jesus Christ in the models of man-made creeds and dogmas. It was a spirit in the life that He stressed on and taught, if I read aright. I know I see it to be so with me. The fundamental truths reported in the four Gospels as from the lips of Jesus Christ, and that I first heard from the lips of my mother, are settled and fixed moral precepts with me. I have concluded to dismiss from my mind the debatable wrangles that once perplexed me and were never absolutely settled. I have ceased to follow such discussions or to be interested in them. If a church would ask for simple assent to the Savior's statement of the substance of the law: 'Thou shalt love the Lord thy God with all thy heart, and with all thy soul, and with all thy mind, and thy neighbor as thyself' — that church I would gladly unite with."

Chapel and Dietrich looked at each other.

"I have no more questions, sir," said Chapel.

Lincoln looked at Dietrich and raised his eyebrows. Dietrich shook his head.

"If you will excuse me now, there are things I must attend to before I set off for Chicago."

Chapel and Dietrich nodded politely and left the office.

Dietrich turned to Chapel and said, "I don't see anything to write about even if I had not given my pledge."

After a brief hesitation, Chapel nodded. "I will tell my editor that he will have to seek elsewhere to find something against Mr. Lincoln. I disagree with much of what Mr. Lincoln stands for, but I can not bring myself to dislike the man himself."

"I would disagree with him over different matters but, like you, I find him to be an admirable person. Will you be going to Chicago to cover Senator Douglas's speech? If so, I propose that we travel together."

20

"We make a strange alliance," said Chapel. "It appears that in order to write about Senator Douglas, a great star in the political firmament, one must also write about the lesser light of Mr. Lincoln. I will travel with you."

CHAPTER FIVE

July 8, 1858
On the train to Chicago

Dietrich studied Chapel as he looked out the window.

"Is there something you want to say to me?" asked Chapel without turning to look at Dietrich.

"How did you know I was looking at you?"

"I could see your reflection in the glass."

"Very observant," said Dietrich. "I'll have to remember that trick. I do have questions. I don't mean to cause you apoplexy, but I have not known many men from the South and I truly do not understand your beliefs on slavery. You strike me as a reasonable man. Can I talk to you about slavery? With all respect, I mean."

Chapel sighed. "Since I've come North, I've had this conversation with many men. I have not convinced a one, and I don't expect to convince you either. Can I, in return, ask you questions about Abolitionism?"

"'Tis fair," answered Dietrich. "I admit that I am not the best representative of Abolitionism, but I will do my best to the limits of my poor abilities."

Chapel turned from the window. His facial expression was neutral. "You open the ball."

Dietrich frowned and started to speak slowly. "You know I am an immigrant to this country. I tried to study the history to understand. Slavery existed before the country did."

Chapel nodded.

"Spanish, Dutch, French. They all had slaves," Dietrich said.

"Don't forget that Indians took slaves from tribes that they raided," said Chapel. "In Mexico and South America Spanish conquistadors exterminated whole populations of Indians and enslaved the rest under conditions that make slavery in the United States look positively benign."

"Yes," Dietrich agreed. "You are correct. One of my ministers compared slavery in this country to original sin. The country was set up by states; almost all of them had slavery. It was allowed from the earliest time. It was, I think you say, a necessary evil."

Chapel nodded cautiously.

Dietrich continued. "Over time things have changed. Many states that allowed slavery in the beginning of the nation later outlawed it. At first, many countries around the world had colonies where there were slaves. But now in most of the civilized world slavery has been outlawed."

"In general, what you say is true. In Brazil slavery continues. Also in the United States."

Dietrich said, "You are, of course, correct once more. In the beginning of the nation the great preponderance of states were slave states. Over time, there has come to be an even balance between slave and free states in Congress. With additional time, that may change, too."

Chapel laughed harshly and said, "Thanks in part to you."

Dietrich blinked.

"I don't mean you in particular," explained Chapel. His facial expression relaxed slightly. "I mean the United States has been flooded with immigrants. The House of Representatives has abandoned the interests of the South in favor of the interests of Germans, Irish and others. Another thing that has changed is that the South used to be, by far, the wealthier part of the country. Our agriculture helped us weather economic panics and money devaluations. Now, we are falling back economically. Tariffs to protect manufacturing and the tax structure add to the costs in the South. How can we pay them? We may do so only by increasing our reliance on slavery. Of course, then the Abolitionists excoriate us more for doing so."

"That is not fair," said Dietrich.

"Fair?" snorted Chapel. "Did you know that it is a capital crime to import a Negro from Africa?"

"Yes, sir," said Dietrich.

"Then it should be at least a felony to import an Irishman."

"But the Irish are almost all members of the Democracy," said Dietrich. "That's your party."

"Not all in the Democracy are members of my party," said

Chapel. "It is not clear that Senator Douglas, for one, really has slave interests at heart. That is part of the reason that my paper sent me here."

"Is it necessary for a man to support slavery for you to support him?" asked Dietrich.

"You mean like in mathematics?" asked Chapel. "What are the necessary and sufficient elements to earn Southern support? That's hard to say. Senator Douglas has said nothing about slavery for the past ten years. His last remarks were more or less negative about our 'peculiar institution.' If he can allow us what we need to survive, I reckon that should suffice despite his personal beliefs. I admit that would not be enough for some of the firebrands."

"Do you really fear a slave revolt?" asked Dietrich.

"Absolutely. Abolitionists have cried for bloody revolt. Do you deny it?"

"Madmen have called for it," answered Dietrich. He looked at Chapel directly. "And John Brown and his lot have done more than just call for it. They have assassinated men in the name of God Almighty. It is the ugly truth. But most who call for the end of slavery are appalled by such blasphemy. Surely we cannot make policy based on the raving of fevered minds. Some in the South have called for the enslavement of the poor free citizens who cannot pay their bills. That, too, is madness."

"Madmen may inspire riot and ruin," Chapel said earnestly. "The poor Negroes may not know that their supposed 'saviors' are mad. On hearing the talk, they may act, learning only later that such actions doom themselves. Sanity, sir, is not the issue. We have been under verbal assault. Words can lead to blows. Blows have been struck. Blood has been spilled and it cries out to us."

Dietrich sat silent for some moments, staring out the window. Finally, he spoke: "I do not believe what you fear will happen. In all the years slavery has existed in this country there was but one slave revolt. It was a pitiful affair that ended in the death of many more slaves than slaveholders. I do not mean to say that your fear is not real. It is. But, surely that is still another reason to end slavery."

Chapel did not respond.

"You cannot believe that it is good to live on another man's labor," said Dietrich. "Your ancestors, at least, did not disguise that slavery is immoral."

Chapel looked out the window at the countryside passing by. Arguments such as this were wearisome. He had engaged in them many times, and each time, the same ideas were posed. Maybe they were stated in a different way, using a different example, attempting to provoke a different response, but each time, his opponent eventually tied together the issues of slavery and immorality as if they were the same side of the coin when in truth such a discussion was so much more complex. He heaved a sigh and spoke: "We could debate if the Negro man is really a man in the way that we are men. I truly believe he is not, although he resembles a man in his form. We could debate if the Negro, as a valued piece of property, might not be better treated than the shabby Irish who fight to keep heart and soul together in the slums like Five Points."

Chapel waited for a reaction from Dietrich. When there was none, he went on: "If your Popish bogtrotter gets too sick or too drunk to work, who cares for him until he recovers? Save he has a family here, no one cares in the least. He is cast aside like a worn cogwheel, perhaps to recover, perhaps to die; another is hired in his place and thrust into the machine."

"We could also debate who it is that flees his situation despite the dangers of branding, beating and death," said Dietrich. "As far as I know, no Irishman, however distressed, has asked if he can please be enslaved."

"Sometimes people under attack strike back with emotion, not logic. It is true that loyal family retainers are cared for long past the time that they are economic benefits. It is true that some slaves love their owners more than anyone else in the world. I cannot swear that all slaves are well treated, but many are."

"I believe you, sir," said Dietrich. "However, it does not change my opinion that slavery is at base immoral."

Chapel spoke in the direction of the window. "Many years ago we took the path of slavery and there is no going back. Tobacco and then cotton became the engines of wealth in the South. Both require slaves." Chapel paused to think and then he turned to

Dietrich. "Are there those who overwork and debase horses in Pennsylvania?"

"Some do so. A few, although it is foolish in the end."

Chapel frowned as he asked, "What if outsiders demanded that, as a result of the mistreatment of the few by foolish horse owners, all horses should be set free to wander and none could be forced to work? Would you oppose them and argue that being owned is good for horses? What would happen if you were forced to abjure? Answer me seriously, sir."

Dietrich was quick to respond. "The economy of the state would be ruined. There would be no way for most to transport what few goods would be produced. Wandering horses would destroy crops and ruin small farms. They would perish in large numbers if we did not care for them."

Chapel looked at Dietrich again. "That's what the South would be like without slaves. White men cannot work in the fields in the heat like Negroes. We would not survive. It would be a disaster. The poor Negroes would starve to death if left to their own devices."

"Mr. Lincoln says we should compensate former slave owners for their financial losses," said Dietrich.

"There is not enough money in the entire United Sates for that," answered Chapel. "Do you know what a prime buck is going for in the most Southern of the states? I grant you that Mr. Lincoln may be willing to discuss compensation, but the Abolitionists and others in the North would not. Mr. Lincoln remembers that the North built the ships and manned the crews that went to Guinea. Northern banks made loans to support the enterprise and reaped profits. New England fortunes, as well as Southern fortunes, were built on the trade routes that carried rum, molasses and slaves. He admits that in similar circumstances people in the North would have done the same as us. He, at least, does not take out after us as spawn of Satan like your churchy Abolitionists."

"He may understand, but, like me, he believes that slavery is wrong."

"Those are fine sentiments," said Chapel with a sneer. "Ending slavery sounds fine. But you Abolitionists forget the slaves."

"What do you mean?" asked Dietrich.

Chapel looked at Dietrich again. "You remember the freed horses we were discussing earlier?"

"Yes."

"Now, imagine that, instead of horses, those are wandering people. They are Niggers — pickaninnies to doddering old mammies. They have no jobs, no schooling and no homes. The Irish hate them because they compete for work at the very bottom rung of the ladder. Where do they go? Should we send them all to Pennsylvania? Can you take care of all of them there?"

Dietrich shook his head.

"We live among them," said Chapel. "To you they are an abstract idea. To us they are Toby, Sally and Gus. We know them as individuals. Some say, 'Send them back to Africa.' Send men, women and children who have lived all their lives in this country to a savage place? What if they don't want to go? What then?"

"I don't know," admitted Dietrich.

"None of you Abolitionists do." Chapel set his mouth in a line and frowned. Silence fell on the coach. After a few seconds Chapel said through clenched teeth, "Now, ask me what you really want to know."

"I beg your pardon," said Dietrich.

"You should," said Chapel gruffly.

"I don't know what you are talking about," said Dietrich.

"Ask the question that all you Yankees really want to ask," insisted Chapel, crossing his arms over his chest.

"You have me at a disadvantage, sir," said Dietrich.

Chapel studied Dietrich in silence for a moment.

"Could I be mistaken?" Chapel asked aloud.

Dietrich looked confused.

"I believe I owe you an apology, sir," said Chapel. "Ever since I have been in the North, men have come to talk to me with a single question in their minds. They have not listened to me with the patience you have shown. They have discounted what I said, and they have not been as honest in reply as you have been. I thought. I assumed you wanted to ask what they wanted to know. I see that I was mistaken."

27

"What did they ask you?" asked Dietrich.

"I am embarrassed to say," admitted Chapel. "But I see no way to avoid the topic now. In one way or another, at one time or another, they asked me what it was like to have a dusky Delilah, a slave woman, on demand for my pleasure."

Dietrich blushed. "I swear, that never occurred to me."

"As you said to me not long ago, sir, I believe you," said Chapel. "Such a question is extremely insulting, and you Northerners do not readily employ the remedy of dueling that we avail ourselves of at home when our honor is threatened."

The silence this time was more amicable.

"I will think on what you told me," said Dietrich. "I admit that I had not thought fully about what the loss of slavery would mean to the South. I further admit that I had not considered in depth what is proper to do with freed slaves. But I must tell you, Mr. Chapel, that one wall is still too high for me to climb. I am still convinced that slavery is wrong. As Mr. Lincoln said once, 'If slavery is not wrong, nothing is wrong.'"

CHAPTER SIX

July 9, 1858
Chicago, Illinois

The city of Chicago was awash in flags — American flags, bunting, streamers and pennants of all colors from hotel windows. Bands in splendid regalia marched through the streets playing patriotic airs, often with more enthusiasm than skill. When Senator Douglas's train was spotted, a battery of one hundred and fifty cannons started firing from Dearborn Park. The booming noise, stench of gunpowder and clouds of smoke filled the city. Smaller batteries firing along the lakeshore and in the western and northern quarters of the city added to the din.

Adam Houston, a gray-haired, bespectacled man dressed in a worn black broadcloth suit, turned to Chapel and Dietrich and spoke enthusiastically. "You see how we welcome our champion home from Washington. My paper, the Chicago Sun, sponsored the banner at the Adams House. It says 'Douglas, the Champion of Popular Sovereignty.'" Houston gestured grandly as he said each word. "One of you is from Virginia. The other is from Pennsylvania. There are reporters from all around this great country covering a state election. In all my years, I've never seen the like. Illinois is the center of attention. What happens here will ring throughout the nation."

He pulled out his pocket watch and peered at it. "We better get along to the Tremont House, where Senator Douglas will be speaking."

Houston dashed off, swerving through the throngs all headed in the same direction. Chapel and Dietrich had to move quickly in his wake.

Houston continued to talk as he moved. "I heard that some son of a bitch in Michigan City spiked the only cannon in town. But that didn't stop us Democrats. Someone found a giant anvil and set it on Main Street. The Democracy hammered it until it sounded like thunder. The welkin echoed from the blows."

Chapel's and Dietrich's remarks were limited to "excuse me"

and "pardon me" addressed to the startled people the reporters passed in an effort to keep up.

"Senator Douglas is the he-coon of the whole country," said Houston, turning his head and shouting without slowing down. "We were stuck in the Missouri Compromise bog until he got us unstuck. Now the territories will be able to become states. Those who want slavery can vote for it and those opposed can vote against it. The people decide. That's the basis of our whole form of government. The will of the majority in each territory and state will decide for that territory and state."

He cackled. "Every step along the way Senator Douglas had to convince a majority of congressmen. He'd get one majority for one piece of the Nebraska Bill and a majority of different members for the next piece. Step by step he log-rolled, called in debts, scratched backs and swapped favors with members of all the political parties until he brought the whole endeavor to fruition. I swear that nobody else in the country could have done it."

The press of the crowd forced Houston to slow down.

"We made it in time," said Houston. "If we stand here, we will be able to hear every word the senator speaks."

Douglas appeared on the balcony, and the crowd roared its approval. Douglas was short and stout. He was dressed in a fine suit and he did not appear in the least tired from his excursions. In fact, he waved energetically. Spotting Lincoln in the crowd, Douglas offered him a chair on the balcony with a courtly gesture. Lincoln accepted, and the men exchanged a few words that could not be overheard in the noise of the assembly.

Douglas then stepped forward and spoke in a slow low-pitched voice that could be heard by the entire crowd: "Mr. Chairman and fellow citizens, I can find no language which can adequately express my profound gratitude for the magnificent welcome which you have extended me. A reception like this clearly shows that there is some great principle involving the rights and liberty of a whole people that has brought you together. I have not the vanity to believe that it is a personal compliment to me."

Several members of the crowd began to shout, "It is!"

Douglas put up his hand to quiet them, nodded to show his

appreciation of the sentiment and then continued, "It is an expression of your devotion to that great principle of self-government to which my life for many years has been and in the future will be devoted. If there is any one principle dearer and more sacred than all others in free governments, it is that which asserts the exclusive right of a free people to form and adopt their own laws, and to manage and regulate their own internal and domestic institutions."

Chapel's pencil raced across the page of his notebook as he recorded Douglas's words.

"When I found an effort being made during the recent session of Congress to force a constitution upon the people of Kansas against their will, I felt bound as a man of honor and a representative of Illinois to resist to the utmost of my power the consummation of that fraud. With others I did resist it, and resisted it successfully until the attempt was abandoned.

"I rejoiced when I found, in this great contest, the Republican Party coming up manfully and sustaining the principle that the people of each territory, when coming into the Union, have the right to decide for themselves whether slavery shall or shall not exist within their limits. My opposition to the Lecompton Constitution was not predicated upon the ground that it was a pro-slavery constitution, nor would my action have been different had it been a free-soil constitution."

Douglas turned to Lincoln and nodded. Lincoln nodded back.

"Mr. Lincoln lays down two distinct propositions upon which I shall take direct and bold issue with him. His first and main proposition I will give in his own language, Scripture quotations and all: 'A house divided against itself cannot stand.' I believe that this government cannot endure permanently half slave and half free. I do not expect the Union to be dissolved. I do not expect the house to fall, but I do expect it to cease to be divided. It will become all one thing or all the other.

"In other words, Mr. Lincoln asserts as a fundamental principle of this government that there must be uniformity in the local laws and domestic institutions of all the states. He therefore invites all the non-slaveholding states to band together and make war upon all of the slaveholding states until slavery shall be exterminated. He then notifies the slaveholding states to stand together and make an aggressive war upon the free states until slavery has been formally established in them all. Mr. Lincoln advocates boldly and clearly a war of sections — the North against the South."

The crowd rumbled with the air of disapproval. Douglas's hands punched through the air.

"Now, my friends, I must say to you frankly that I take bold, unqualified issue with him upon that principle. I assert that it is neither desirable nor possible that there should be uniformity. Uniformity is the parent of despotism the world over, not only in politics, but in religion also. How could uniformity be accomplished, if it was desirable and possible? By abolishing state legislature, blotting out state sovereignty and vesting Congress with the plenary power."

Douglas glanced at Lincoln and continued, "The other proposition discussed by Mr. Lincoln in his speech consists in a crusade against the Supreme Court of the United States on account of the Dred Scott decision. On this question, I also take direct and distinct issue with him. The right and the province of construing the law is vested in the judiciary as established by the Constitution. What security have you for your property, for your reputation and for your personal rights, if the courts are not upheld and their decisions respected when once firmly rendered by the highest tribunal known to the Constitution?

"I am aware that once an eminent lawyer of this city, now deceased, said that the state of Illinois had the most perfect judicial system in the world, subject to but one exception, which could be cured by a slight amendment, and that amendment was to change the law to allow an appeal of the decisions of the Supreme Court of Illinois, on all constitutional questions, to a Justice of the Peace."

People in the crowd laughed. Douglas tilted his head toward Lincoln, listened and then chuckled.

"My friend, Mr. Lincoln, who sits behind me, reminds me that that proposition was made when I was Judge of the Supreme Court."

The laughter grew louder.

"Be that as it may, I do not think that fact adds any greater weight or authority to the suggestion."

Douglas waited for the laughter to die down.

"The reason assigned by Mr. Lincoln for resisting the decision of the Supreme Court in the Dred Scott case is because the decision declared that a Negro who is descended from African parents who were brought here and sold as slaves is not, and cannot be, a citizen of the United States. He thinks it wrong because it deprives the Negro of the privileges, immunities and rights of citizenship, which pertain according to that decision only to the white man.

"In my opinion, this government of ours is founded on the white basis. It was made by the white man, for the benefit of the white man, to be administered by the white man, in such manner as they should determine. The words in the Declaration of Independence, that 'all men are created equal,' refer to all white men of English descent being fully equal to Englishmen. It is also true that a Negro, an Indian, or any other man of an inferior race to a white man, should be permitted to enjoy, and humanity requires that he should have all the rights, privileges and immunities, which he is capable of exercising — consistent with the safety of society.

"I am opposed to Negro equality and I am in favor of preserving not only the purity of the blood, but also the purity of the government from any mixture or amalgamation with inferior races. I have seen the effects of his mixture of superior and inferior races — this amalgamation of white men and Indians and Negroes; we have seen it in Mexico, in Central America, in South America, and in all the Spanish-American states. Its results have been degeneration, demoralization and degradation below the capacity for self-government.

"My friends, my gratitude for the welcome you have extended to me on this occasion knows no bounds. It not only compensates me for the past, but it furnishes an inducement and incentive for future effort."

As Douglas waved to the crowd, several bands struck up a variety of patriotic songs. People cheered. In short order cannons began to boom in the distance. Dietrich covered his ears with his hands, and Chapel had a pained look on his face. Houston led them more slowly through the crowded streets away from the hotel until the noise diminished sufficiently that they could converse.

"That speech was a pip!" exclaimed Houston. "That skinny-as-the-rails-he-used-to-split Lincoln will be up all night trying to answer that."

"Could you speak a little softer?" asked Dietrich, wincing.

"You ain't used to a Douglas rally," said Houston with a smile. "We usually raise a howl. I don't know why the crowd was so restrained today."

"It was impressive," said Chapel.

The men turned a corner and saw a group of six men jeering at a Negro man they had trapped against a wall. Two men swayed as they tried to stay erect. The odor of alcohol came from all of them. The Negro edged away from the wall and his eyes swiveled from side to side.

"Where are you going, boy?" asked a balding man in shabby clothing who seemed to be the ringleader. "We ain't had our fun yet."

"Looks like a party," said Houston, his eyes bright. He stopped.

Chapel stepped quickly toward the group, and Dietrich followed him.

"It appears that you gentlemen have a great fear of that Nigger," said Chapel.

"What do you mean?" asked one of the men in an unsteady voice.

"Why there are six of you and one of him," answered Chapel. "I guess it takes six Chicagoans to confront one Nigger."

"Watch him," said the ringleader, pointing to the Negro. "Murphy and me will deal with this runt."

"Teach him some manners, Cletus," said one of the men.

Four of the men moved closer to the Negro. Cletus and Murphy, a large man with a crooked nose, stepped toward Chapel.

"I guess two Chicagoans can deal with a runt of a Southerner," said Cletus.

Chapel stared Cletus in the eyes and then quickly smashed his

34

fist into Murphy's nose. Murphy sat down and grunted in surprise as blood gushed from his nostrils.

"Five against one," mused Chapel. "The odds are improving."

Dietrich stepped to Chapel's side and slammed his fist into Cletus's belly. Cletus doubled over and began to retch onto the street.

"How about four against two?" asked Dietrich.

The men surrounding the Negro stood stunned. The Negro burst out of the circle and fled.

"Cuffee is gone," said Chapel. "Do you want to try and tree us?"

One man backed into the wall and fell in a drunken heap. Muttering to themselves, the men gathered their wounded colleagues and stumbled off.

"Thank you, Mr. Dietrich," said Chapel. "I never have seen the sport in a group of men beating a man who cannot defend himself."

"You're welcome, Mr. Chapel," answered Dietrich.

"They were just funning," complained Houston, scowling. "There was no reason for violence."

"Do you think they were going to ask that Negro to a dance?" asked Dietrich in a loud voice. "I think you're talking to the wrong men about being violent."

"They've not gone far, Houston," said Chapel, feigning a move in the direction the men went. "If you like, we can set them up in a circle with your back against the wall. Then you can take the Nigger's place and they can party all they like."

Houston shook his head.

"That was a nice move, staring at one man and striking the other on the nose. I would be afraid I'd miss and maybe hurt my hand on the bones in his face."

"I have practiced a good deal," said Chapel. Then, turning to Dietrich, he said, "Your fisticuff skill was evident as well. One punch let the wind out of his bellows."

"I've practiced, too," said Dietrich. "Some men like to find the biggest man around to tussle with. I had to learn."

"Other men like to scrap with the smallest man around. I, too, had to learn," Chapel laughed.

Dietrich put out an open hand. "My friends call me August."

Chapel took the proffered hand and shook it vigorously. "My friends call me Thaddeus."

"You can continue to call me Mr. Chapel," said Chapel to Houston coldly. "You may address my friend as Mr. Dietrich. You may be the kind of man who enjoys cutting the shell off a live turtle or pulling the wings off flies, but I am not."

"It was just a little Nigger bashing," protested Houston, shaking his head. "You two have tender feelings, like a woman or like old Abe Lincoln. That's another reason I support Senator Douglas. We in the Sucker State need a real man to represent us."

"I do not support Mr. Lincoln," said Chapel. "But I think it speaks well of him that he bears malice for no man."

Houston snorted. "It's easier to admire a man from afar. His faults don't show so much. If you two lived in Illinois, you'd have greater doubts about him."

Dietrich frowned. "What do you mean? Doubts about what?"

Houston mumbled to himself, "There are several things. For one, he works for the railroads. Soulless corporations."

"We all work for newspapers," answered Chapel. "They're soulless monsters that demand that we use up gallons of ink every day even when there's nothing in particular that merits it."

Dietrich chuckled.

Houston glanced down at his shoes for a moment. "There have been charges of infidelity."

"Which Mr. Lincoln answered for us directly," said Dietrich. He smiled. "Even the Richmond Enquirer did not find that worth reporting."

Houston reddened. "What about falsifying evidence and getting a witness to lie in the Duff Armstrong murder trial?"

CHAPTER SEVEN

July 10, 1858
Chicago, Illinois

Dietrich muttered to himself as he paced the street in front of the Tremont House. Chapel stood still and silent, watching him.

"This disquiets me almost beyond measure," said Dietrich. "If Houston told me it was raining while carrying a wet umbrella and wearing muddy boots, I would not believe him until I personally saw that it was raining."

"If it is humbug, we will discover it soon. We promised only to listen to the editor of the Sun. Would we not do the same if the crimination was about Senator Douglas?"

"We would."

"I think even Mr. Lincoln would approve then," said Chapel. "We are pulling the reins with even hands."

Dietrich continued to mutter to himself.

"How would you compare this crowd to the crowd Senator Douglas spoke to?" asked Chapel.

Dietrich looked around with calculation.

"I would say it is about a quarter smaller than the Douglas crowd," answered Dietrich.

"Just about what I would estimate," said Chapel.

At that moment Lincoln stepped out on the balcony. His supporters shouted and stomped their feet. Lincoln smiled broadly and waved, allowing the crowd time to cheer and then gradually quiet.

"My fellow citizens, on yesterday evening, upon the reception given to Judge Douglas, I was furnished with a seat very convenient for hearing him and was otherwise very courteously treated by him, and his friends, and I thank him and them. During the course of his remarks, my name was mentioned in such a way as renders it proper that I should make some sort of reply to him.

"Popular sovereignty! Everlasting popular sovereignty! Let us inquire into this vast matter of popular sovereignty. What is popular sovereignty? Vast credit is taken by our friend, the judge, in regard to his support of it, when he declares the last years of his life have been, and all the future years of his life shall be, devoted to this matter of popular sovereignty. What is it? Why, it is the sovereignty of the people!

"Can you get anybody to tell you that the people of a territory have any authority to govern themselves, in regard to slavery, before they form a state constitution? No more than a year ago it was decided by the Supreme Court of the United States that if any one man chooses to take slaves into a territory, all the rest of the people have no right to keep him out. The judge approves. He says he is in favor of it, sticks to it and expects to win. When that is so, how much is left of this vast matter of squatter sovereignty?

"When they come to make a constitution, they may say we will not have slavery. But from the beginning of the settlement of a territory until there are enough people to make a state constitution — all that portion of time popular sovereignty is given up. Has there ever been a time when anybody said that anyone other than the people of a territory itself should form a constitution? I suppose that Judge Douglas will claim in a little while that he is the inventor of the idea that people should govern themselves."

Laughter rose up from the crowd.

"We remember that in the Declaration of Independence, it is said, 'We hold these truths to be self-evident that all men are created equal; that they are endowed by their Creator with certain inalienable rights, that among these are life, liberty and the pursuit of happiness; that to secure these rights, governments are instituted among men, deriving their just powers from the consent of the governed.' There is the origin of popular sovereignty, Judge."

Several in the crowd hooted their approval.

"Judge Douglas made two points upon my recent speech at Springfield. He says they are to be the issues of this campaign. I said, 'A house divided against itself cannot stand.' I believe this government cannot endure permanently half slave and half free. I do not expect the house to fall, but I expect it will cease to be divided. It will become all one thing or all the other.

"That is the paragraph in which Judge Douglas thinks he discovers great political heresy. If you read that passage over, you see that I only said what I expected would take place. I made a prediction only — it may have been a foolish one. I did not even say that I desired that slavery be put in the course of ultimate extinction. However, I do say so now.

"I know that the government has endured eighty-two years half slave and half free. I believe it has endured because, during that time, until the introduction of the Nebraska Bill, the public mind rested in the belief that slavery was in the course of ultimate extinction. I have always hated slavery, I think, as much as any Abolitionist.

"Why did those old men decree that slavery should not go into the new territory, where it had not already gone? Why declare within twenty years the African slave trade, by which slaves are supplied, might be cut off by Congress? These are but two of many clear indications that the framers of the Constitution intended and expected the ultimate extinction of slavery.

"I have said a hundred times that I believe there is no right and ought to be no inclination in the people of the free states to enter into the slave states and interfere with the question of slavery at all. I have said that always. Judge Douglas has heard me say it. I have said, very many times, in Judge Douglas's hearing, that no man believes more than I in the principle of self-government. I believe that each individual is naturally entitled to do as he pleases with himself and with the fruit of his labor, so far as it in no wise interferes with any other man's rights.

"I have said, as illustrations, that I do not believe in the right of Illinois to interfere with the cranberry laws of Indiana, the oyster laws of Virginia, or the liquor laws of Maine. How is it then that Judge Douglas infers? I suppose there might be one thing that at least enabled him to draw such an inference that would not be true of many others, that is because he looks upon this matter of slavery as an exceedingly little thing — this manner of keeping one sixth of the population of the whole nation in a state of oppression. He looks upon it as being something on a par with the question of whether a man shall pasture his land with cattle or plant it with tobacco. It so happens that there is a vast portion of the American people who do not look upon that matter as being this very little thing. They look upon it as a vast moral evil. However, we agree that, by the Constitution we have no right to interfere with slavery and we are, by both duty and inclination, to stick to that Constitution from beginning to end.

"Another issue is upon his devotion to the Dred Scott decision, and my opposition to it. I have expressed heretofore and I repeat my opposition to the Dred Scott decision. If I wanted to take Dred Scott from his master, I would be interfering with property. But all I am doing is refusing to obey it as a political rule. If I were in Congress and a vote should come up on a question whether slavery should be prohibited in a new territory, in spite of that Dred Scott decision, I would vote that it should.

"Judge Douglas said last night, that before the decision he might advance his opinion and it might be contrary to the decision when it was made; but after it was made he would abide by it until it was reversed. Just so. We'll abide by the decision, but we'll try to reverse that decision peaceably. The sacredness that Judge Douglas throws around this decision is a degree of sacredness that has never been thrown around any other decision before. It is a first of its kind; it is an astonisher in legal history. It is based upon falsehood as to the facts, and no decision made on any question under so many unfavorable circumstances has ever been held by the profession as law. It has always needed confirmation before the lawyers regarded it as law.

"We were often in the course of Judge Douglas's speech last night reminded that this government was made for white men. Well, that is putting it into a shape in which no one wants to deny it, but the judge then goes into his passion for drawing inferences that are not warranted. The judge presumes that because I do not want a Negro woman as a slave, I do necessarily want her for a wife.

"We meet together once a year on the fourth of July to celebrate that are now a mighty nation. We are about thirty millions of people, and we own and inhabit about one fifteenth part of the land of the whole earth. We run our memory back over the pages of history for eighty-two years. We find a race of men living in that day that we claim as our fathers and grandfathers; they were iron men. They fought for the principle they were contending for. Perhaps half our people are not at all descendents of these men — German, Irish, French and Scandinavian. When they look through that old Declaration of Independence they find that those old men say that, 'We hold these truths to be self-evident, that all men are created equal.' They have the right to claim it as though they were blood of the blood and flesh of the flesh of the men who wrote that Declaration.

"Judge Douglas holds that the Declaration of Independence means only the descendents of the English are equal to the people of England. According to his construction, you Germans are not connected with it.

"Inferior races, he said, are to be treated with as much allowance as they are capable of enjoying. These are the arguments that kings have made for enslaving the people in all ages of the world. They always bestrode the necks of the people, not that they wanted to, but because the people were better off being ridden. This argument of the Judge is the same old serpent that says you work and I eat; you toil and I enjoy the fruits of it. Taking this Declaration of Independence, which declares that all men are equal on principle, and making exceptions to it — where will it stop? If one man says it does not mean a Negro, why not say it does not mean some other man?

"My friend, the judge, has said to me that I am a poor hand to quote Scripture. I will try it again, however. It is said in one of the admonitions of the Lord, 'As your Father in Heaven is perfect, be you also perfect.' The savior, I suppose, did not expect that any human creature could be as perfect as the Father in Heaven. He set that up as the standard, and he who did the most toward reaching that standard attained the highest degree of moral perfection. So, I say in relation to the principle that all men are created equal, let it be as nearly reached as we can. If we cannot give freedom to every creature, let us do nothing to impose slavery upon any other creature.

"I leave you, hoping that the lamp of liberty will burn in your bosoms until there shall no longer be a doubt that all men are created free and equal."

The crowd cheered and applauded Lincoln's sentiments as he stepped from the stage.

Later, in the Sun newsroom Chapel and Dietrich could hear the poetry of the proofreaders — "mumble, mumble, occasion, mumble, mumble, creation" —punctuated with an occasional mutter, "Thinks he's a damned reporter, but he couldn't spell cat if you gave him the 'c' and the 'a.'" Off to one side, two telegraph keys clattered. Transcribers translated the clicks into English and scribbled messages onto sheets of paper that they tossed on sloppy piles of similar messages. Occasionally, a copy editor would run up, grab a pile, glance at each sheet and toss most of those into a barrel. With a few sheets in hand, the copy editor would then run off shouting. Those sensations, the distant rumble of the presses, and the odors of a cheroot, ink, chemicals and scorched paper gave Dietrich and Chapel an unexpected sense of familiarity and reassurance.

Jason Woodward, the editor, stood nearby, surveying his employers. His hooked nose and clear black eyes reminded those who met him of a hawk. He held a battered cigar in his mouth.

"Houston can be a bit huffy, but he sinks his teeth into a story like a bulldog and he shakes it till he gets the whole thing. I appreciate you two coming here to meet me about this Lincoln story. I'd like to get the whole of that."

"You are, I take it, a Douglas partisan," said Chapel.

"Democrat to the bone," answered Woodward.

"I see in your paper's article about the judge's speech that you report that 30,000 men heard him speak," Dietrich said. "Isn't that more than the entire population of men in Chicago?"

"Some came from out of town just to hear him," insisted Woodward.

"Are you telling us that not one man in Chicago missed the speech and more men came to listen?" asked Chapel.

Woodward waved off the comment. "I am an editor, not an arithmetician. If my admeasurement of the crowd was a little off, I'll print a retraction."

"On an inside page in small type next to the obituaries?" asked Dietrich.

"Certainly not," said Woodward. He smiled, showing nicotine-stained teeth. "Too damned many people read the obituaries. They're the only reason some people buy the paper. I'd put it close to the advertisements for ladies' bangles. Republicans might see it there, but no Democrat would."

Chapel and Dietrich chuckled and relaxed their posture.

Woodward exhaled a foul-smelling cloud of smoke and led the reporters to his office. He gestured to two chairs, into which Chapel and Dietrich settled. Woodward himself moved around to the well-appointed chair behind his desk and sat down. Folding his hands on a small stack of papers on a blotter, he looked at the men, smiled and began to speak.

"Although you two are from different states, I'm certain you know the history of our local hero. Mr. Douglas arrived from Massachusetts to make his fortune with little more than the clothes on his back. He worked at what he could find, becoming a schoolteacher, among other things. He became a lawyer, then a circuit court judge, and then a judge of the state Supreme Court. He went into politics and ended up a United States senator. For years he has been the biggest man among the Democracy. He is able to work with the South and the North. Many of our settlers came from southern states, and Senator Douglas understands them."

Chapel and Dietrich nodded.

"You probably do not know the history of Mr. Lincoln," said Woodward. He briefly removed the cheroot from his mouth and exhaled another stream of rancid smoke. "You need to so you can understand. In a way, Mr. Lincoln's history is even more remarkable than that of Senator Douglas. He comes from farming stock, although I believe one of his ancestors was a weaver. His family moved from Kentucky to Indiana and then to Illinois, always in search of better land. With little schooling, he became a grocer and chopped wood to make ends meet. When his store busted, he became a surveyor and then he read the law. He served in the state legislature and held one undistinguished term in Congress."

Woodward chuckled. "He opposed the war in Mexico and did more damage to the Whigs than we in the Democracy were ever able to do. For years he has been out of office and practicing law quite successfully. He argues before the Illinois Supreme Court, litigates contract disputes, debt collection, medical malpractice, patent violations and railroad work. He has even argued before the United States Supreme Court.

"While Senator Douglas does the heavy work in Washington, plowing the national fields, Mr. Lincoln walks behind and criticizes him. That is the only reason Mr. Lincoln is known. Senator Douglas will surely be the next presidential candidate if he survives that idiot Buchanan."

"Are you saying that you don't see the conspiracy that Mr. Lincoln talks about?" asked Dietrich.

Woodward nearly choked on his cigar.

"Conspiracy? When the president set out to crush the senator? I admit that James Buchanan fed the flames of rumor when he wrote to the Supreme Court judges as president-elect and annoyed both our opponents and the Northern wing of the Democracy. But that was not a conspiracy; that was just his usual bad judgment at work. Then he appointed Robert Walker as Kansas territorial governor. Walker offended the Southern wing of the party. Presented with a mockery of popular sovereignty, in the form of the Lecompton Constitution for Kansas, Buchanan continued to act like a jackass and urged its adoption by Congress, which tore the Democracy into two factions. Senator Douglas opposed him out of principle, united with the Republicans on that one issue and won. Kansas voted to stay a territory rather than accept a spurious constitution."

Woodward took a breath and continued.

"To punish Senator Douglas, Buchanan stripped government jobs from every man the senator had recommended. The president replaced Douglas supporters with Douglas opponents. The national Democracy offers support to these new damned Republicans. If Senator Douglas does not become president, it will be because the current president, elected by Senator Douglas's own party, split the party into sections and gave popular sovereignty a bad odor. James 'Jackass' Buchanan took the only truly national party, the Democracy, ruined his own administration, and threatens to ruin the chances of the party for years to come. If there is a conspiracy, it is against the Democracy, and its chief architect is the president, who is a Democrat himself, the accursed man. Mr. Lincoln talks about a conspiracy to force slavery into states where the people do not want it? There is no such a thing. It is impossible."

Woodward paused.

"You were telling us about Mr. Lincoln," said Chapel calmly.

"So I was. No one questions Mr. Lincoln's honesty. His friends call him 'Old Abe' and 'Honest Abe.' Likewise, no one questions his loyalty to old friends, especially those who helped him when he was penniless. But what happened is that the one virtue opposed the other virtue. When he first came to Illinois, he was tested by a bunch of hard cases in New Salem known as the Clary's Grove boys. Their leader, Jack Armstrong, challenged Mr. Lincoln to a fight. Armstrong wanted an anything-goes scuffle. Mr. Lincoln, being the challenged party, insisted on wrestling instead. Apparently, the two went at it for some time, and, when Armstrong felt himself weakening, he broke the rules to achieve a throw. Mr. Lincoln did not object or complain. He acted in such a way that he earned the support of the toughs forever after. Armstrong knew he would have been beaten and knew that Mr. Lincoln made light of his cheating to spare his feelings and reputation with the others. Those roughnecks have been his prime supporters ever since."

"That's quite a tale," said Dietrich, smiling. "It reflects well on Mr. Lincoln."

"It does," said Woodward. "Nobody ever made money betting against Mr. Lincoln. He is a formidable opponent in any arena. Anyway, while he was destitute, Mr. Lincoln frequently slept and ate at the Armstrong farm. Hannah fixed him a pair of pants so he could survey through briars and brambles without losing his skin. He played with their children and helped them any way he could. Mr. Lincoln eventually moved to Springfield, read the law and rose in the world. The Armstrong family stayed on their farm and advanced little in the way of worldly achievement."

"Sir," said Chapel, "I fail to see what this has to do with the question at hand."

"Indulge me, if you would," said Woodward. "My tale may need some editing to bring it to newspaper standards, but not much is left to tell. Mr. Lincoln became an honest attorney. It is well known that he has withdrawn from cases upon discovering that his client lied to him. It is also well known that he has refused more than one winning case when he believed that the potential client was legally correct but morally in the wrong."

"And in the particular?" asked Dietrich, raising his eyebrows.

"I feel some sympathy for Mr. Lincoln. He is a good man, albeit horribly politically unsound. Imagine his moral conflict. He was asked to defend the son of Jack and Hannah Armstrong against a charge of murder and learned that Jack Armstrong's deathbed request was that Mr. Lincoln save Duff from hanging. Naturally, Mr. Lincoln promised that he would. Then he learned that the young man was — beyond any doubt — guilty."

Chapel cleared his throat before he said, "I wonder that you did not publish the story yourself. If you can prove it, it would create a great sensation. And it would not hurt Senator Douglas in the election, either."

Woodward laughed. "I would if I could. I know it happened, but you do not accuse an attorney of malfeasance unless you can cite chapter and verse. I admit that I cannot. Ever since the trial ended, there have been odd rumors and second-guesses blowing around the prairie about it. Houston went at it with a will, but those involved would not talk to him. Despite his best efforts, the investigation was bootless. As soon as people heard that a reporter from the Sun was asking questions, they became as quiet as the grave."

"So, why should we disinter this ancient mystery for you?" asked Dietrich. "Obviously, if we find something, it will help Senator Douglas. I see how you benefit from our labors, but what is the benefit for us?"

"We?" asked Woodward, looking from one man to another. "That's interesting. I didn't expect that. I had hoped to appeal to a rivalry. Now, I perceive an unusual alliance. That's all the better for me. To answer your question, first, it is not ancient. Duff Armstrong was acquitted in early May of this year. Second, didn't the two of you come to Illinois, in part, to take the measure of the men contending for senator? What better way to take the measure of

Mr. Lincoln than this? A man under pressure, torn between two conflicting personal moral imperatives — what that man does will tell you a great deal about him. Third, 'tis one hell of a story. Any reporter would give his eye teeth to have it."

Dietrich and Chapel looked at each other in silence. Then Chapel shrugged.

"If we decide to look into it, what information do you have so far?" asked Dietrich.

Woodward smiled. He exhaled a stream of smoke toward the ceiling. "I have a list of names and locations of people who were involved in the trial. I have Houston's notes, if you can read them. I can set the scene for you. It begins nearly one year ago, on August 29, 1857, at Walker's Grove."

Woodward settled back in his chair and spun the narrative that combined Houston's reporting, court records and a bit of hearsay.

***

James Preston 'Press' Metzker was a responsible and an impressive man when he was sober. Approaching six feet in height, Metzker weighed well over two hundred pounds, with a deep chest, long muscular arms and massive legs. He took pride in his strength, his family and friends, and in meeting his responsibilities. He was quick to volunteer to help his neighbors. Metzker worked without stinting from first light until it was too dark to see to make his farm successful. If you needed a meal or a joke, he was the man to come to. Metzker loved and provided well for his wife and his three children. By ten o'clock at night, however, Metzker was not sober.

On this particular night, he walked unsteadily toward a sutler's wagon. A religious tent meeting was going on a half-mile away. Metzker and others who had different ideas about what constituted a good time came to the races and to drink instead. Metzker looked in what he imagined to be the direction of the tent meeting, but because of the legally required distance between the religious gathering and the horse races, he could not see a thing.

Metzker saw the sutler and managed, just barely, to speak without slurring his words, "Don't they preach against the demon

47

alcohol?"

The sutler noted the size of the man who addressed him and answered politely, "I reckon so."

"But you sell it anyway, don't you?" asked Metzker.

"That I do," answered the sutler.

"Maybe you should repent," suggested Metzker in a hopeful tone.

"Maybe so," agreed the sutler. "It would make my mother happy."

Metzker wandered away from the wagon and spotted Duff Armstrong, a somewhat distant neighbor he had a pleasant nodding relationship with. Armstrong, who was stretched out on a bench softly snoring, stood about five feet four inches tall and weighed at most 140 pounds. Metzker contemplated his neighbor for a few moments. Then, without much thought, Metzker grabbed Armstrong's ankles and spilled him onto the ground. Armstrong could not be considered sober either. He hit the cold ground with an audible thump and awoke in pain. Confused and hurt, he struggled erect to search for whoever had interrupted his sleep.

Metzker decided the situation was funny and started to laugh.

"Do you want to go at it?" asked Armstrong, making fists.

"No, I'd probably hurt you," answered Metzker seriously. "You're a little 'un and all."

Armstrong had spent a lifetime being teased about being the runt of the litter. His father was known as a no-holds-barred fighter, and all of his brothers, even the younger ones, were considerably bigger than he was. He gritted his teeth and almost threw himself at the bigger man. A lifetime of losing fights to bigger opponents restrained him.

"You shouldn't have done that," said Armstrong.

"You're right," said Metzker, hanging his head. "I was lonely and wanted company. I'll buy you a drink to make up for it."

Although neither man needed more alcohol, they went to the sutler's wagon. Metzker purchased whiskey for both of them. Armstrong drank the whiskey, but he continued to glare at his neighbor. At length, Metzker blundered onward and Armstrong retreated to the bench and tried to get back to sleep.

Ordinarily, that would have been the end of things, but as ill luck would have it, as Metzker wandered through a group of men seated around a fire, he noticed another small man who was also a distant but friendly neighbor, Jimmy Norris. Norris was nodding off to sleep against a section of sawn tree trunk. Without considering, Metzker walked up and kicked the section of wood out from beneath Norris. The wood gouged Norris in the back and shoulder as it flew away. He was dumped onto the ground.

Norris jumped up. "Why did you do that? Do you want to fight?"

Again Metzker slowly wondered why he had done something he had only half thought out. "I guess I thought it'd be funny, but nobody laughed."

Although Jimmy Norris was about the same size as Duff Armstrong, he was a different type of man entirely. Norris had never been able to count on his brothers or his father to back him up in a fight. He had been fighting his own battles for as long as he could remember. Although a devoted husband and a loving father, Norris was not a man who forgave easily. One way or another he always got back at anyone who temporarily bested him. In fact, Norris had been charged with murder some years earlier when he killed a man in a fight. His attorney was to successfully argue self-defense, but it had been a close thing.

"Nobody laughed when I woke up Armstrong either," said Metzker sadly.

Norris smiled to himself and put his fists down. He set off determinedly toward the closest sutler's wagon.

Less than an hour later, close to eleven o'clock at night, Armstrong confronted Metzker. While Metzker's attention was centered on Armstrong, Norris skulked up behind Metzker and smashed the back of his skull with terrible force with a wooden club about three feet long and two inches thick. It was later identified as a neck yoke from a wagon frame. Armstrong struck Metzker in the face with what at least one witness later described as a "slungshot." There was no doubt about who the attackers were. At least ten men saw the assault.

A lesser man might have died on the spot. However, Metzker

hauled himself onto his horse and headed home. By his account, on the ride home he got dizzy and fell to the ground a couple of times. He reached home a few minutes before midnight. He told his wife he was in a fight and who it was with. He said Norris hit him with a club and he did not know what Armstrong hit him with. When the doctor was called the next day, he discovered that Metzker's right eye was bruised and swollen shut. Metzker had bruises and scrapes on much of his body. More seriously, Metzker's skull was fractured in the back and in the front near the corner of his right eye. Metzker lingered for the rest of the day and then slipped into a coma. There was nothing the doctor could do for him. They sent for a minister. Metzker died on the afternoon of September 1, leaving a grieving widow and three sad and confused fatherless children.

***

Woodward paused for dramatic effect.

"I don't understand," said Dietrich. "Duff Armstrong attacked Press Metzker with a children's toy — a slingshot?"

"No!" answered Woodward. "You may not have such a thing in Pennsylvania, but we have it here. A slungshot is a metal ball sewed into a leather cover and attached to a strong rope so it can be swung like a whip or used in the hand as a bludgeon. It is a terrible weapon and can easily split a skull like a ripe watermelon. It is for close-in fighting."

Chapel asked, "Where did this information come from?"

Woodward pointed to a pile of papers on his desk. "I have a copy of the grand jury report in addition to Houston's notes. I'll let you take it with you. A short time after Press Metzker died, Jimmy Norris was arrested at his home, and Duff Armstrong was taken from the Armstrong farm. They were jailed at the county seat, Havana, to wait for the October term of the Mason County Circuit Court so a grand jury could be called."

"Is that when Mr. Lincoln became involved?" asked Dietrich.

Woodward shook his head. "Not yet. The grand jury is just charged with determining whether or not there is sufficient evidence for a person to be held for a trail."

"The legal system in Germany is different," said Dietrich. "I don't understand."

Woodward exhaled a cloud of smoke before he spoke: "If the grand jury decides there is enough evidence for a man to be bound over for trial, then a trial is scheduled. If the jury decides that there is not sufficient evidence, the man is released without a trial. Of course, the prosecuting attorney has all the advantages at a grand jury hearing. It is a recitation of the evidence against the person charged. The person charged has no legal representation at this event. Lawyers say that a good prosecutor could get a cheese sandwich indicted for murder."

"In addition to the cheese sandwich, did the grand jury indict Jimmy and Duff for murder?" asked Chapel.

"They did indeed," replied Woodward. "On October 26, the grand jury commenced its deliberations into the matter of the untimely death of Press Metzker. Upon subsequent days the 'good men and true' heard from ten men who had witnessed the fight. They also heard from B.F. Stephenson, the physician who attended Press Metzker about the skull fractures Press sustained."

Woodward picked up the grand jury indictment and started to read it. He flipped through the pages. "Here it is. State of Illinois; the October term of the Mason County Circuit Court, in the year of our Lord one thousand eight hundred fifty seven. The grand jurors chosen, selected and sworn in for the for the County of Mason, in the name of and by the authority of the people of Mason County, Illinois, upon their oath present that James H. 'Jimmy' Norris and William 'Duff' Armstrong, late of the County of Mason and the state of Illinois, by reason of not having the fear of God before their eyes and seduced by the instigations of the devil, on the twenty ninth day of August in the year of our Lord one thousand eight hundred and fifty seven, with force and arms at and within the County of Mason and the State of Illinois in and upon one James Preston 'Press' Metzker did unlawfully, feloniously, willfully, and of their malice aforethought make an assault on the said person of James Preston Metzker which resulted in and caused grievous bodily insult and injury. Such grievous bodily insult and injury resulted in and caused his demise. May God Almighty have mercy upon his soul."

Woodward mumbled under his breath and then he read aloud: "James H. Norris used a certain stick of wood three feet long and of the diameter of two inches. The unlawful assault caused and produced on the back part of the head of him, the said James Preston Metzker, one mortal bruise resulting in the death of the afore mentioned James Preston Metzker."

Woodward turned the pages of the document.

"William Armstrong at the time of or shortly after the initial assault by James H. Norris utilized a certain hard metallic substance commonly called a slungshot in front of or to one side of the heretofore mentioned James Preston Metzker. The blow, which fell in and upon the right eye, caused the victim to sustain one other mortal bruise. Heroic efforts of the physician came to naught. The combination of assaults by James H. Norris and William Armstrong did result in and cause the demise of said James Preston Metzker who perished after languishing for three days."

Woodward looked at Chapel and Dietrich expectantly.

Dietrich looked at Chapel and shook his head. "This has been a very long day and I know not what to think."

"Yes," agreed Chapel. "There is too much to think about for us to make a rational decision about anything."

"Young men have no stamina these days," said Woodward. He exhaled another rank cloud of smoke. "Houston would never let a little thing like a long day put him off the scent. Take a copy of the grand jury report and Houston's notes with you. You'll also find a series of local newspaper articles about Norris's trial and about Armstrong's trial. Note the difference between the two."

Chapel picked up the papers from Woodward. He and Dietrich headed toward the door.

"So Mr. Lincoln claims that all men are created equal, including the Negro, does he?" asked Woodward. "I reckon that makes the Negro his brother, don't you?"

"In a sense," answered Dietrich.

"With his coloration and hair," sneered Woodward, "Old Honest Abe just might be a brother to a Nigger." Woodward's laughter followed the men out of the office and into the street.

CHAPTER EIGHT

July 11, 1858
On the train to Springfield

Blinking away sleep, Dietrich carefully carried two cups of steaming coffee down the aisle of the swaying train. He spotted Chapel in a seat at the end of the car, studying the papers he had been given by Woodward. He sat down on the seat across from him.

"Here, Thaddeus," said Dietrich, reaching across the aisle with a cup in his hand.

"August, I owe you my life." Chapel seized the cup and started sipping.

The men sat in companionable silence for a moment.

"I could not fall asleep right away last night," said Chapel. "I gave these a quick perusal. I must say that, despite what I think of them as people, Houston and Woodward may be on to something deep."

"I will read the papers in detail, of course," said Dietrich. "Can you give me a brief summary?"

Chapel drained the cup in one long swallow and put it down on the seat beside him.

"In brief?" asked Chapel. "Well, you heard the report of the grand jury."

"It did not sound good for Norris and Armstrong," answered Dietrich.

"It did not," agreed Chapel. "In a short trial soon after the indictment Norris was convicted of manslaughter and sentenced to eight years of hard labor."

"That sounds justified," said Dietrich. "He was at risk of hanging."

"Norris was provoked," said Chapel. "Obviously, that does not justify what he did, but it could have been an action made in anger without fully thinking through the consequences. I've seen duels fought for less cause. The tragedy is that two families are left bereft."

"And Armstrong?" asked Dietrich, sipping from his cup.

Chapel replied, "Duff Armstrong's attorneys applied for a change in venue and a delay. When the prosecutor heard that Mr. Lincoln would be involved, he applied for an additional delay. Mr. Lincoln was successful in Duff's defense."

"You mean Duff was convicted of a lesser charge?" asked Dietrich. "Assault with a deadly weapon, assault causing bodily harm, or something of that nature?"

"Acquitted of all charges."

"How?" asked Dietrich. Then he pointed toward the window. "Look there. We could ask him."

Through the sooty window, Chapel and Dietrich could see Abraham Lincoln sitting with a group of men in the next railroad car.

"I would prefer to gather some additional information first," said Chapel. "And you have not yet studied on the papers, but I agree that we should join him."

Chapel and Dietrich walked through the gap between cars and entered the car as Lincoln and the men he was with burst into laughter.

"Gentlemen, welcome," said Lincoln to Chapel and Dietrich. "Please join our little group. I think you know Samuel Anthony."

Anthony rose to shake hands with the men.

"Pleased to see you again. I hope your editors are happy with the articles you've written so far. Gentlemen, we are joined by reporters from Virginia and Pennsylvania. This is Donald Isaac Arnold, Leonard Swett and Judge David Davis, all friends of Mr. Lincoln."

Each man rose and shook hands with Chapel and Dietrich. Lincoln had shed his coat and collar. He was down to his shirt and yarn suspenders. One strap of his braces had slipped completely off his shoulder. Lincoln sprawled over one entire seat. His legs angled over to the seat opposite him. Lincoln's boots, mismatched socks and his large bare feet occupied that seat.

Noting the reporters' glances at his feet, Lincoln commented, "When I get the opportunity, I like to let my feet breathe. I have to stand for so long when I speak that my feet complain."

Everyone chuckled.

"You seem comfortable enough now," commented Anthony. "This means of locomotion has to be easier than what you used in the early days when you rode with the circuit court."

"That is true," answered Lincoln. "And it reminds me of a story. As you may know, the lawyers and the judge rode around the counties in a circle dispensing justice and settling cases in each county. We rode on horseback or in buggies with a few law books and one change of clothing. We forded streams and followed bad roads, where there were any roads at all. I remember once during an especially rainy circuit when my poor nag and I came across a hat sitting in the middle of a puddle. From idle curiosity, I picked it up and discerned that it was occupied. There was the top of a man's head under the hat. I immediately fell to digging away the mud from the head. First the forehead, then the eyes and nose appeared. After that I was able to uncover the man's mouth. As soon as he could speak, the man piped up. 'Go it, stranger,' he said. 'There is a whole horse beneath me.'"

Lincoln wrapped his long arms around his knees and threw his head back, laughing. The men found the sight and sound of Lincoln laughing even funnier than the story. Soon everyone was laughing.

"Did you hear the speeches?" Lincoln asked Dietrich and Chapel. "I should, mayhap, explain to the rest of you that Mr. Chapel's paper holds with the extension of slavery. Mr. Dietrich's paper holds with immediate abolition of slavery. Yet, here they are as friends. I swear that our beleaguered nation could take a lesson from these two gentlemen."

Lost for words, Dietrich and Chapel looked at each other.

"What did you think of Judge Douglas, our 'Little Giant'?" asked Lincoln.

"He's a formidable opponent," answered Chapel.

"Sit down, gentlemen," invited Lincoln. "We were just doing a post-mortem on the speeches. I am interested in your opinions."

Chapel and Dietrich found an open bench and sat down.

"I still say that recognition is a concern," said Anthony. "The judge is much better known than you are all around the state. I have my doubts about following him around and speaking after he finishes."

Lincoln shrugged. "At least recognition is not a problem after they see me. With a face like mine, no matter how hard they try to forget, they cannot. Besides, I am not convinced that being known is automatically an advantage. I once was involved in picking a jury when my opponent objected to seating a juror just because he knew me personally. The judge did not allow a challenge on that basis. So, thereafter, I started asking each prospective juror if he were acquainted with my opponent. Since the prospective jurors and the attorney all lived locally, all of them answered, 'Yes.' I challenged none of them. Finally, the judge asked me why I kept asking each one if he knew my opponent and then never making a challenge. I had to explain, 'Your Honor,' I said, 'when I find a man who does not know my opponent, I will challenge him. When a man tells me he knows my opponent, I reckon that's to my advantage.'"

Lincoln and the other men laughed.

"You both heard the speeches. What do you gentlemen think?" Lincoln asked, looking in the direction of Chapel and Dietrich.

"What?" interrupted Anthony. "Are you interested in the opinion of those ink-stained scribes? You would listen to those penny-a-line scribblers?" His tone and the reddish tint to his cheeks suggested that he had already been imbibing despite the early hour.

"Yes, indeed," answered Lincoln. "I once defended a newspaper editor charged with libel for a two-dollar fee and a one-year subscription to his newspaper. I regularly annoy Billy Herndon by reading the papers from around the country aloud in the office before conducting any other activity. I've read articles that each of you has written and I deem them fair and honest. I would like to hear your opinions."

"'Tis true," said Anthony, raising his eyebrows and opening his mouth wide in mock astonishment. "Unlikely as it sounds, Mr. Lincoln will listen to a Paul Pry, a Jenkins, a Johnny Busybody, and a Jimmy Keyhole Snooper as if their opinion had the merit of honest men. I fear he will ruin the current breed of ne'er-do-well reporter entirely."

The men laughed.

Anthony went on. "Mr. Lincoln listens still, even after getting the sage advice of the great New York editor Horace Greeley. The esteemed editor once suggested that the Illinois Republicans nominate the Illinois Democrat, Judge Douglas, as our candidate for the Senate. No doubt he thought the best way to advance the party was to turn it over to our opponent. Surely, if Mr. Greeley is not as steadfast in his support as the northern star, he is at least as steadfast as the northern lightning bug."

"You must admit that our Republican candidate would have won, since the Republican Douglas and the Democrat Douglas would have been one and the same," said Lincoln. "That the Republican Party would have ceased to exist thereafter is but a minor quibble."

"Ah, the great Mr. Greeley," said Anthony, raising one finger into the air. "He's a self-made man who worships his creator."

The men laughed.

"I have to admit that I am jealous of the great editor," said Anthony. "He hires managing editors who are strangers to remorse and reporters who save him from completely embarrassing himself. That leaves him free to editorialize by recommending both sides of any issues of interest in subsequent days. Thereafter he can always claim he advocated whatever side proves to be the popular one. However, that is enough frivolity. We are interested in what you two journalists think."

Dietrich looked at Chapel and started to speak slowly.

"I thought you did well, Mr. Lincoln," said Dietrich. " I think reminding people of the founding fathers, most of them Southerners, created the ideas of the republic."

"I beg to disagree," said Chapel. "Not that your speech did not stir people. It did. However, I thought Judge Douglas had the more enthusiastic listeners. It appeared to me, sir, that the practice of following him yields the first strike to the judge. In a fight the man who strikes first usually wins and the one who only reacts to the first strike usually loses."

"Some of my most discerning advisors agree with you," said Lincoln thoughtfully.

"Also, sir, many in the crowd when Judge Douglas spoke were stirred by his talk about miscegenation."

"I know," answered Lincoln, smiling. "If the judge and his friends could just control their amorous feelings for Negro women, they might become more rational about other things also."

The men chuckled.

"Have you, sir, no objection to the mixing of the races?" asked Chapel.

"Personally, I have no desire to marry a Negro woman," answered Lincoln, leaning back comfortably. "Of course I am already well supplied in the wife department, and so I need no other. If a white man wants to marry a Negro woman I say he should do so, as long as the Negro woman is willing to put up with him."

The men laughed. Chapel's cheeks became red.

"Please understand, Mr. Chapel, that we are not mocking you or laughing at you. I own that I do not understand Southerners' sensitivity to even the discussion of slavery. I also do not understand the influence of slave traders on Southern political doctrine. Such men are despised in Southern society. You would never admit them into the parlor, but they rule you in political doctrine as surely as you rule your own slaves. Why should small farmers and tradesmen support the slave system that depresses their own wages? They outnumber the few slaveholders many times over. Surely someday they will realize that."

"We are united, sir, in opposition to allowing outsiders to determine how we should live," said Chapel.

Lincoln nodded.

"Truly, I value your advice," Lincoln said to the reporters. "I will think on it seriously."

Lincoln paused and then regarded Chapel.

"Mr. Chapel, you support slavery, correct?"

"I do," answered Chapel.

"With your permission, sir, I would like to pose a question to you," said Lincoln. "I invite you to ponder it. You need not answer immediately. In fact, you need not answer at all."

"Fire away," said Chapel.

"As a supporter of slavery can you prove conclusively the right to enslave? If A can enslave B, why cannot B snatch up the same argument and prove equally that B should enslave A? You say that A is white and B is black. Is it color then? Take care. By this rule you are to be the slave of the first man you meet with a fairer skin than your own. You say that it is not color exactly. You say the whites are intellectually the superior of blacks and therefore have the right to enslave them. Take care again. By this rule you are to be the slave of the first man you meet with an intellect superior to your own. You say you have a legal claim to enslave another. Very well, another can make a legal claim to enslave you."

Chapel pondered Lincoln's question while the others continued to talk about the events of the day before.

CHAPTER NINE

July 12, 1858
Springfield, Illinois

Chapel knocked on the door of the Myers and Caldwell Boarding House early in the morning. A small attractive woman with white hair answered the door.

Chapel removed his hat and addressed her. "I'd be obliged if I could speak with Mr. Dietrich, Ma'am."

"He'll be down to breakfast directly," she said. "Mr. Dietrich does not miss many meals. If you have not eaten yet, we have room at the table for another. Ten cents for all you can eat and all the coffee you can drink."

"It smells wonderful, and August has bragged to me about the quality of your victuals, Ma'am. I am delighted to accept."

The woman opened the door and escorted him to the dining room.

"I am Elsie Myers," she said.

"I am Thaddeus Chapel."

"I run this establishment with the help of Nellie Caldwell, who does most of the cooking, and my son Israel," said Mrs. Myers. "When my husband, Dutch, passed away, he left me with the house paid for and no debts to speak of. I suppose I could rattle around in this big old place with only Israel and me taking up the space, but whatever would I do then? 'Tis cheery having boarders to cook and clean for. I'd rather wear out than rust out, I always say."

The dining room was starting to fill up with men who yawned and stretched as they headed for the table. Mrs. Myers intercepted one man and spoke quietly to him, pointing to his hands. He shrugged and left the room, only to return shortly with damp but cleaner hands. The conversation was amiable and only moderately loud.

Dietrich came in blinking. His eyes were slightly reddened. He caught sight of Chapel and smiled. He came over and sat next to him.

"Gentlemen," said Mrs. Myers, over the din of the conversations, "Mr. Dietrich, would you lead us in a brief prayer?"

"We thank you, Lord, for the food that sustains our physical beings and the grace that sustains our souls. Let us remember the author of our bounty and the final judge of our lives. May we find forgiveness through Christ Jesus. Amen."

"Thank you, Mr. Dietrich. That was well said," said Mrs. Myers. "Israel, you can bring the food in now."

A tall and hefty young blond man with blue eyes carried in platters of fried eggs and potatoes. He quickly followed that with two pots of piping hot coffee. Fresh baked bread arrived and was passed down the table. Fresh butter and preserves followed that. Corn and tomatoes from the garden came next. Conversation stilled as the men went about the serious business of eating. As the men took the edge off their hunger, conversations started again.

"I read over the papers last night," said Dietrich to Chapel. "It is a most curious thing how Mr. Lincoln won an acquittal for Armstrong, when the other man, Norris, was sentenced to eight years of hard labor."

"Houston managed to offend some he interviewed and to annoy all the rest," said Chapel. "Mr. Lincoln is more nearly your champion than he is mine. Do you think this is worthy of further scrutiny?"

"Mr. Lincoln?" asked Mrs. Myers from across the room. "Are you gentlemen discussing politics?"

"No, Ma'am," answered Dietrich. "We were talking about one of his legal cases."

"His railroad work?" asked Mrs. Myers. "I am told that he has been involved in some essential case law."

"Actually, it is his criminal defense work we were discussing," remarked Chapel.

"Oh, I should have known," said Mrs. Myers. "Mr. Dietrich is a reporter, and you appear to be one also. How would you sell papers with boring articles about transportation litigation and the imposition of taxes?"

"Our readers do prefer red meat," admitted Dietrich.

"Mr. Lincoln is a particular favorite in this house," commented Mrs. Myers, smiling. "Once a boarder in this house, a good man sadly now departed this world was accused of murder. Mr. Lincoln defended him. It was a remarkable event. If my husband were still alive, you would not escape without a lengthy discussion of the Trailor murder case and Abraham Lincoln for the defense. We played a very small role in that event, you know. If you really want to know about Mr. Lincoln as a criminal defense attorney, you might ask Marshal Jim Maxey."

"I would think that a marshal and a defense attorney might have different objectives in mind in legal matters," said Chapel.

Mrs. Myers laughed. "Not Marshal Maxey and Mr. Lincoln. They're good friends and as good men as any I know." Mrs. Myers paused. "This wouldn't have anything to do with Mr. Lincoln's Senate bid, would it?"

When Chapel and Dietrich hesitated, she laughed again.

"Well, much as I support his actions about the fraudulent Lecompton Constitution, nobody ever called our current senator 'honest Stephen Douglas.' You young men look into any action Mr. Lincoln was involved in all you like. I can tell you, you won't find any stain on his character because there won't be any stain to find."

"I hope some day to have defenders as loyal as Mr. Lincoln's," said Chapel.

"Off with the two of you," said Mrs. Myers, making a shooing motion. "I have work to do and it sounds like you do, too."

Outside the boarding house, Chapel and Dietrich conferred hastily.

"You certainly found more commodious lodgings than I did," said Chapel. "Do you think Mrs. Myers has a spare space?"

"I doubt it," said Dietrich. "I happened to ask about boarding there immediately after a boarder was suddenly called out of town. There have been no vacancies since then. Most of the men who board here are long-time lodgers. I would be happy to recommend you if a place comes open."

"Thank you. Now that you have read the papers, do you think there is something to investigate?"

"I do," answered Dietrich. "If there were something like this in Judge Douglas's past, I would be interested in finding out more about it. Mr. Lincoln asked us to hold the reins equally and steer down the middle. I believe we are doing that."

"How do we start?" asked Chapel.

"I've made a list of names of people to interview and places where they live," answered Dietrich, showing Chapel the list. "One of them is in Springfield now."

Chapel hesitated. "I do not know that we should start with Mr. Lincoln."

"I concur," answered Dietrich.

Chapel relaxed.

"At this point we don't know enough to formulate questions for Mr. Lincoln," said Dietrich. "And he is busy running for the senate. We should not waste his time. I've always found Mrs. Myers to be a source of excellent advice. Why don't we start with the marshal?"

Marshal Jim Maxey was a tall man with broad shoulders and a deep chest. His sandy hair was starting to turn gray. He had a face as weather-beaten as any farmer's. Despite his age, he appeared to be no one to trifle with. He was in his office, leaning against a wall as he spoke with a remarkably pretty woman with hair the color of copper.

"Can I help you gentlemen?" he asked.

"I believe you can, sir," answered Chapel. He nodded to the woman. "Ma'am."

"I can leave you gentlemen if you wish," said the woman.

"Please don't depart on our account," said Dietrich. "This is not an official matter. We would like to ask you, if we could, where we might locate a man."

Dietrich consulted his list. "Mr. Tom Edwards."

"I can help you with that," answered Maxey, crossing his arms. "Mr. Edwards is a friend of ours."

He looked the men over without saying a word.

"Jim, not every man is a fugitive or a bail jumper," said the woman.

"I'm sorry," said Maxey, relaxing his posture. "My wife, Cassie, is correct. In my job I see many people who are not quite what they appear to be and it makes me unduly suspicious. I do apologize."

"Besides, I feel certain that these men were about to tell us just why it is that they want to see Mr. Edwards," said Cassie with a smile.

Dietrich looked at Chapel. Chapel shrugged.

"We are reporters," started Dietrich. "We were sent to cover the race for senator, due to the national interest in Judge Douglas and his likely run for president two years hence."

"If he survives the senate race," interrupted Chapel.

Dietrich nodded. "Since arrival we have developed an interest in his lesser known opponent, Mr. Lincoln."

"Who commands unusual loyalty in his friends," continued Chapel.

Dietrich frowned. "Am I telling this or are you, Thaddeus?"

"My apologies," said Chapel to Dietrich.

"We have learned of an unusual criminal case that Mr. Lincoln defended and we would like to talk with Mr. Edwards about it."

"It can't be the Trailor murder case," said Cassie, frowning. "Mr. Edwards was not involved in that."

"That was a long time ago," said Maxey. "William and Arch Trailor are deceased. Attorney General Josiah Lamborn is no longer with us, either."

"He was never the same after the conclusion of the trial," mused Cassie.

Maxey reached out and touched Cassie's hand. They smiled knowingly at each other.

"Bob Cassell might have been complaining again," said Cassie brightly. "You know how steamed he got."

Maxey smiled broadly. "I thought his boiler was going to burst like a paddlewheel steamboat. Did you gentlemen want to hear about Melissa Goings?"

Dietrich and Chapel looked at each other blankly.

"Melissa Goings was a seventy-year-old woman married to Roswell Goings, who was seventy-seven. He was a sot who had mistreated his wife for years. Sober, he was a meek man, but drunk he was a brute. And he was very rarely sober. One day he got drunk and during an argument with his wife he started to choke her. Mrs. Goings somehow got hold of a piece of stove wood and struck him once on the side of his head. After four days, he died from the injury.

"Of course, Mrs. Goings was arrested and charged with murder. Mr. Lincoln was engaged to defend her. Stories vary on the details, but as best I can tell, Mr. Lincoln was left alone with her in a room of the courthouse to talk about her defense. When the bailiff returned, Mr. Lincoln was there alone, reading the newspaper. Asked about the whereabouts of his client, Mr. Lincoln assured Cassell that he did not know. Cassell asserted that Mr. Lincoln had told her to leave the state to avoid prosecution. Mr. Lincoln swore that it was not true. 'She asked me where she could get a drink of water,' Mr. Lincoln said. 'I merely told her that I had heard that there was mighty good water in Tennessee.'"

Dietrich and Chapel looked startled, but when Maxey and Cassie started to laugh, they joined in.

"I don't reckon that you two are out to do Mr. Edwards any harm," said Maxey. "I can't be certain where he is right now, but I believe you'll be able to find him clerking at the front desk of the Illinois Hotel this afternoon."

Dietrich and Chapel thanked him and left.

"If you wander over to the hotel, I'll meander over to the courthouse," said Maxey to Cassie.

When Chapel and Dietrich entered the Illinois Hotel that afternoon, they saw behind the front desk a stout spectacled man with a florid complexion and thinning red hair. He was dressed in a ruffled white shirt and a bright crimson vest.

"Can I help you gentlemen?" asked the man, smiling. "I can offer you either one room or two. How long do you expect to stay in our fair city, capitol of the state of Illinois?"

Chapel returned his smile. "Actually, sir, my friend and I are looking for Tom Edwards."

"You have found him, sir," answered Edwards. "This humble child of God is in fact Tom Edwards. I am the youngest son of the late, lamented Hilda and Edward Edwards. How may I be of service to you?"

Dietrich and Chapel exchanged a glance.

"I am a reporter for the Penn Statesman," said Dietrich. He nodded at Chapel. "This worthy gentleman is a reporter for the Richmond Enquirer. We would like to talk with you about Mr. Lincoln and one of his legal cases if you have the time."

"Regretfully, sir, I am bound to this desk and my employer likes to see that I am attentive to our guests. I cannot engage you gentlemen in conversation at present, pleasant as that would be." He thought for a moment.

"I will have thirty minutes free at seven for supper," said Edwards. "Ordinarily, I would rush home, snatch a bite to eat and rush back since the fare at the hotel is somewhat beyond my modest means. However, if you gentlemen would care to join me in the dining room at that time, I could perhaps provide satisfaction."

"Only, sir, if you will permit us to purchase your meal so as to not strain your modest means," said Chapel.

Edwards almost glowed with pleasure. "Oh, I could not accept."

"We insist," answered Dietrich firmly.

"Well, in that case, what can I do?' asked Edwards, speaking rapidly. "I accept your generous offer."

At seven when Chapel and Dietrich returned, they found Edwards dressed in a fine black frock coat. He led them into the dining room where they were seated in a quiet corner.

"I can heartily recommend the roast beef with potatoes and greens. The bread is fresh baked, and the cakes are marvelous. Of course, if you prefer chicken or fish, there are several excellent alternatives."

"I feel certain that your recommendations will be top notch," answered Chapel. "Why don't you order for all of us?"

Edwards signaled for a waiter.

"Of course, I do not ordinarily imbibe while I am working," said Edwards.

"If we get a pitcher of beer, you could just wet your whistle while Mr. Chapel and I consume the rest."

"An excellent suggestion," said Edwards. "I will take your

sage advice."

When the food arrived, Edwards ate with perfect manners but so efficiently that he finished long before the reporters did. Edwards tossed down two glasses of beer and in short order the pitcher was empty.

"I must apologize," said Edwards, signaling to the waiter for another pitcher of beer. "As I mentioned, I usually rush home and eat quickly so I can return to work on time. I fear I have developed the habit of eating quickly, and I hope you are not disaccommodated."

"Not at all," answered Chapel. "I admire your devotion to your work."

Between rapid bites of cake, Edwards asked, "How is it that I may be of service to you?"

"As my friend Mr. Dietrich mentioned, we are reporters. Although we each came to report on Judge Douglas initially, we have become interested in a legal case that Mr. Lincoln was involved in. We were informed that you played a minor role in the case so we decided to talk to you directly."

"Fortunately for me I have not been in such straits that I have needed an attorney, although I would certainly hire Mr. Lincoln if I did. You may not know it, but I have known Mr. Lincoln since he first appeared in New Salem. I witnessed his titanic wrestling match with Jack Armstrong. Despite my corpulent appearance now, back in the day I was one of the Clary's Grove boys. I never thought any man could give Jack a run for his money. Then this odd-looking tall drink of water came along. It was the custom for newcomers to be put up against Jack to test their mettle. If a man lost after a fair effort and made no complaint or excuse, he was thought to be a good man. If he managed to postpone his defeat by dint of exceptional effort, he was thought to be an exceptional man. None of us thought that anyone would ever match our local champion. Imagine our surprise when a tall, gawky stranger showed that he could have beaten Jack."

"Then, when Hannah Armstrong needed to contact Mr. Lincoln to defend her son, she thought of you," said Dietrich.

"Oh, that legal case," said Edwards. "That would have been

my guess. Over the years Mr. Lincoln became an attorney and a leading light in Illinois politics. I became a hotel desk clerk. In America, a man may become anything." He winked at the reporters. "If Mr. Lincoln ever comes to see the light and wants instruction in the science of hotel keeping, I stand ready to teach him."

Dietrich and Chapel chuckled.

"I kept in touch with Jack and Hannah over the years. I was honored that, when she needed help, Hannah asked her neighbor to write to me."

"What did the letter say?" asked Dietrich.

Edwards became sober immediately. "There was one letter wrapped in another letter. The outer letter gave me permission to read the letter enclosed, which was addressed to Mr. Lincoln, and I did. In the inside letter Hannah said that she had recently become a widow. I still find that hard to believe. Jack Armstrong was like a force of nature, a twister maybe, or a blizzard. It did not seem possible that he would ever take sick and die. I know that is the fate in store for all of us, but it was a shock."

Edwards shook his head before continuing. "The letter said that her son, Duff, was in terrible trouble. She mentioned that Jack had made her promise to contact Mr. Lincoln to ask him to defend Duff against a charge of murder. She said she was willing to mortgage the farm, if needed, to pay Mr. Lincoln's fees."

Edwards shook his head again. "Things looked really bad for the boy according to what Hannah wrote, but to tell the truth, the details were pretty sketchy. Apparently, a second man had already been convicted over the incident. Hannah apologized for her boldness in writing to Mr. Lincoln. She said she knew he was awfully busy. She said if Mr. Lincoln did not have the time, she would understand. She was certain that there would be others who she could find to help Duff."

"What did you do next?" asked Dietrich.

"I am a poor sort of Christian but I bowed my head and I prayed for the soul of my oldest friend, Jack Armstrong," said Edwards. "Then I went looking for Mr. Lincoln. I went to his office and said, 'Mr. Lincoln, I sure am happy to see your face.' Mr. Lincoln put on a look of pretend disgust and answered, 'For all your faults, Edwards, I always thought you were at least an honest man. Look at my visage and tell me if you are honestly glad to see this.' He added that I should change my ways or I might end up like the old farmer Mr. Lincoln knew who was such a habitual liar that, if he wanted his dog to come to him, he had to get another man to whistle to it."

Edwards smiled. "After I finished laughing, I told him that I was truly glad to see him. I assured him that I did not need his legal assistance, but another old friend did. I handed him the letter from Hannah and in his slow and careful way he read it thoroughly. When he read about Jack's death his features took on a sadness. When he read about Duff's troubles, his eyes became alive again. Finally, he finished and stood in silence. I waited and eventually he looked at me again. He said he would help, of course. He said he would do anything he could. He told me he would write to Hannah through her neighbor at once."

Edwards took a deep breath. "I knew that a lawyer of Mr. Lincoln's standing charges fees commensurate with his skills. He has argued cases before the United States Supreme Court. His railroad cases can run into thousands of dollars. I knew Hannah was willing to borrow against her farm, as Jack implored her to do, but I did not know if that would generate enough money to cover the tariff. I have been fortunate in a business venture or two. I even got involved in some financial matters with Mr. Lincoln as a partner. I tried gently to bring up the matter of his fees. Mr. Lincoln's eyes flashed. In all the years I have known him, I had never seen him so angry before."

Edwards looked directly at the two reporters. "Don't let people tell you Mr. Lincoln does not have a temper. For all his temperate language under provocation today, in his younger days he had a terrible struggle with his temper. He has mastered it these past several years, but it has not disappeared. For just a second, he looked like he would strike me. Then he did rebuke me. 'You ought to know me better than to think I'd take a fee from any of Jack Armstrong's blood,' Mr. Lincoln said. He recited to me all that Hannah and Jack had done for him when he was young and poor. He said, 'I danced that boy on my knee a hundred times down in Menard County.' He told me about their open hearts and the many kindnesses they showed him when he was a penniless young man with debts to pay and no sense of direction. Finally he told me to tell Auntie Hannah not to worry. He said to go to her and tell old Hannah to keep up a good heart and we'll see what can be done."

"Do you know what took place after that?" asked Dietrich.

"When Hannah came to visit Mr. Lincoln, she stopped by to thank me for my help, such as it was," said Edwards. "It was good to see her. I could tell that she was still concerned about Duff, but she told me she worried a lot less after talking with Mr. Lincoln. Quite a while later, I received a note from her neighbor writing for Hannah again saying that Duff was safe at home and wasn't Mr. Lincoln wonderful."

"Did you ask Mr. Lincoln about it?" asked Dietrich.

"I did, and he waved my question off." Edwards waved one hand in the air. "He was never given to braggadocio."

"Have you heard any rumors about the trial?" asked Chapel, putting down his fork.

"A new country is heard from. I've rarely known a trial to generate so many stories. I've heard that Duff shot the man dead on the spot, that he beat the man to death, and that it was a mistaken identity, that Duff was never present at the assault. I heard that Mr. Lincoln fabricated evidence, withheld evidence, and persuaded a witness to lie under oath."

Edwards smiled. "Come to think on it, you should have heard the rumors about the Trailor murder case. Those speculations make the rumors here sound like nursery rhymes. You should have seen Abraham Lincoln on that occasion."

Dietrich and Chapel looked at each other.

"May we ask one last favor?" asked Chapel.

"If I can be of additional service, please let me know," said Edwards.

"Would you be willing to write to Hannah Armstrong and ask if we could speak with her about these matters?" asked Chapel.

In the following silence, all three men sat without moving.

"There was another reporter a while back, a most irritating fellow, who demanded that I write a letter of introduction to Mrs. Armstrong," said Edwards, frowning. "I advised him that, while I might be amenable to helping him, he was asking me to impose on a recently widowed woman who also had a very recent fright that her son might be hung. Naturally, I declined."

Edwards lapsed into silence again. Neither reporter said anything.

"On this occasion, however, you gentlemen have explained your reason for asking. I do not believe you would willingly cause distress to Auntie Hannah. I am inclined to oblige you. I would strongly advise you to wait until I hear back from Hannah before imposing your presence on her person. The Armstrong family is law abiding and honest. They are also, however, very protective of their own. If you appear unannounced, I could not answer for what the sons and Hannah's neighbors might do."

CHAPTER TEN

July 17, 1858
Springfield, Illinois: The Lincoln home

Mary Todd Lincoln slapped her hands over her ears and screamed. Tears ran down her face in a torrent. With her reddened complexion and contorted face, she looked scarcely human.

As the thunder rolled again, Lincoln came striding up to the house and thrust himself through the front door. He took in the scene in a few seconds. Mary was screaming in the middle of the room. Two boys were huddled together in one corner.

"Bobby and Willie, Momma will be all right. You know she is afraid of the thunder and lightning. This is a big storm. As soon as it is over, she will start to feel better. You boys go play. I'll take care of Momma."

While the boys left the room, Lincoln guided Mary over to a chair. He lifted her off the floor and sat down in the chair with Mary in his lap. He rubbed her back with his hands as he rocked her gently.

"The th-thunder," said Mary through her tears.

"Shh, it's all right now," whispered Lincoln. "I'm sorry I was late. I was discussing the election, and the storm blew in quicker than I thought it would."

"You are never here," insisted Mary. "Little Bobby scarcely knows who you are."

"I'm sorry about that, too," said Lincoln. "I cannot make a living as an attorney staying in Springfield. I regret that I spent so much time away when he was younger. He's become more of a Todd and less of a Lincoln. I promise that I will try to spend more time with the boy."

"You can't spend time with him now," argued Mary. "You're too busy running for the senate. There is always something coming up that keeps you away from home. There are speeches you need to make or legal cases to argue. It's always something, isn't it?"

"It is," admitted Lincoln. "You know I have to go to every

balloon launch, every barn raising and every cattle auction in the state to speak to anyone who won't run me out of town on a rail."

"I know," said Mary. "I want you to be a senator, too. Probably more than you do."

Lincoln continued to rock Mary.

"I don't know why you put up with me," she sobbed. "Thunder and lightning terrify me. They sound like distant cannons, and I swear the rain smells like blood. I know terrible things are coming. I just don't know what."

"I don't know why you put up with me," answered Lincoln. "When the 'hypo' comes over me I can sit and brood for hours on end."

"I have a terrible temper," said Mary.

"I'm hardly ever home," said Lincoln.

"When someone betrays me I cannot forgive them, although I know I should," said Mary.

"I'd rather tell a joke than face a disagreement with you," said Lincoln.

Mary started to relax a little.

"Talk to me, Father, so I can ignore the thunder."

"Do you remember when we first met?" asked Lincoln softly. "Do you remember when I told you that I wanted to dance with you in the worst way?"

"Yes." answered Mary. "After you stepped all over my new shoes during the dance, I told you that you had succeeded beyond all imagining. You had danced with me in the very worst way."

Mary sighed. Lincoln continued to rock her.

"Shortly after that my friend, Julia, asked why I gave a cold shoulder to a rich man who came courting. I told her that I would rather marry a good man with a good mind and prospects for fame and power than a man with all the gold coins in the world."

"I don't know how you saw that in me," answered Lincoln. "I think I was pretty poor clay to work with."

"You've never seen in yourself what I and others can see," answered Mary.

"And handsome I'm not," said Lincoln.

"What good is handsome?" asked Mary, her eyes flashing. "I

know the Bible says 'Vanity, thy name is woman.' But the author of that verse never met the men that courted me."

Lincoln chuckled.

"You've done wonders," said Lincoln. "You gave up a life of ease when you married a poor man with few prospects. Still, it has not been all bad, I hope."

"Do you know what I said to Billy Herndon the other day?" asked Mary. "I told him that you may not be a handsome figure, but people are perhaps not aware that your heart is as big as your arms are long."

Mary giggled. "He expected more hectoring and vexation from me. The man was quite confused."

"I wish you would not torture him so," said Lincoln. "He thinks the worse of you for your treatment of him."

"I know I should not," said Mary. "I do not like the man. He has no feeling for the practice of law like you do. I don't doubt his ability at it, but he is a worker without joy in his labor and it makes him a small man. Besides, I get jealous when you spend time in the office when you could be at home. I own it is foolish of me."

"I worry that his impression of you may be conveyed to others," said Lincoln.

"I can not imagine how," said Mary.

"Nor can I," admitted Lincoln. "Perhaps it is a foolish thought on my part. Will you at least concede that he is a more religious man than I am?"

"I do not stipulate to that, counselor," snapped Mary. "He has more of the forms of religion, but he lacks your natural poetry in worshiping Providence."

Lincoln and Mary exhaled in unison and broke into laughter.

"Stay with me, Father, for the rest of the day," Mary pleaded.

"Judge Douglas will speak in Springfield later this afternoon," said Lincoln. "I need to hear him."

"Why?" asked Mary, blinking away tears. "You have the transcript of the speech he made in Bloomington yesterday. He won't change it much and there are others you can trust to listen. Stay with me, please."

"Very well. I shall."

***

Late in the afternoon, Douglas arrived in Springfield on a special train that had been donated to him by the Illinois Central Railroad and Chicago and Southern Lines for the duration of the canvass. The massive engine's smokestack belched black smoke, soot and fiery embers. A small cannon named "Popular Sovereignty" fired from a flatcar while the train whistle shrieked. Douglas bounced down the steps of his specially appointed personal sleeping car and walked through ankle-deep mud toward the speakers' platform. Benjamin S. Edwards, a Republican who had announced his conversion to the Democracy, slogged along by his side.

Douglas bounded up the steps to the platform and scrutinized the crowd, looking for Lincoln. Lincoln was not present. Douglas noted with approval that several reporters crowded in close enough to take notes. He remembered that in Bloomington the day before, his arrival had been triumphant. Accompanied by the Bloomington Rifles and the town band, Douglas rode through the streets in an open carriage and waved to an adoring and noisy audience of supporters. However, Douglas's two-hour-long speech in the courthouse square lacked decisiveness and focus. Since then, Douglas had been refining and polishing his words. He was determined to do better in the state capitol and the home of his opponent.

Moving close to the platform, Chapel tried to avoid the worst of the mud puddles to spare his fine English Walking Shoes. Nearby, Dietrich moved through the muck, unconcerned that his sturdy Donelson boots were getting covered in mud. Samuel Anthony waved and then waded over to the two men.

"I'll make your job easy," said Anthony, handing each man a sheave of papers. "This is what Judge Douglas said in Bloomington. You'll see it isn't much different than what he said in Chicago."

As Douglas's deep voice rose in slow cadence, Dietrich and Chapel looked at the papers and followed along. After a few minutes, Dietrich commented, "He's prettied up his language."

"It's a nice speech," agreed Chapel.

"But he has not changed his tune," said Anthony as Douglas

spoke from the stage.

"Now, Mr. Lincoln says he will not enter into Kentucky to abolish slavery there, but will fight slavery in Kentucky from Illinois. I do not think he would. Mr. Lincoln is a very prudent man. Mr. Lincoln is going to plant his Abolition batteries all along the banks of the Ohio River and throw his shells into Virginia, and Kentucky, and Missouri and attack the institution of slavery. I believe that the Union can only be preserved by maintaining inviolate the Constitution of the United States as our fathers have," said Douglas, his eyes scanning the crowd.

"Mr. Lincoln will wage warfare upon the Supreme Court because of the Dred Scott decision. He is going to appeal to the people to elect a president who will appoint judges who will reverse the decision. Suppose you get a Supreme Court composed of such judges. What confidence would you have in such a court?

"But, my friends, Mr. Lincoln says that this Dred Scott decision destroys popular sovereignty. It is true that the court has decided that Congress had not power to prohibit slavery in the territories. That is interesting as a matter of theory, but of no importance in practice. If the people of a territory want slavery, they will have it, and if they do not, they will drive it out. Local police regulation must support slavery, else it cannot flourish."

The Douglas supporters applauded.

"Mr. Lincoln's main objection to the Dred Scott decision is that it was intended to deprive the Negro of the rights of citizenship. He is in favor of Negro citizenship. I am not. He believes the Negro should be able to vote, to hold office, to serve in the legislature so that thereafter they can have the right men for U.S. senator. He will make them eligible to the office of judge or governor or to the legislature. When he gets the Nigger Cuffee elevated to the bench, he will certainly not refuse his judge the privilege of marrying any woman he may select!

"We have decided in Illinois that we do not want slavery, but we do not want the Negro to be a citizen. No other state can tell the people of Illinois what to do with the Negro. If the people of Maine desire to be put on an equity with the Negro and allow that he has the right to come and kill their vote by a Negro vote, they have the right to think so, I suppose. Passing over to New York, we find in that state a Negro may vote provided he holds $250 worth of property. In New York they think a rich Negro is equal to a white man. Well, that is a matter of taste with them. If they think so in that state and do not carry the doctrine outside of it, I have no quarrel with them.

"Mr. Lincoln says that the Declaration of Independence contains this language: 'We hold these truths to be self-evident, that all men are created equal.' He goes on to argue that the language 'all men' included the Negroes, Indians and all inferior races. I do not doubt that he believes that the Almighty made the Negro equal to the white man. He thinks that the Negro is his brother. I do not believe that the Negro is any kin of mine at all. I hold that the white race, the European race — I care not whether Irish, German, French, Scotch, English or what nation they belong to so they are the white race — to be our equals."

Someone in the crowd shouted, "Down with Niggers!"

"I do not anticipate any personal collision between Mr. Lincoln and myself. You all know that I am an amiable, good-natured man and I take great pleasure in bearing testimony that Mr. Lincoln is a kind-hearted, amiable, good-natured gentleman with whom no man has the right to pick a quarrel, even if he wanted one. He is a worthy gentleman I have known for twenty-five years, and there is no better citizen, no kinder-hearted man. He is a fine lawyer, possesses high ability, and there is no objection to him, except the monstrous revolutionary doctrines with which he is identified and which he conscientiously entertains and is determined to carry out if he gets the power.

"It must be a contest of principle — Either the radical Abolition principles of Mr. Lincoln must be maintained, or the strong, constitutional, national democratic principles with which I am identified must be carried out. I shall be satisfied whatever way you decide. I leave the question in your hands and again tender you my profound thanks for the cordial and heartfelt welcome tendered me this evening."

Douglas received a mighty cheer and was escorted to the train by a large group of followers. The train whistle shrieked and the cannon sounded as Douglas boarded. People streamed to both sides of the track. Douglas supporters waved banners and cheered as the train slowly began to pick up speed. The Little Giant could be seen saluting the crowd and moving from one window to another, acknowledging the people supporting him. Steam spurted from the pistons turning the wheels with chugging noise. Black coal-fired smoke and sparks shot out of the smokestack.

"Judge Douglas manages the fuss and feathers of campaigning as well as any man," remarked Anthony to Dietrich and Chapel. "I wish Mr. Lincoln showed his colors as well, but he's as plain as an old shoe."

"So now Mr. Lincoln's opposition to the Dred Scott decision means he is in favor of full Negro citizenship," said Dietrich. "That's a stronger charge than the judge has made before."

"According to the judge, Mr. Lincoln is now more than an Abolitionist," said Chapel. "He's an Immediatist, wanting slavery to vanish at once. In every speech the judge makes, Mr. Lincoln gets more radical and more dangerous."

"Where was Mr. Lincoln?" Dietrich asked Anthony.

"He was needed elsewhere," answered Anthony, looking away from the reporters. "He will speak this evening instead."

"Did you attend his answer when he said slavery could be excluded from a territory by local regulation if the residents opposed it?" asked Dietrich. "Doesn't that contradict the Dred Scott decision as much as anything Mr. Lincoln ever said?"

Chapel looked up from contemplating his muddy shoes. "I did attend to that."

Anthony said, "Judge Douglas has given those remarks before, but I do not think he has said that in the southern states."

"That would not pass muster in the south," said Chapel.

"Will Mr. Lincoln answer Judge Douglas's speech?" asked Dietrich, turning to Anthony.

"Mr. Lincoln will answer all the judge's challenges," said Anthony. "For your edification he shall provide you with the circumstances that he labors under in this election."

That evening Lincoln appeared well rested and calm as he started to speak.

"Another election is approaching and I believe the Republican Party will, without much difficulty, elect their state ticket. But in regard to the legislature, which, after the election, will vote upon who will be Senator from Illinois, we, the Republicans, labor under some disadvantages. In the first place, we have a legislature to elect based upon an apportionment made several years ago, when the population was far greater in the south than it is now. Our opponents hold almost entire sway in the south as we do in the north. In the year 1855, according to the law, a census was taken for the purpose of reapportionment of representation in the two branches of our state government. If fairly done, we would gain six to ten more members. Our opponents, holding control of both branches of the legislature, steadfastly refused to give us such an apportionment.

"There are one or two Democratic senators who will be members of the next legislature and who will vote for the election of senator, who are holding over in districts in which we would win, if we only had the chance. There are but twenty-five senators in all.

"There is still another disadvantage under which we labor. Senator Douglas is of worldwide renown. All anxious politicians of his party have been looking upon him certainly at no distant day to be president of the United States. They have seen in his round jolly, cheerful face jobs in post offices, land offices and cabinet appointments, and foreign missions, bursting and sprouting out in wonderful exuberance, ready to be laid hold of by their greedy hands."

Laughter rang out throughout the assembled throng as Lincoln pretended to snatch something from the air.

"We have to fight this battle upon principle, and upon principle alone. So I hope those with whom I am surrounded have principle enough to nerve themselves for the task and leave nothing undone that can fairly be done to bring about the right result.

"After Senator Douglas left Washington, he tarried a considerable time in the city of New York. Like another Napoleon, it was published in the Union that he was framing his plan of going to Illinois to pounce upon and annihilate the treasonable and disunion

79

speech which Lincoln made here on the sixteenth of June. I shall point out the main points.

"The first is popular sovereignty. It is to be labeled upon the cars in which he travels; put upon the hacks in which he rides; to be flaunted upon the arches he passes under, and the banners which wave over him. It is to be dished up in as many varieties as a French cook can produce soup from potatoes."

People applauded and laughed.

"If we examine only a very little, and do not allow ourselves to be misled, we shall be able to see that the whole thing is the most arrant quixotism that was ever enacted before a community. The judge is not sustaining popular sovereignty, but absolutely opposing it. He sustains the court decision that declares that the popular will of the territories has no constitutional power to exclude slavery during their entire territorial existence.

"Well, with so much being disposed of, what is left? Why, he is contending for the right of the people, when they come to make a state constitution, to make it for themselves, and precisely as best suits themselves. I declare that the judge can find no one to oppose him on that proposition. What is Judge Douglas going to spend his life for? Is he going to spend his life maintaining a principle that nobody on earth opposes?

"As to the Lecompton Constitution, Judge Douglas with the Republicans and some of the American Party had the argument against the administration. I wish to know what there is in the opposition of Judge Douglas to the Lecompton Constitution that entitles him to be considered the only opponent to it. I agree to the rightfulness of his opposition. In the House of Representatives, there were about twenty anti-Lecompton Democrats. It took one hundred and twenty to defeat the measure. Why is it that twenty shall be entitled to all the credit of doing that work, and the hundred none?"

The Lincoln supporters cheered.

"He says I have a proneness for quoting Scripture. If I should do so now, it occurs perhaps he places himself somewhat upon the ground of the parable of the lost sheep which went astray in the mountains, and when the owner of the hundred sheep found the one that was lost and threw it upon his shoulders and came home rejoicing, it was said that there was more rejoicing over the one sheep that was lost than over the ninety and nine in the fold.

"The application is made by the Savior in this parable thus, "Verily, I say unto you, there is more rejoicing in heaven over one sinner that repenteth, than over ninety and nine just persons that need no repentance. And now, if the judge claims the benefit of this parable, let him repent."

Lincoln's supporters hooted and laughed.

"When he was planning his campaign, Napoleon-like, in New York, he gave special attention to a speech of mine delivered here on the sixteenth of June. He charges in substance that I invite a war of sections, that I propose all local institutions of the different states shall become consolidated and uniform. I said in that speech that I believe this government cannot endure permanently half slave and half free. I simply expressed my expectation. Cannot the judge perceive the distinction between a purpose and an expectation? I have often expressed an expectation to die, but I have never expressed a wish to die."

Members of the audience laughed and applauded.

"Now, as to the Dred Scott decision, I am opposed to the decision in a certain sense, but not in the sense in which he puts it. I say that in so far as it decided in favor of Dred Scott's master and against Dred Scott and his family, I do not propose to disturb the decision. I reminded him of a Supreme Court decision which he opposed for at least several years. I shall read from a letter written by Mr. Jefferson in 1820: 'You seem in pages eighty four and one hundred eighty six to consider the judges as the ultimate arbiters of all constitutional questions — a very dangerous doctrine indeed and one which would put us under the despotism of an oligarchy. Our judges are as honest as other men, not more so. They have, with others, the same passions for party, for power, and the privilege of their corps. Their power is more dangerous as they are in office for life. The Constitution has more wisely made all departments co-equal and co-sovereign within themselves.' I am sustained by Mr. Jefferson.

"The plain truth is this: Judge Douglas is for Supreme Court

81

decisions when he likes them and against them when he does not like them. He says this Dred Scott case is a very small matter at most — that it has no practical effect; it is but an abstraction. I submit the proposition that the thing which determines whether a man is free or a slave is rather concrete than abstract. I think you would conclude that it was if your liberty depended on it, and so would Judge Douglas if his liberty depended on it.

"One more thing. Judge Douglas has tormented himself with horrors about my disposition to make Negroes perfectly equal with white men in social and political relations. He did not stop to show that I have said any such thing. I adhere to the Declaration of Independence. If Judge Douglas and his friends are not willing to stand by it, let them come up and amend it. Let them make it read that all men are created equal except Negroes. Last week he said it meant only that Americans in America were equal to Englishmen in England. Then, when I pointed out to him that by that rule he excludes the Germans, the Irish, the Portuguese and all other people who have come here since the revolution, he reconstructed his construction. He tells us now that it means Europeans.

"I now press him a little further, and ask if it meant to exclude the Russians in Asia? Or does he mean to exclude that vast population from the principles of the Declaration of Independence? I expect ere long he will introduce another amendment to his definition."

Lincoln paused to let the applause recede.

"I have said that I do not understand the Declaration to mean that all men were created equal in all respects; but I suppose that it does mean that all men are equal in some respects; they are equal in their right to 'life, liberty and the pursuit of happiness.' Certainly the Negro is not our equal in color — perhaps not in many other respects. Still, in the right to put into his mouth the bread that his own hands have earned, he is the equal of every other man, white or black. In pointing out that more has been given you, you cannot be justified in taking away that little that has been given him. All I ask for the Negro is that if you do not like him, let him alone. If God gave him but little, that little let him enjoy."

The people in the audience stood and applauded. Nice cheers

82

were raised to Lincoln.

Anthony turned to Chapel and Dietrich. He was almost glowing with happiness.

"There you see the candidate," said Dietrich.

"It was a good speech," conceded Chapel.

"One of his best," agreed Dietrich, smiling.

"He did not cover another disadvantage," said Anthony. "On election day you will see trains full of the Irish pulling in and pouring them out to vote Democrat. They ship them in from out of state. It happens every time."

Anthony shook his head. "At times he is too high minded for his own good."

CHAPTER ELEVEN

August 1, 1858
Springfield, Illinois

Dietrich and Chapel were sitting on the front porch at the Myers and Caldwell Boarding House, drinking beer and arguing good naturedly about whether Lincoln or Douglas would benefit most from the newly announced debates between them when Tom Edwards appeared. He was carrying a letter.

"Gentlemen, I am the bearer of glad tidings. Hannah Armstrong has acceded to your request for an interview. I gather from the tone of the reply that she had doubts and sought the counsel of others before agreeing to see you."

"Hallelujah," shouted Chapel, almost spilling his beer. "I had lost hope in the enterprise entirely."

"Oh, ye of little faith," responded Edwards. "She has some reservations still and she makes some requirements, but I feel certain that two fine gentlemen of the press like you can allay her concerns."

Dietrich drained the last of his beer and asked, "What are her conditions?"

Edwards opened the paper and read, "She asks that you come to her farm within the next week while her son, Duff, is away helping his brother construct a new barn. She asks that you do not contact him directly. She wants my assurance that you are not interested in assailing Duff or Mr. Lincoln in the newspapers but are only interested in finding out what occurred at the trial."

Chapel said, "I give you my word, sir…."

Edwards waved Chapel's statement away. "I feel quite certain of your honesty, of the honesty of both of you, or I would never have agreed to contact Hannah. Please do not think that you purchased my assistance at the cost of one dinner."

Dietrich answered, "We did not think that."

"Of course, if you choose to invite me to a celebratory repast, I would feel bound to accept."

"My editor would roast me over a red-hot fire before he'd approve another expenditure of the magnitude incurred at the Illinois Hotel," said Dietrich. "However, I believe that I can persuade him to cover the cost of a libation at Key's Tavern."

The next morning on the train to Petersburg, Dietrich noted that Chapel was unusually quiet and withdrawn.

"Is something wrong?" asked Dietrich.

Chapel hesitated before replying. "I got a letter from my editor. He praised my coverage of Judge Douglas's speech in Springfield."

"That makes you glum?" asked Dietrich. "Heaven forefend that he should give you a raise, then."

"Oh, there is very little chance of that," said Chapel, smiling despite himself. "It is just that he commented on my writing that Judge Douglas stated that slavery would not flourish where the majority of citizens oppose it. He asked me to listen with particular attention for other such remarks. He wrote that Judge Douglas has not been forthcoming with such remarks in southern states."

"Anthony said as much at the time," answered Dietrich.

"Yet, I also recall that Woodward, the editor of the Chicago Sun, said that the Democrats are the only national party," said Chapel. "If we Southerners reject Judge Douglas on the basis that he says there are any kind of limitations on slavery, then all political parties will be regional and we will have no national consensus of any sort."

Dietrich nodded, "That could end in a war of sections, like Judge Douglas talks about."

"I can not refrain from reporting what is said," Chapel mused. "Even if I did, others would report it. I do not regret writing the truth, but I worry about what the effect of writing the truth may ultimately be."

"I share your concern. However, what people choose to do about what we report is the responsibility, I believe, of those who take action. I would not ignite a war of sections, and I know you would not either. Like you, I am sadly coming to believe that a war is more likely. Perhaps our reporting will inform the public mind about the risk. At least I pray it is so."

CHAPTER TWELVE

August 3, 1858
On the road to Petersburg, Illinois

With delays and changing between trains, it took two days before the men arrived in Petersburg. Renting a buggy and getting directions to the Armstrong farm from suspicious local people took longer than either man anticipated. They rented a room at the local hotel and resolved to set off in the morning. While eating supper in the dining room, Chapel and Dietrich were approached by a broad-shouldered man with brown hair and a long oval face with a sharp nose. He walked decisively to the table and stopped.

"Would you care to join us, sir?" asked Chapel.

The man pulled out a chair and sat down.

"You look like a scrapper," he said, tilting his head as he looked at Dietrich.

"I can be when the need arises," answered Dietrich.

"I heard you was a Dutchman," said the man.

"I'm guessing that you are one of the Armstrong family," said Dietrich.

"Got it in one shot," agreed the man. "I'm Jacob. I'm here to see why it is that you want to bother my mother. She's been through a lot, what with the trial and my father dying and all. You want to stir up memories that I'd just as soon were left alone."

Dietrich and Chapel looked at one another.

"It's not our intention to bother your mother," stated Chapel.

"You could leave her alone, then," snapped Armstrong.

Dietrich spoke slowly: "It is an imposition, I know. We may stir painful memories, much as we would try not to. We are reporters, and we are investigating stories about Mr. Lincoln and his defense of your brother. Mr. Lincoln is becoming a known man around the country. It is understandable that our respective readers are curious about him. We mean no harm to your mother and we mean no harm to your brother's reputation. We only want to know what happened."

"It appears that Mr. Lincoln conducted a remarkable defense," said Chapel. "Your brother was acquitted."

"It's not remarkable to get an innocent man off," Armstrong said, frowning.

"But another man was convicted and sent to hard labor," said Dietrich.

"I reckon he was not innocent," Armstrong responded.

"Were you present at the altercation?" asked Chapel.

Armstrong shook his head. "I was at the revival, where Duff should have been. Had I been present at the horse races, Duff would not have been involved in a fight."

"Your mother has agreed to see us," said Chapel. "I regret the discord that we may cause your family and I respect your efforts to protect it, but we will, with her consent, speak to Hannah Armstrong."

Armstrong put his hands on the tabletop. They looked gigantic. His fingers were scarred and slightly gnarled.

"Would you tussle with me for the privilege?" asked Armstrong.

Dietrich put out his hands. They looked strong and massive. "If it were necessary, I would. But Mrs. Armstrong has freely given her permission, so it is not necessary. Tomorrow, if you like, we will travel with you. If you do not like, we will travel without you. Either way, we will meet with your mother and talk with her. I hope you choose to guide us there."

Armstrong studied Dietrich's hands.

"The Bible warns us about scribes," said Armstrong. "I do not approve, but I admit that it is not my place to approve or to disapprove. I will meet you here at daybreak. Be ready then, or I will leave you behind."

Armstrong pushed his chair back and rose to his feet. He stood for a moment glowering in silence and then walked off.

The countryside around Petersburg had farms with neat fields, well-maintained fences and sturdy comfortable-looking houses. The animals looked healthy, and most gardens had flowers as well as tidy rows of tomatoes, corn and beans. Hannah Armstrong's farm was in no way remarkable. Clean clothing and quilts hung from lines in the sunlight. At Armstrong's direction, Dietrich unhitched the horse from the buggy and led it into a stall in the barn. Chapel brought a bucket of water from the well to let the horse drink.

"It appears you two have done honest work at some time in your lives," commented Armstrong as he led the men toward the house.

Chapel and Dietrich nodded but did not reply.

"I'm here with the two strangers," called Armstrong as he approached the steps at the porch.

"Invite them in," came the response.

Armstrong pulled the door open and motioned for Dietrich and Chapel to go inside. Chapel and Dietrich doffed their hats as they entered. The front room of the house was simple but clean. Hannah was dressed in a gingham dress and a white apron. She nodded pleasantly.

Chapel made a shallow bow. "If I may, Ma'am, my name is Thaddeus Chapel and this is August Dietrich. We are very much obliged to you for seeing us."

Hannah Armstrong had her grey hair pulled back. Although her face was wrinkled, her features were strong and well formed. Her back was straight and she looked at the men with clear brown eyes.

"I thank you, sirs, for responding to my invitation so promptly," said Hannah in a strong voice. "I needed persuasion to see you, but I have been advised that you are honest men, not out to take advantage of a simple farm woman. I pray that is so. Foolishly perhaps, I will trust you not to seek out William, my son. He had a hard time and I will not have him further troubled by these tragic events."

"On my honor," said Chapel, putting his hand over his heart. "I swear that we will not seek him out."

Hannah looked at Dietrich, who nodded his agreement.

"I'm so nervous that I am forgetting my manners," said Hannah. "Please, gentlemen, sit down. Can I offer you coffee? How about you, Jacob?"

Dietrich and Chapel wisely accepted her offer. Hannah bustled into the kitchen and returned, using her apron to protect her hands as she carried hot cups to the men. Chapel and Dietrich commented on the neatness of the house and the beauty of the flowers in the garden to put Hannah at ease. Hannah declined any praise for herself but proudly told the men that her sons kept the farm in good shape and looked after her well following the death of her husband. Jacob eased into a chair at the edge of the room and fell silent, watching but making no comment. Finally, Hannah brought up the trial.

"Jack and I were shocked when Duff was arrested," said Hannah. "We knew from the way he acted that something bad had happened at Walker's Grove, but we had no idea that Press had been killed. How terrible for his wife and children."

Hannah shook her head sadly. "We went down to Havana for the grand jury. I had never been there before. I was surprised by how pretty it was along the river there, not that I had much leisure for such. The sheriff told us that Duff should have a lawyer. Local folks thought highly of old Mr. Dilworth and his partner Mr. Campbell, so we hired them. I didn't understand it all, but they tried to get the charges thrown off for one reason or another. The judge would not have it. They did get the trial moved away from Press's angry neighbors and they got the whole trial delayed."

"From what happened in the Norris trial, that was a help to your son," said Chapel.

Hannah sighed, "I hate to think badly of any man. The Norris family is suffering just as much as Press's. But it appeared to me that he killed Press. His lawyer was little more than a boy. He did not think to get things moved or delayed."

Hannah's eyes filled with tears.

"It was after we got back from Havana that Jack really started to fail. He had been feeling poorly before that, but the sight of his first-born son in jail hit him hard."

Hannah smoothed her apron with her hands.

"As a young man, Jack was handsome and strong. We girls all set our caps for him, whether or not we would admit it. Unlike some, I knew he would be a good provider and a good father. Underneath the bluster that he wore like a coat, I could tell that he had a heart of gold."

89

Hannah smiled. Her eyes were focused on something far away that nobody else could see.

"He used to say he had the strongest team, the best tracking hound, the fastest horse and the prettiest wife in the county. When other men came to the region, it was Jack who took their measure. He was never bested. Until Mr. Lincoln came, he was never matched."

Dietrich opened his mouth, but a look from Chapel silenced him.

"Where have the years gone? I'm left an old woman and a widow alone. It seems like only yesterday that Jack came courting and my mother chased him away, saying I was too young. How I cried then. But Jack waited for me."

Hannah looked at the reporters.

"You are kind to listen to a lonely old woman and her memories," Hannah said, smiling at Dietrich and Chapel. "It makes me sad, but it makes me happy, too, to remember. Jack remained a powerfully strong man physically even as he started to fail. He begged me not to let Duff hang. He forced me to promise I would contact Mr. Lincoln and ask him for help, regardless of the cost. Finally, just to quiet his mind, I assured him that I would."

"You had to be persuaded," said Dietrich softly.

"I did," said Hannah, nodding. "I remembered how much the lawyers in Havana charged. Mr. Lincoln was much bigger than they were, and I could only guess at how much he would charge. Besides, he was going to run for the senate. Everybody said so. Would he even remember simple people like Jack and me? If he did, would he have time to help us, even if he was willing? If he did and he would, how ever could we pay his fees?"

"You had your doubts," said Chapel.

"Yes," said Hannah, nodding again. "I had my doubts. In the end, I had to promise Jack that I would mortgage the farm if need be. He could not rest easy in his mind worrying about Duff. It is a terrible thing for a parent to contemplate the death of a child. As strong as he was physically, Jack could not face that. I did not want to make the promise, but, in the end, I had to."

Dietrich commented, "You eased your husband's last days."

"I knew his time was coming," said Hannah, looking off into the distance. "Like always, once set in his mind, Jack could not be moved. I could never deny that man anything. Like many times before, my fears were groundless and Jack's trust was sound. After Jack passed on to heaven, I had my neighbor write to Tom Edwards. I soon got back a letter from Mr. Lincoln, inviting me to Springfield and assuring me that he would do all he could. Jack's heart was wiser than my head. Tom told me that Mr. Lincoln would not charge me."

Hannah leaned toward the reporters. "I think Tom had it in mind to pay Mr. Lincoln from his own money. Mr. Lincoln would not even discuss the matter with me."

"You met him in Springfield," ventured Dietrich.

"Yes," agreed Hannah. "I told him what little bit I could and he asked me many questions I could not answer. Then he bought me lunch at a very fancy hotel where Tom Edwards works and told me he would do all that he could. I heard Mr. Lincoln spent quite some time in the countryside around Walker's Grove, but he did not stop by. There was supposed to be a trial. The attorney trying to put my son in prison heard that Mr. Lincoln would oppose him. Then that attorney got the judge to delay things. Duff was upset, not wanting to be in jail so long, but I got a note from Mr. Lincoln saying that Duff was safe enough where he was and that the delay just gave Mr. Lincoln more time to prepare for the trial. He told me he would do everything that he could."

She had a faraway look in her eyes as she continued.

"Finally the trial came," said Hannah. "I didn't know whether I should be glad it was finally going to happen or be sad and scared about the climax. Mr. Lincoln promised me he would not let Duff hang. They had a lot of fuss over who could be on the jury. That took longer than the trial."

"What happened at the trial?" asked Dietrich.

"There were lots of questions and answers," said Hannah. "I did not understand the half of it. It was like a tug of war with each side pulling its hardest. First one side was ahead and then the other side came back. Just when I thought I could not stand it any more, they stopped for dinner. I waited outside. Mr. Lincoln came to see me and told me Duff would be set free. After dinner they all talked some more. Finally, the jury told Duff he could come home."

Hannah dabbed at her eyes with her apron.

"After the trial I talked to Mr. Lincoln and thanked him for giving my son back to me. I asked him again about his fee and he told me sternly never to mention it to him again. He said he hoped Duff had learned his lesson and would stay away from drink and fighting. He warned me that, although Duff got to come home this time, it could never be done again. Duff must stay away from trouble, for nobody would forget that Press had died."

Hannah looked at Chapel and Dietrich squarely. "He gave me my boy back, Mr. Lincoln did. I don't know how and I don't know if anybody else could have. I don't think so, though. Now, I hope you gentlemen do not use what I told you to do Mr. Lincoln a disservice. He is much respected in these parts and I would sorely regret if I was the cause of any harm to him."

Chapel and Dietrich exchanged a look.

"All that you have told us adds credit to Mr. Lincoln," said Chapel. "I promise you that nothing you have said is in any way a detriment to him."

Jacob accompanied the men outside to see them on their way. He helped them harness their horse to the buggy and reminded them of the way back into town. He stood and watched for as long as they were in sight.

Dietrich held the reins easily in his hands as he spoke. "I would say that Mr. Lincoln showed admirable loyalty to his old friends."

"True enough," answered Chapel. "I would say that he had a powerful reason to get Duff off, regardless of what it took to achieve an acquittal."

CHAPTER THIRTEEN

August 8, 1858
Havana, Illinois

Sheriff I.F. West of Mason County was a short man with unremarkable features who prided himself on controlling his temper under aggravating circumstances. It was, he thought, the lot of the lawman that law-abiding citizens were uncomfortable in his presence and law breakers naturally saw no reason to treat him with the respect that all men deserve. He had been involved in many strained conversations in the past, but none had been like this. The two men before him — one obviously a Southern dandy and the other clearly a Dutchman and an immigrant — were testing his patience beyond all reason.

"I don't see what good it will do to rake the ashes of that dead fire," groused West. "The less said the better for all concerned, as far as I can see."

Chapel and Dietrich shrugged.

"We don't mean to stir up old antagonisms," explained Chapel. "We are interested in Mr. Lincoln and his conduct in the trial. He is becoming a person of national interest, and his lawyering will interest our respective readers."

"Hannah Armstrong approves of your digging around," stated West, drumming his fingers on his desk. "You are certain of that? It would not do to try to deceive me."

"Yes, sir," answered Dietrich. "We have spoken to Mrs. Armstrong and we have her blessing, so to speak."

"I don't suppose Mrs. Metzker has a say in this," said West. "She and Mrs. Norris are two people that I don't see any reason to disturb. Would the two of you agree?"

"Certainly, Sheriff," said Chapel. "Both women, along with Hannah Armstrong, suffered the consequences of the actions of others. I imagine that is often the case in such affairs."

West regarded the men. "You imagine rightly. Very well. I will loan you Deputy Starks for the day. He was part of the investigation and is well acquainted with what happened. If you have questions for me at the end, I will do my best to answer them. If you plan to talk to anyone else around here, I would appreciate it if you would let me know."

Seeing the looks on the faces of Dietrich and Chapel, West added, "I do not plan to hinder your investigation, gentlemen. I just like to know what is going on in my jurisdiction that might result in trouble. This might cause trouble and I would like to be prepared for it."

Deputy Gabriel Starks proved to be the physical opposite of Sheriff West. Starks was a tall, muscular man with abundant wavy blond hair and blue eyes.

"Deputy, what are you working on at the moment?"

"Nothing I cannot postpone," replied Starks.

"Good. Then I would like you to take these two reporters to Walker's Grove and show them where Metzker got himself killed," West said. "Show them anything they want to see and answer any questions they have."

Starks did not appear distressed or surprised by the assignment given him by the sheriff. "Gentlemen, do you have mounts of your own or do we need to find some for you?"

"We were using a buggy rented from the livery stable," answered Dietrich.

"Horses would be better," said Starks.

"The hostler will rent you horses that Mrs. Metzker is aiming to sell," said West. "She'd get a little money, and the horses could use the work."

"Metzker certainly won't mind," said Starks.

The hostler led a leggy roan mare with white stockings and a bay mare with a strong physique out of the barn. He tied the horses to the top outside rail of the corral and left the tack near the horses.

Dietrich approached the bay, which looked uneasily at him with the white of her eye showing. He spoke softly to the horse in German and moved slowly but steadily as he put the saddle blanket and then the saddle on her back. He cinched the saddle tightly and then waited patiently. At last the horse had to exhale and Dietrich quickly tightened the strap under her belly an additional four notches.

"It's a nice trick," said Dietrich to the horse. "You breathe in deeply when I start to tighten the trap under your belly. Later, when you breathe out, the saddle slides around and you dump me to the ground. Lucky for me and unlucky for you, I've seen that trick before."

Dietrich adjusted the stirrups and swung up easily into the saddle.

Chapel's horse did not resist him putting on the saddle. However, when he put one foot in the saddle, she sidestepped. Chapel completed his mount in one movement, pulling strongly with his arms. He slipped his foot into the other stirrup and was solidly mounted. The roan spun in a circle and bucked half-heartedly before settling down. Chapel rode as if he were part of the horse.

"The sheriff was right," said Chapel. "These horses do need to be ridden."

Starks, who had been watching from atop his horse, led them out of town at a lope. Once outside of town, Chapel gave his horse her head and allowed her to run. They came pounding back the other direction and then settled into a steady trot.

"She is one sweet animal," said Chapel. "I have a stallion back home I could breed her with. If I lived in these parts, I would inquire about buying her."

"Deputy Starks, you could have told us about the tricks these horses play before we got on them," said Dietrich.

"I could have," agreed Starks.

Within an hour, Starks, Chapel and Dietrich reached Walker's Grove. At the reporters' request, Starks used a stick to sketch a rough map of the area in the dirt.

"The race track was here," said Starks, pointing with the stick. "That area is flat and the ground is soft but not muddy. It's easy on the horses' hoofs. There is a hill close by so everybody can watch the races from along the track or from a higher vantage on the hill. The sutlers' wagons were located in a semicircle on higher ground. None were closer than half a mile from the revival. That's the law and it is enforced. Scattered around them, in no particular order, men pitched tents or built temporary wooden shelters. A few were for rent, but most were personal."

"And the fight?" asked Dietrich, peering at the map.

"That took place close to the sutler's wagon at the top of a hill over here."

"I would like to see that area in detail," said Chapel.

"Fair enough," answered Starks. "I suggest we walk there from here so you get a feel for the lay of the land."

Starks, Dietrich and Chapel led their horses up a gradual incline, over the hilltop and then up another slight incline.

"The wagon was there at the top," said Starks, pointing. "That's the highest point in this area so even the drunks could see it and find their way there. Besides, some men work up a thirst walking uphill."

They continued, this time heading downhill.

"The witnesses were between the wagon up there and the flat place at the bottom of the hill," said Starks, indicating a large open space.

"Did the men camp on the side of the hill?" asked Dietrich, stopping to survey the area.

"A few men did, but not many," said Starks, giving the reins he held one sharp pull downward. "Not many men want to sleep on the side of a hill. There were campfires around, and the area at the bottom is a known local scuffle ground. The men not passed out from drink and not yet asleep gathered here, expecting some entertainment."

"Did they expect that Norris and Armstrong would take on Metzker?" asked Chapel quickly.

"A good question," commented Starks. " I asked that myself. According to everyone I spoke with, there was no particular expectation who would be in the tussle. Several men told me that they had noticed Metzker acting like the bull of the herd. They more than halfway thought someone would try to pin his ears back."

"This hillside reminds me of the remains of a Roman amphitheater I saw in France," said Dietrich. "Everyone has a view of the action even without being close."

"How close were the witnesses?" asked Chapel.

"Another good question," said Starks. "I asked that also. The closest person said he was about twenty yards away."

"But he said he could see clearly?" asked Dietrich.

Starks nodded, "He said the moon was bright, almost overhead and nearly full. He said he saw the entire action. The witness said Armstrong confronted Metzker face to face. He said he saw Norris open the ball with a vicious strike with a wooden club to the back of Metzker's head. The witness stated that Norris came from behind Metzker and that Metzker never saw him coming. The witness reckoned that Armstrong hit Metzker with a slungshot after the blow from Norris."

Chapel and Dietrich stared at the scuffle ground, trying to imagine what had happened there.

"It would have been over almost as soon as it started," said Starks. He shook his head. "If they had waited until morning or until they sobered up, it would never have happened. Two families would have fathers at home, a mother wouldn't be worried, and there would have been one less widow in the world."

"Can we go down to the bottom?" asked Dietrich.

"At your service," answered Starks with a slight bow.

Starks showed the reporters where he thought the fight took place.

"Remember I did not see it myself so I could be off to some extent. We found the slungshot right about here."

Chapel and Dietrich placed themselves and Starks in the positions of Norris, Metzker and Armstrong. They alternated in the three positions. Chapel and Dietrich also took turns and climbed the hill to the approximate location of the witnesses and peered at the other two men who pretended to fight.

On the way back to Havana, they discussed what they had learned.

"The witnesses were not close and they had to look through the trees to see," said Dietrich.

"But there would have been fewer leaves on the trees than there are now," said Chapel. Also, the witnesses all agreed that the moon was bright that night."

Starks remained silent.

"It strikes me that instead of a Roman amphitheater, that ground became a Greek theater where the tragedy was played out," said Chapel.

Dietrich and Chapel turned the horses in and paid the fees. They thanked Starks for his help and headed back to the hotel.

Starks returned to the sheriff's office.

"What did you think of those two?" Sheriff West asked Starks.

Starks leaned against the wall of the office and considered. "Good horsemen, especially the Southerner. They appear intelligent enough, although not experienced in looking over the scene of a crime. They asked good questions. They could learn to be lawmen with a little work."

West looked out the window. "It took the three of you long enough."

Starks threw back his head and laughed. "Long enough? You must have forgotten what happened when Old Abe Lincoln came here. He asked so many questions that I can't even remember all of them. These men only wanted to go out once. Mr. Lincoln had me out there time and again and at all hours. He pure wore me out chasing up and down the hills. Those long legs of his covered ground a lot easier than mine did."

CHAPTER FOURTEEN

August 10, 1858
Havana, Illinois

Chapel and Dietrich knocked on the office door that bore the inscription "Walker and Lacey Attorneys At Law." They heard muffled sounds and a scraping noise before a high-pitched voice with a Southern accent called out, "Enter, please."

Inside, the office was small, narrow and deep. An unwashed window let in light over a small bookshelf overflowing with books. Two tables were nearly completely covered in neat piles of paper. There was a wooden chair by each table.

A man about Chapel's size and build was seated at the far desk. He was writing on a parchment with orderly swift strokes of his pen. Chapel and Dietrich paused to size him up. The man had on a starched white shirt but no collar. His sleeves were rolled up. When he looked up, they could see that he had an unlined face and an open countenance. His hazel eyes were smiling and his auburn hair was neatly combed and cut short.

"I must apologize once more for disobliging you," he said in a soft drawl. "I know you have been patiently endeavoring to meet with me for some time. Unfortunately, I have been busier than a one-armed wallpaper hanger. And that is unlikely to change soon."

The man sat back abruptly. "I am forgetting my manners. My parents would be mortified and my old mammy would haul me off by my ears if they saw this. We have not even been properly introduced, and here I am prattling away about my problems."

He stood and bowed slightly. "I am William Walker, attorney at law, and I am, however briefly, at your service."

"I am Thaddeus Chapel," replied Chapel, matching Walker's bow. "May I present my colleague and associate August Dietrich."

Dietrich started to put out his hand and then dropped it to his side when he saw that Walker was not paying attention to him.

"As you know, we are reporters who are interested in talking with you about the Norris and Armstrong trials and about Mr. Lincoln's role in them," said Chapel.

Walker resumed his seat. "Mr. Lincoln had no role at all in Jimmy Norris's trial; more's the pity. He was the leading counsel in the Duff Armstrong trial and I merely observed. Part of the reason I have been so confounded busy is that I am helping to organize his political appearance in town, which will occur shortly."

"You are a supporter of Mr. Lincoln?" asked Chapel. "From your speech and the mention of your mammy, I thought you might be a Douglas man."

"I might have been and was," answered Walker. "However, that was before I had the distinct pleasure of working personally with Mr. Lincoln. Oh, it is not wholly a personal matter, although I am pleased to count myself in that legion of young lawyers who benefited from his personal kindness and instruction. When I took the time to study on his ideas and principles, I surprised myself by finding that I could not in good conscience oppose them. Have you met him and spoken with him?"

"I have," said Chapel.

"Then you know that he can challenge a man's thinking without giving offense or contention."

"In fact I can personally attest to what you say."

"If I may ask, would you be willing to talk to us about the trial?" asked Dietrich.

"Willing, I am," answered Walker, "but my time is grievously short at this juncture. I have to file these papers by noon. Then, I have a meeting on preparations for the speech. I urge you gentlemen to attend the speech. I can give you half an hour's time now. I could be more forthcoming after Mr. Lincoln departs from this area of the state, if you could manage to wait so long and if you are willing to tolerate my rude behavior."

"Agreed," said Dietrich. "We have talked with Hannah Armstrong. We were shown the scuffle ground by Deputy Starks. I would like to hear about the indictment and the trial of Jimmy Norris."

"You mention the two together," said Walker. "They happened nearly together. The grand jury read out the indictment. I have a copy here somewhere if you need it."

"Thank you, no," replied Dietrich. "We have a copy."

"They read out the indictment and I knew that trials of the accused would be forthcoming. It was a certain thing. The whole community had been buzzing about what happened. Mr. Dilworth, representing Duff Armstrong, prepared a motion to quash the indictment. He was kind enough to ask for my assistance in reviewing the motion before it was presented, although it was clear that he had done a better job than I could have. He brought up ten points. Seven were technical, and three were about the merits of the case."

Dietrich pulled out his notebook and began to write.

"I will not bore you with the legal technicalities," said Walker, "but I will recount the arguments on the merits of the case. First, he argued that the head wounds Press Metzker received were not adequately described. Second, he contended that the indictment did not specify whether or not the two men acted in concert. Third, he argued that it was not stated which of the two wounds actually caused the death of Press Metzker. It was a well-reasoned and well-written document. Of course, it had no realistic chance of approval, and the judge rejected it without comment. Part of an attorney's role is to attempt every means of protecting a client, however unlikely the means is to succeed."

Walker hesitated.

"Following the unsuccessful attempt to have the indictment quashed, didn't Mr. Dilworth ask for a delay and a change of venue?" asked Chapel.

Walker glanced down at his desk. "He did. I did not. Foolishly, I might add. My only excuse, and I own it is a poor one, is that Jimmy Norris wanted to get the business over with. Due to my inexperience, I did not wholly recognize the importance of the matter. The prosecutor, Joseph Harding, played successfully upon my youth and naiveté."

Dietrich pointed to the door. "But you are the senior partner. Your name appears first."

Walker gave a shaky laugh. "When Mr. Lacey and I were enrolled as attorneys, we each had prospects to enter into practice under the tutelage of an experienced attorney until we learned the ropes. However, we soon discovered that we both had prospects with the same attorney. In fact, the man had barely enough business to feed himself. He simply found it easier to allow each of us to imagine that we could work with him than to disappoint our expectations. Mr. Lacey then proposed that, instead of starving separately and competing between us for the dregs of local legal business, we should combine our meager talents and starve together, splitting whatever fees we could scrape up. He suggested that, having a name earlier in the alphabet, his should be listed first. I contended that, being by far the more handsome of the two of us, my name should be listed first. In the end, we flipped a coin to determine who could choose the leading name. Mr. Lacey won and promptly picked my name as the senior."

Chapel and Dietrich laughed.

"You will understand that the defense of a man who attacked and killed a popular member of the community by sneaking up behind him and clubbing him to death was not a highly sought-after prize in the local legal fraternity," said Walker. "Remuneration for defending those unable to pay for their own defense is quite minimal. My firm was chosen when no other could be compelled to participate. Because, as you say, my name was first on the door, I was given the assignment. My skills were not up to the task, albeit given the evidence and the popular feeling against poor Norris, I am not certain that a more skilled lawyer would have done substantially better."

Walker grimaced.

"One day after the indictment, the venire men were called and selection of the jury began. I was able to exclude relatives of the victim, but I allowed a number of his friends to serve, not thinking to exclude them. The prosecutor, Mr. Harding, called only five witnesses: Grigsby Metzker, brother of the deceased; three of his friends who had witnessed the fatal assault — Charles Allen, William Killion and James Walker; and a medical expert, Doctor B. F. Stephenson."

Chapel and Dietrich started writing in their notebooks.

"Can you spell the names of the witnesses?" asked Dietrich.

Walker complied with his request.

"Grigsby and his friends all testified that they saw Norris attack Metzker from behind with a club. They claimed they stood forty feet away or so. I challenged them on standing farther back, but they all said the moon was bright enough that, even at eleven at night, they could see clearly. A check of the almanac for that date showed that they were correct. Charles Allen said he stood closer than the rest. I challenged the witnesses about having been drunk, but they denied it. Mr. Allen, in particular, said he had drunk very little. Mr. Allen was a very credible witness. The doctor testified that the posterior head wound could have been fatal by itself. I got them to admit that Metzker had been bothering Norris, but that is about all I accomplished with the prosecution witnesses."

Chapel looked up from writing and said, "I don't know what else you could have done. Perhaps you are being too hard on yourself."

"You have yet not heard about the so-called defense," Walker said. "I could not find any defense witnesses so, in desperation, I put Norris on the stand to defend himself. He admitted fighting with Norris, but claimed he used only his fists. Even I did not believe that. He talked about Metzker starting the fight earlier and that might have helped a little bit. Then came the cross examination."

Walker remained silent for some moments.

"The prosecutor, Mr. Harding, started by saying to Norris, 'This is not the first man you have killed, is it?' I should have been on my feet objecting, but I was so surprised that I just sat there. He got in more information. Unknown to me, some years ago Norris had been in a fight in which a man died. He was tried and acquitted by claiming self-defense. The jury should never have been allowed to hear about it because Norris was acquitted. According to the law, Norris should be considered innocent. It had nothing to do with the current case, and as soon as I objected, the judge told the prosecutor he had to stop talking about it. Of course, by then, it was too late. You cannot unring a bell. The judge told the jurors to completely disregard the remarks. Naturally, they could not. Mr. Harding made Norris sound like a liar, which he probably was. The jury scarcely left the room before deciding that Norris was guilty. Fortunately, they found him guilty of manslaughter and not murder so he did not hang. No thanks to me."

Walker looked off into space. Chapel and Dietrich looked at each other.

"Mr. Walker, with the evidence against him, the finding of guilty was a foregone conclusion. Whatever mistakes you made from inexperience, you convinced the jury that he was somewhat provoked and they took that into consideration," said Dietrich.

Walker looked at Dietrich and smiled grimly. "Thank you for your kind thoughts, but I know I failed to defend my client adequately."

"Could we talk about Mr. Lincoln's defense of Duff?" asked Chapel. "It appears that Duff was in much the same circumstance as Norris, but Mr. Lincoln got him off."

"Gentlemen, I think this might be a good time to end our present discussion. My involvement with Mr. Lincoln and Duff Armstrong would take some time to discuss, and, regretfully, time is what I have little of at this moment. Can we reconvene after the speeches scheduled for the next week in this area? I will be better able to satisfy you then."

"You've been more than generous with us, Mr. Walker," said Chapel with a slight bow. "With your consent we will meet again."

Chapel and Dietrich moved toward the door.

"I have one thing more to say," said Walker with a half smile. "When you think about the two trials and the two different verdicts, remember Duff Armstrong had a much better lawyer than Jimmy Norris did."

CHAPTER FIFTEEN

August 17, 1858
Havana, Illinois

Chapel and Dietrich knocked on the door of Walker's office. A hoarse and tired voice called out, "Enter at your own risk."

When the reporters walked in, they found Walker in a very different state than they had seen him last. He was unshaved and his hair was mussed. The suit he wore was wrinkled and dirty. Walker was slumped in his chair. A half-empty bottle of whiskey and a glass with a splash of whiskey in it sat on his desk.

"Gentlemen!" called out Walker. "I say to meet me in a week and here you are. You are veritable bulldogs and I commend you." He saluted the reporters.

"I know I must look a sight," Walker chuckled.

"Obviously we have come at a bad time, sir. Let us retire and meet another time," said Chapel.

"No, no," said Walker. "Come in and pull up a chair. I invited you, gentlemen, and I must act the gracious host."

Walker poured whiskey into the glass and sipped it. "May I offer a libation to you? There must be glasses around here somewhere."

Dietrich spied glasses on a bookshelf and brought two of them to the desk. Chapel and Dietrich pulled chairs over toward Walker.

"Did you hear the speeches?" asked Walker. "Wasn't Mr. Lincoln wonderful? You can see why the Little Giant does not want to debate him any more than he has to."

Dietrich leaned forward and answered, "His speech on the Declaration of Independence was truly remarkable."

Walker took another sip and motioned with his other hand. "Did you know that, when I first saw Mr. Lincoln, he was dressed like I am now? His suit looked like he had slept in it. Later, I learned that he actually had. His eyes were red from the lack of sleep and he had not shaved in days. He was not drinking whiskey, of course, but even Mr. Lincoln is not perfect."

Chapel and Dietrich laughed politely.

"He was in a state," continued Walker. "He told me that he accepted the defense of Duff Armstrong only to discover that he had a bare ten days to prepare. I was able to give him my detailed notes about the Norris trial and he had a four-page summary that had been prepared for the Cass County prosecutor. In great detail, he led me through all I could remember of the testimony that had condemned Jimmy Norris. He took notes at points I could not fathom. Then he rushed out of my office saying he had to locate defense witnesses. Defense witnesses to what, I could not imagine."

Walker took another sip of whiskey.

"Out of curiosity, I showed up in the courtroom at Beardstown on the day the trial was to begin. There was Mr. Lincoln looking rested and calm and with him were ten witnesses, whose purpose I could not even begin to guess. He stated that he was ready to proceed. It was as if he had worked for weeks, or even months, to prepare — not just ten days.

"At that point, the state's attorney, Hugh Fullerton, who was to prosecute the case, asked for a continuance to better prepare. Mr. Lincoln concurred. The case was set aside until the spring court term of 1858. Personally, I think Mr. Fullerton took one look at Mr. Lincoln, and ten witnesses, and decided that he was not nearly as ready to try the case as he had been when he thought he was going up against an attorney appointed by the court, such as myself."

Walker picked up his glass.

"Mr. Lincoln seemed genuinely pleased to see me. When I asked if he was disappointed with the delay, he assured me that he was not. He said he would be much better prepared for the trial this way. I asked if he regretted the energy he expended preparing. He said it just gave him a solid grounding in the basic facts that he would need whenever the trial took place.

"Maybe it's his training as an attorney that makes him such a formidable campaigner. He has endless energy on the stump. He is constantly ready to give a speech, and his voice is unaffected by bad food or little sleep. I have been with him for a week and I am exhausted. Mr. Lincoln is as sharp as ever. He responds to people in the crowd. He shakes hands with the multitude, smiles at the ladies, and listens to the ramblings of old people, never showing fatigue or boredom."

"And after the continuance in Beardstown?" asked Chapel.

Walker yawned and wobbled in his chair. "Mr. Lincoln introduced me to friends of his in the courtroom. I met Abram Bergen, a young attorney, who told me he observes as many of Mr. Lincoln's trials as he can and learns from every one. He also introduced me to Henry Shaw, an attorney who thought he would be asked to assist with the prosecution. Mr. Lincoln told me he wanted to talk with me at length and asked that I write down everything I could remember about the Norris trial. I agreed, of course. I met Hannah Armstrong, who evidenced complete trust in Mr. Lincoln. I knew the case and so I was worried for her."

Walker's last words came out in a slur. He leaned forward and his head came to rest on the desktop. Walker's breathing slowed and he began to snore.

Chapel looked at Dietrich. "I believe that our interview with Mr. Walker is over."

Dietrich nodded. "We need to get to Ottawa for the debate. After that, perhaps we can find one of the people who participated in or observed the trial."

CHAPTER SIXTEEN

August 21, 1858
Ottawa, Illinois, Washington Square: The First Debate

With Dietrich in the lead and Chapel following close behind, the two dodged and pushed their way through masses of people. Twelve thousand came to hear the candidates debate. A dozen military bands and two twelve-pound brass cannons seemed determined to leave people unable to hear at all. The dust in the air from the commotion made the city look like a smokehouse. When they arrived at the city square, Dietrich and Chapel found the speakers' platform occupied by people. Even the roof was full of onlookers. Broken shingles dangled and dropped to the floor of the stand. The reporters forced their way onto the platform, but even the best efforts of both party loyalists could not force all the spectators off.

Dietrich noticed that a drunk, losing his balance on the speakers' platform, was forcing Chapel perilously close to the edge. He reached out his long arm and gripped Chapel's pleated shirtfront in one hand. Dietrich maneuvered Chapel around the drunk and pulled him further back from the edge. Dietrich then released Chapel and pushed the drunk, who teetered on the edge before plunging unharmed to the ground below.

"This is chaos," said Chapel, straightening his shirt. "Hell must resemble this place. No one anticipated such a crush of humanity."

"'Tis so," agreed Dietrich, shading his eyes from the glaring sun. "On one hand, well-liquored Democrats pound their arguments with fists into the faces of barely sensible Republicans. On the other hand, intoxicated Republicans express their doctrines with kicks on Democrats so drunk that they feel no pain. When the marshals wearing partisan party sashes try to intervene, members of the opposing party join the battle against them. No wonder the enterprise is running late. If the speakers do not start soon, the mob may reduce this little town to splinters."

Finally, in the searing heat, Douglas stepped forward. Cheers and boos began to echo through the audience. Douglas waited patiently until the noise started to diminish. Then he began to speak in his slow bass voice.

"Ladies and gentlemen, I appear before you today for the purpose of discussing the leading political topics which now agitate the public mind. By an arrangement between Mr. Lincoln and myself, we are present here today for the purpose of having a joint discussion in regard to the questions dividing us."

Dietrich stood poised, pencil in hand, but during the early part of the speech he took no notes. He noticed that Chapel was not writing either.

"If he continues to serve up leftover oration," said Chapel to Dietrich, "we shall save a quire of paper."

Douglas rumbled on.

"I have the resolutions from the first mass convention ever held in Illinois by the Black Republican Party and I now will read a part of them: 'We unite ourselves as the Republican Party to restore Nebraska and Kansas as free territories, to repeal the fugitive slave law, to restrict slavery to those states in which it exists, to abolish slavery in the District of Columbia and all the territories forever. We will support no man for office who is not positively and fully committed to the support of these principles.' I desire to know whether Mr. Lincoln stands today as he did in 1854, in favor of these Black Republican principles."

Douglas paused and wiped his brow with a silk handkerchief while his supporters cheered and clapped.

"In the remarks I have made on this platform, I mean nothing personally disrespectful or unkind to Mr. Lincoln. I have known him for twenty-five years. There were many points of sympathy between us when we first got acquainted. We were both comparatively boys and both struggling with poverty in a strange land. I was a schoolteacher in the town of Winchester, and he, a flourishing grocery-keeper in the town of Salem. He sold whiskey in his store. Lincoln is one of those peculiar men who perform with admirable skill everything they undertake. Lincoln was always more successful in business than I. He was then just as good at telling an anecdote as now. He could beat any of the boys at wrestling, or running a footrace, in pitching quoits, or tossing a copper. He could drink more liquor than all the boys of the town together."

Douglas's supporters laughed heartily. Lincoln's supporters booed.

"Whilst in Congress he distinguished himself by his opposition to the Mexican war, taking the side of the common enemy against his own country. Lincoln objected that the war had begun on the wrong spot and thereafter became known as Spotty Lincoln. The indignation of the people followed him and he was submerged or obliged to retire into private life, forgotten by his friends."

"That is new," Chapel said softly to Dietrich. "Not exactly the truth, but new."

For much of the rest of the speech neither man took any additional notes.

"We are told by Lincoln that he is utterly opposed to the Dred Scott decision for it deprives the Negro of the rights and privileges of citizenship. I ask you, are you in favor of conferring upon the Negro the rights and privileges of citizenship?"

From the mass of people came calls of "No" and "Never."

"Do you desire to strike out of our state constitution that clause which keeps slaves and free Negroes out of the state, and allow the free Negroes to flow in?"

Again voices from the audience called out, "No. Never."

"Do you desire to turn this beautiful state into a free Negro colony, in order that when Missouri abolishes slavery she can send one hundred thousand emancipated slaves into Illinois to become citizens and voters equal with yourselves?"

From the crowd came strong shouts of "Not while I live" and "Keep the Niggers out of here."

"Mr. Lincoln, following the example of all the little Abolition orators who lecture in the basements of schools and churches, reads from the Declaration of Independence that all men were created equal and then asks how can you deprive a Negro of that equality which God and the Declaration of Independence awards to him. I do not question Mr. Lincoln's conscientious belief that the Negro was made his equal and hence is his brother."

Many in the gathering laughed.

"For my own part, I do not regard the Negro as my equal, and positively deny that he is my brother or any other kin to me whatsoever. I do not believe that the Almighty ever intended the Negro to be the equal of the white man. If he did, he has been a long time demonstrating the fact.

"For thousands of years the Negro has been a race on the earth and during all that time he has been inferior and must always occupy an inferior position. If we only adhere to the principle of popular sovereignty, we shall be the North Star that guides the friends of freedom throughout the civilized world."

Lincoln rose and his supporters gave him applause that went on for some time. He had to wait for some minutes before he could be heard.

"My fellow citizens, when a man hears himself somewhat misrepresented, it provokes him — at least, I find it so with myself; but when the misrepresentation becomes very gross and palpable, it is more apt to amuse him.

"As to those resolutions as being the platform of the Republican Party in 1854, I had nothing to do with them, and I think Trumbull never had. There was a call to form a Republican Party at Springfield, and I think my friend Mr. Lovejoy, who is here upon this stand, had a hand in it. He tried to get me into it and I would not go in. I went away from Springfield when the convention was in session to attend court in Tazewell County. It is true they did place my name, though without authority, upon the committee, and afterwards wrote me to attend, but I refused. This is the plain truth."

Lovejoy nodded solemnly.

"In regard to that general Abolition tilt that Judge Douglas makes, I hope you will permit me to read a part of a printed speech that I made at Peoria."

A voice in the crowd called out, "Put on your specs."

"Yes, sir, I am obliged to do so. I am no longer a young man." Lincoln began to read. "As for the spread of slavery, I cannot but hate it. I hate it because of the monstrous injustice of slavery itself. I hate it because it enables the enemies of free institutions with plausibility to taunt us as hypocrites, causes real friends of freedom to doubt our sincerity, and especially forces many really good men amongst ourselves into an open war with the very fundamental principles of civil liberty — criticizing the Declaration of Independence and insisting that there is no right principle of action but self-interest."

The Lincoln supporters applauded. Lincoln acknowledged the response and then continued reading. "I have no prejudice against the Southern people. They are just what we would be in their situation. If slavery did not exist amongst them, they would not introduce it. If it did now exist amongst us, we should not instantly give it up. We know that some Southern men do free their slaves, go north and become tip-top Abolitionists, while some Northern ones go south and become most cruel slave-masters.

"When Southern people tell us they are no more responsible for the origin of slavery than we, I acknowledge the fact. When it is said that the institution exists and that it is very difficult to get rid of it, I can understand and appreciate that. I surely will not blame them for not doing what I should not know how to do myself.

"When they remind us of their constitutional rights, I acknowledge them, not grudgingly, but fully, and fairly; and I would give them any legislation for the reclaiming of their fugitives, which should not be more likely to carry a free man into slavery than our ordinary criminal laws are to hang an innocent one. But all this, to my judgment, furnishes no more excuse for permitting slavery to go into our free territory than it would be for reviving the African slave trade."

Lincoln took off his glasses, folded them up and returned them to his vest pocket.

"This is the true complexion of all I have ever said in regard to the institution of slavery and the black race. Anything that argues me into his idea of perfect social and political equality with the Negro is but a specious and fantastic arrangement of words, by which a man can prove a horse chestnut to be a chestnut horse."

At this the entire multitude broke into laughter. Chapel muttered, "There are ladies present."

"I have no purpose directly or indirectly to interfere with the institution of slavery in the states where it exists. I believe I have no lawful right to do so, and I have no inclination to do so. I have no purpose to introduce political and social equality between the white and the black races. There is a physical difference between the two, which in my judgment will probably forever forbid their living together upon the footing of perfect equality. I, as well as Judge Douglas, am in favor of the race to which I belong having the superior position. Notwithstanding all this, there is no reason why the Negro is not entitled to all the natural rights enumerated in the Declaration of Independence, the right to life, liberty and the pursuit of happiness.

"I hold he is as much entitled to these as any white man. I agree with Judge Douglas he is not my equal in many respects — certainly not in color, perhaps not in moral or intellectual endowment. But in the right to eat the bread, without the leave of anybody else, which his own hands earn, he is my equal and the equal of Judge Douglas, and the equal of every living man.

"Now I pass on to consider one or two more of these little follies. The judge is woefully at fault about his early friend Lincoln being a grocery-keeper. I don't know as it would be a great sin if I had been, but he is mistaken. Lincoln never kept a grocery, nor ran a tavern selling whiskey anywhere in the world. It is true that Lincoln did work the latter part of one winter in a small still house up at the head of a hollow."

Lincoln's supporters laughed and mimicked drinking whiskey.

"My friend the judge is equally at fault when he charges me at the time when I was in Congress of having opposed our soldiers who were fighting the Mexican war. When the Democratic Party, the Democracy, tried to get me to vote that the war had been righteously begun by the president, I would not do it. But whenever they asked for money, or land warrants, or anything to pay the soldiers there, during all that time I gave the same votes that Judge Douglas did."

"The judge has read from my speech in Springfield, in which I say that, 'a house divided against itself cannot stand.' Does the judge say it can stand? I don't know whether he does or not."

Lincoln turned to face Douglas, who ignored him.

"The judge does not seem to be attending to me just now, but I would like to know if it is his opinion that a house divided against itself can stand. If he does, then there is a question of veracity, not between him and me, but between the judge and a somewhat Higher Character."

These remarks were followed by laughter and applause. A minister held up a Bible for those around him to see. "Amen!" shouted the minister. "Smite him mightily, Brother Lincoln, in the hip and thigh."

"I believe that there was a tendency, if not a conspiracy, among those who have engineered this slavery question for the last four or five years to make slavery perpetual and universal in this nation. My friend, Judge Douglas, took hold of this Springfield speech of mine, complimented me as being a 'kind able and intelligent gentleman' and he drew out from my speech this false idea to set the states at war with one another, to make all institutions uniform, and set the Niggers and white people to marry. So I went to work to show him that he misunderstood the whole scope of my speech. I claimed no right under the Constitution, nor had I any inclination, to enter into the slave states and interfere with slavery.

"Next, he said Lincoln will not enter the slave states but will go to the banks of the Ohio and shoot over the river! Then in the Springfield speech he said, 'Unless he shall be successful in firing his batteries until he shall have extinguished slavery in all the states, the Union shall be dissolved.' Now, my friends, I don't think that was exactly the way to treat a 'kind, amiable, intelligent gentleman.'"

Many people laughed uproariously.

"My friends, that ends the chapter. The judge can take his half hour."

Douglas rose and addressed the crowd once more.

"Fellow citizens, I will now occupy the half-hour allotted to me in replying to Mr. Lincoln. The first point to which I will call your attention is, as to what I said about the organization of the Republican Party of 1854, and the platform that was formed on the fifth of October of that year and I will then put the question to Mr. Lincoln whether or not he approves of each article in that platform.

"I did not charge him with being a member of the committee which reported that platform. I charged that that platform was the platform of the Republican Party adopted by them. The fact that it was the platform of the Republican Party is not denied, but Mr. Lincoln now says, that although his name was on the committee which reported it, that he did not think he was there, but thinks he was in Tazewell, holding court."

An argument broke out in the back of the crowd between supporters of Douglas and supporters of Lincoln. The men engaged in a bit of shouting and shoving, and one man took a swing at another and missed. The crowd jeered as a Marshal led the fighter away from the ruckus.

"Gentlemen, I ask your silence, and no interruption. Now, I want to remind Mr. Lincoln that he was in Springfield when the convention was held, and those resolutions were adopted."

An audience member shouted, "He was not there." Someone else called out, "You can't do it."

Mr. Glover, chairman of the Republican Party, stood and walked to the edge of the speaking stand. "I hope no Republican will interrupt Senator Douglas. The masses listened to Mr. Lincoln attentively, and as respectful men we ought to now hear Senator Douglas without interruption."

Douglas continued. "The point I am going to remind Mr. Lincoln of is this: after I made my speech in 1854 during the fair, he gave me notice that he was going to reply to me the next day. I was sick at the time but stayed over to hear his reply, and then, to reply to him. He spoke in the House. As I took the stand to reply, Mr. Codding gave notice that the Republic State Convention would meet instantly in the Senate chamber. He called upon the Republicans to retire there instead of listening to me.

"Gentlemen, Mr. Lincoln tells me that he went along with them. I do not know whether he did or not."

Members of the Republican committee went over to Lincoln and prevented him from interrupting further.

"Mr. Lincoln does not want to avow his principles. I avow mine as clear as sunlight in midday. Mr. Lincoln was selected by the very men who made the Republican organization to reply to me. He spoke for them. He was the leader preaching up this same doctrine of Negro equality under the Declaration of Independence. I have here a newspaper printed at Springfield, Mr. Lincoln's own town, in October, publishing these resolutions, charging Mr. Lincoln with entertaining these sentiments."

Douglas held up a newspaper and waved it through the air.

"This denial that he did not act on the committee is a miserable quibble to avoid the main issue. Does he support the Black Republican Party principles espoused? He is afraid to answer it. He knows I will trot him down to the Southern part of our fair state, which we call Egypt, and I intend to make him answer the question there."

Douglas supporters raised three cheers for their champion. Douglas waved to the audience. When Douglas stepped back and began to shake hands with the men on the platform, bands struck up patriotic tunes. The men surrounding Lincoln began to pound him on his back and praise his words. The crowd started to disperse.

As Lincoln stepped to the ground, four young farm boys rushed toward him. Lincoln reached out his hand to shake hands, but one of the boys seized his extended right arm. Another boy grabbed his other arm. Lincoln, frowning, said something to them that was lost in the din when two brass twelve-pound cannons fired. The other two boys each grabbed Lincoln's legs. They made an uncoordinated effort to lift Lincoln off the ground like he was a sack of potatoes. The boy holding Lincoln's left leg lost his grip for a moment while the other three held him aloft. In regaining his grip the boy pulled Lincoln's pant leg up exposing his pantaloons. Shouting and laughing, the boys carried Lincoln through the audience while Lincoln tried to put a pleased expression on his face.

Several minutes later, Lincoln's advisors joined him in the home of one of his supporters. Lincoln looked at their grim faces gathered around the table in the kitchen. Judd looked angry. Anthony looked stunned. Walker just looked tired.

"I thought I did passably well," said Lincoln. "From the expressions on your faces, I take it that you disagree."

Walker sighed. "Until Judge Douglas's response, you were holding your own. Your reaction to the continued charges made you appear ungentlemanly. People do not like a thin-skinned man."

"You spent the entire time reacting to Douglas's false allegations," snarled Judd. "He called the tune and you danced to it. If you are to be the first man in Illinois, you need to show less deference to the judge. If he knows he can bite through your hide and draw blood, he'll be all over you like a bluetail fly."

"I never did like that damned house divided speech," Anthony grumbled. "There is something wrong with those Republican propositions that Douglas spouted."

"I was not there when they were adopted," said Lincoln, looking hard at Anthony.

"Not that," said Anthony, looking off into space. "There's something else. I just can't quite put my finger on it right now."

A man with a round red face and sparse gray hair stuck his head into the kitchen.

"I don't mean to intrude, but there are two reporters — a big Dutchman and a little Southerner — asking if they can talk with Mr. Walker when he is free."

"Invite them in," said Lincoln. "I know them and they gave good advice about a speech I gave in Chicago."

After a brief time, Chapel and Dietrich entered the kitchen.

"Welcome, gentlemen," said Lincoln. He introduced them to Judd. Anthony and Walker greeted them.

"We were doing a post-mortem of my speech," said Lincoln. "At first I thought I had done an adequate job, but these gentlemen have convinced me that I was skinned like a rabbit. What do you think?"

Dietrich and Chapel glanced at each other.

"I think you're still counterpunching," answered Dietrich. "When Judge Douglas ignored your explanations and continued his attacks, you got too hot under the collar."

Lincoln nodded. "I agree. What do you think, Mr. Chapel?"

"I think Judge Douglas scored when he read the Republican platform adopted in Springfield," said Chapel. "That is a radical

117

document and he means to tie it to your tail like young boys tie tin cans to the tails of dogs. You have to disavow it."

"Can I ask you a question, Mr. Lincoln?" asked Dietrich. "I don't mean to disrespectful, but what did the judge mean by 'Spotty Lincoln?' Was it something that happened during the Mexican War?"

"I had only one term in Congress," said Lincoln, glancing at his friends in the room. "I was foolish enough to criticize President Polk for his role of initiating the war, just before the conflict ended and the United States greatly expanded its territory. The president announced that he was about to victoriously conclude the war, which he said Mexico had started by invading Texas and 'shedding the blood of our citizens on our own soil.' In a manner more befitting an attorney in court than the congressman of a district where the war was quite popular, I demanded that the president tell Congress whether the spot of soil on which the blood of our citizens had been shed was actually part of Texas or, as the Mexican government claimed, if it was a part of Mexico. I asked if the people in the area had ever been proved to be under the government of Texas by voting, or paying taxes, or if they were in active rebellion against Mexico. Later on, with eighty-five others, I voted to support a resolution that said in part that the war was unnecessarily and unconstitutionally begun by the president."

Lincoln paused.

"I compared the president to an ant on a hot stove and a man in a fever-dream. In Washington, my remarks elicited a response they richly deserved. They were completely ignored."

Lincoln smiled. "At home, however, I discovered that I had embarrassed my friends and united my enemies against me. Even Billy Herndon thought I was wrong. I failed to make the point that the president, not Congress, initiated the war by sending American troops into an area claimed by both governments and occupied by the Mexican army. It was inevitable that American and Mexican forces would clash. Congress declared war only after the first battle. Of course, constitutionally, only Congress can declare war. I thought President Polk had been dangerously provocative. In truth, I still think so."

Several of Lincoln's friends nodded.

"I also failed to convey that, although I opposed the war, I supported every piece of legislation that aided the soldiers and their families. I believe it was the Peoria Press that first called me 'Spotty Lincoln.' I had agreed to serve only one term, and it is well that I did. I should have heeded the words of Justin Butterfield, a Whig, who had earlier opposed the War of 1812. His opposition to that war caused his temporary political retirement. Asked if he opposed this war, he answered, 'No, indeed! I opposed one war and it ruined me. From now on I am for war, pestilence and famine."

The men in the kitchen laughed.

"Even as a legal argument my remarks constituted a shoddy piece of work. I know to plead not what I need not. I failed to do that and found I had committed myself to prove what I could not."

"Springfield!" shouted Anthony, slapping his hand on the table.

Everyone turned to look at him.

"That's it," exclaimed Anthony. "Springfield. Look, Judd. Do you know every Republican document written in the convention in Chicago?"

"Of course I do."

"Chapel, Dietrich, would you recognize any political document written by any organized political party in your home cities?"

"Without doubt," answered Chapel.

Dietrich nodded.

Anthony straightened his jacket cuffs. "You see, that's what is odd about the platform Judge Douglas read. It sounded familiar, but I could not recall the particulars. I'm certain that it is an anti-Democracy platform of some sort; the judge would not be wrong about that. But it was not one written in Springfield, or like Judd, Chapel and Dietrich, I would know the document nearly word by word."

"The son of a bitch lied," snapped Judd. "We have to track the document to its source to show that Mr. Lincoln was not involved in the writing of it. By the implication that it was written in his home city, Douglas is hanging it around Mr. Lincoln's neck."

Lincoln held up a hand to stop Judd. "We don't know that

Judge Douglas lied. He might have been mistaken about its origins."

Judd stood up. "We have enough Republican Party officials here that one of them will be able to recognize it and tell us its paternity. Nice work, Mr. Anthony."

Judd rushed out of the kitchen.

"Sit, gentlemen," said Lincoln to Chapel and Dietrich. "You have already been of service and I would like to know what else you think."

"Just don't expect Mr. Lincoln to do everything you recommend," said Anthony. "I tried to advise him that a speech he wanted to make would raise people's hackles, but he went and did it anyway."

Lincoln looked at Anthony and smiled.

"Mr. Anthony reminds me of a man I met when I first arrived in New Salem," said Lincoln, leaning back in his chair. "He ran flatboats down the river to New Orleans, and he had a reputation as a strong man and a wrestler. I was sort of known for wrestling at the time so we arranged to have a match. He was strong and he was a good wrestler, but I was on my home ground. The Clary's Grove boys cheered me wildly and drove me to greater efforts. After a time, I was able to wear him out and then to throw him. I lined up for the second fall, but the man just sat on the ground. First, he said that he should have taken a different grip. Then, he said he should have made a feint before he tried lifting me up. After that, he talked about shifting his balance from one foot to the other too quickly. While he talked, the crowd got restless. Finally, I did, too. I told him if he had figured out how to beat me, we ought to go at it for the second fall. He looked up at me and said, 'Take it easy, Lincoln. I ain't finished with the first fall yet.'"

Lincoln led the laughter.

"Mr. Anthony," said Lincoln, smiling, "the first fall is over. I gave the house divided speech and we have to go on from here. So, what do you journalists recommend?"

"Wherever the Republican platform was written," said Dietrich, "you will need to respond to it lest Judge Douglas continue to say that you are dodging and refusing to respond."

"And the questions Judge Douglas asked, you need to address those, too, for the same reason," Chapel added.

Dietrich nodded, "But you cannot just react. You need to have questions for the judge to answer to justify his positions. With respect, Mr. Lincoln, I think you need to lay the lumber to the judge when you have the opportunity."

Lincoln nodded, "I reckon so. Do you gentlemen have additional advice?"

Chapel hesitated and then responded, "I don't believe that the way you were carried from the field of battle enhanced your reputation for dignity."

"Nor do I," answered Lincoln. "Thank you both for your honesty. Is there anything else you would like to add?"

Dietrich and Chapel shook their heads.

"I think I could spare Mr. Walker for a few minutes," said Lincoln.

Walker, Dietrich and Chapel left the room while Lincoln and Anthony conferred quietly.

"We won't keep you long," said Chapel to Walker. "We know the next debate is coming up soon. We just need to know what Mr. Lincoln did during the time between court dates."

"What didn't he do?" asked Walker. "He talked to Duff. He interviewed the neighbors to find out who would testify about Duff's character. He tracked all over Walker's Grove. He interviewed me and went over the notes I wrote. He wanted to know every question asked and every answer given during the Norris trial. He checked every assertion and every fact six ways from Sunday. Mr. Lincoln didn't tell me his strategy, but I was honored when he asked me to assist him during the second trial."

"Did you get a fee?" asked Dietrich.

Chapel smiled, "I got a legal education and the distinct honor of working with Mr. Lincoln. One thing he taught me was to work at being an attorney. Right now, I would like to work at being his political advisor. If you have no more immediate questions, I would like to return to that work."

"Thank you, sir," said Dietrich.

"Much obliged," said Chapel.

CHAPTER SEVENTEEN

August 26, 1858
Freeport, Illinois: The Second Debate

Douglas stepped from the platform of the special train on which he rode and was greeted with shouts and cheers. A crowd with a thousand torches escorted him to the Brewster House. About one third more people than had seen the first debate were assembled to witness the second.

Not long after, Lincoln arrived on the regular train. People carrying banners supporting his campaign numbered even more than the Douglas supporters. They sang and shouted as they accompanied him to the Brewster House.

Standing in the square before the second debate Dietrich asked Chapel, "Do you think that Judge Douglas calculated putting the first two debates into northern, Republican strongholds so that he would have the advantage in the later debates?"

"Of that I have no doubt," replied Chapel, pulling his coat closed in the chilly breeze. "We must be nearly into Wisconsin. Senator Douglas reckons everything. Did you notice that when Mr. Lincoln rode up in a Conestoga wagon with farmers, Judge Douglas uncharacteristically walked?"

"Mr. Lincoln in his rumpled suit and stovepipe hat looks like a farmer's son. Judge Douglas with his blue suit with shiny buttons, ruffled shirt and wide-brimmed hat would fit in on a Southerner's plantation."

"Yes, I wonder who his tailor is," mused Chapel. "I also wonder if Mr. Lincoln is resolved to answer fire with fire. I trust we will soon discover that. He is about to speak."

Lincoln stood and walked to the speakers' stand.

"Ladies and gentlemen, on Saturday last, Judge Douglas and myself first met in public discussion. In the course of his opening argument Judge Douglas proposed to me seven interrogatories. I answered one of the interrogatories then. I then distinctly told him that I would answer the rest on condition only that he would agree to answer as many for me. He made no answer, but spent at least half of his reply in dealing with me as though I had refused to answer. I now propose to answer any of the interrogatories, upon condition that he will answer questions from me."

Lincoln looked over at Douglas.

"I give him an opportunity to respond. The judge remains silent. I now say to you that I will answer his interrogatories, whether he answers mine or not; and after I have done so, I shall propound mine to him.

"I do not now, nor ever did, stand in favor of the unconditional repeal of the fugitive slave law. I do not now, nor ever did, stand pledged against the admission of any more slave states into the Union. I do not stand pledged against the admission of a new state to the Union with such a constitution as the people of that state may see fit to make.

"I do not stand today pledged to the abolition of slavery in the District of Columbia. I do not stand pledged to the prohibition of the slave trade between the different states. I am pledged to a belief in the right and duty of Congress to prohibit slavery in all the United States territories.

"I am not opposed to honest acquisition of territory, and, in any given case, I would not oppose such acquisition unless it would aggravate the slavery question among ourselves.

"Now, it will be perceived that so far I have only answered that I was not pledged to do this or that. The judge has not asked me anything more. But, I am disposed to take up some of these questions and state what I really think upon them."

A person in the audience cried out, "Go it, Mr. Lincoln."

"In regard to the fugitive slave law, I have never hesitated to say, and I do not hesitate to say now, that under the Constitution, the people of the southern states are entitled to a congressional fugitive slave law. If the people of a territory shall, having a fair chance and a clear field, when they come to adopt the constitution do such an extraordinary thing as to adopt a slave constitution, uninfluenced by the actual presence of the institution among them, I see no alternative but to admit them into the Union.

"I should be exceedingly glad to see slavery abolished in the

District of Columbia. I believe that Congress possesses the constitutional power to abolish it. I should not, however, be in favor of endeavoring to abolition it, unless it would be gradual, based on a vote of the majority of qualified voters, and include compensation for unwilling owners. Then I would be exceedingly glad, in the words of Henry Clay, to 'sweep from our capitol that foul blot upon our nation.'"

Lincoln's admirers applauded loudly for some minutes. Someone called out, "That's sound doctrine."

"I now proceed to propound to the judge the interrogatories, so far as I have framed them. I will bring forward a new installment when I get them ready." He turned his glance toward Douglas.

"Question 1: If the people of Kansas shall adopt a state constitution and ask admission to the Union under it before they have the requisite number of inhabitants according to the English Bill — some ninety three thousand — will you vote to admit them?

"Question 2: Can the people of a United States territory, in any lawful way, against the wish of any citizen of the United States, exclude slavery from its limits prior to the formation of a state constitution?

"Question 3: If the Supreme Court of the United States shall decide that states can not exclude slavery from their limits, are you in favor of acquiescing in, adopting, and following such a decision as a rule of political action?

"Question 4: Are you in favor of acquiring additional territory in disregard of how such acquisitions may affect the nation on the slavery question?"

Lincoln paused for a moment and then turned again to face the crowd. "Judge Douglas read a set of resolutions in which he said Judge Trumbull and myself had participated in adopting in the first Republican State Convention held at Springfield in October of 1854. He insisted that I and Judge Trumbull and the entire Republican Party were responsible for them. He used the resolutions as a sort of authority for those questions. Mind, I do not answer his interrogatories because of their spring from that set of resolutions. I answer them because Judge Douglas thought fit to ask them.

"I do not now, nor never did, recognize any responsibility upon myself in that set of resolutions. I assured him that I never had anything to do with them. I repeat that here today. In fact, it turns out that those resolutions were never passed in any convention in Springfield."

Cheers and laughter came from the people assembled. Dietrich looked up from taking notes, caught Chapel's eye and nodded. Both men then returned to writing notes.

"It turns out that they were never passed at any convention or public meeting that I had any part in. In addition to all this, that there was no Republican State Convention held in Springfield in the fall of 1854."

People in the audience cheered again.

"There was an assemblage of men calling themselves a convention at Springfield then. They did pass some resolutions. But I knew so little of the proceedings or the resolutions passed that, when Judge Douglas read them, I thought they must have been the Republican Party resolutions adopted. For, I could not bring myself to suppose the Judge Douglas could say what he did upon this subject without knowing that it was true.

"It turns out he got hold of some resolutions passed at some public meeting in Kane County. I am just as responsible for the resolutions in Kane County as those at Springfield, the amount of responsibility being exactly nothing in either case; no more than there would be in regard to a set of resolutions passed on the moon.

"Judge Douglas did not make his statement upon that occasion as matters he believed to be true, but he stated them roundly as being true. When we consider who Judge Douglas is, a distinguished senator, that he has served nearly twelve years as such — that his name has become of world-wide renown — it is most extraordinary that he should so far forget all suggestions of justice to an adversary or prudence to himself to venture upon the assertion of that which the slightest investigation would have shown him to be wholly false."

Lincoln supporters cheered, and two men danced a jig in the street.

"Another extraordinary feature of the judge's conduct in this canvass, made more extraordinary by this incident, is that he is in the habit in almost all the speeches he makes of charging falsehood upon his adversaries. I now ask whether he is able to find anything that Judge Trumbull or I have said a justification at all compared with that sort of vulgarity."

The Lincoln supporters in the crowd shouted, hooted and whistled. It was some time before order could be restored.

Douglas looked out at the wind-blown dark clouds and muttered that the weather would not help his scratchy throat.

Dietrich turned to Chapel. "We may now have to take notes."

Douglas spoke. "I am glad that at last I have brought Mr. Lincoln to the conclusion that he had better define his position on certain political questions to which I called his attention at Ottawa. There, he showed no inclination to answer them."

The Douglas supporters cheered.

"I laid the foundation for those interrogatories by showing that they constituted the platform of the party whose nominee he is. I desired simply to know, inasmuch as he had been nominated as the 'first, last and only choice of his party', whether he concurred in the platform, which that party had adopted. I will first respond to the interrogatories, which he has presented me. Mark you, he has not presented interrogatories which have ever received the sanction of the party and he has no foundation for them save his own curiosity."

Douglas partisans chuckled.

"First, he desires to know, should the people of Kansas form a constitution by means entirely proper and unobjectionable and ask admission into the Union as a state before they have the requisite population for a member of Congress, whether I will vote for that admission. Well now, I regret exceedingly that he did not answer that interrogatory himself before he put it to me. But I will answer his question. In reference to Kansas, it is my opinion that as she had population enough to constitute a slave state, she has people enough for a free state.

"Can the people of a territory in any lawful way against the wishes of any citizen exclude slavery from their limits prior to the formation of a state constitution? I answer emphatically, as Mr.

Lincoln has heard me answer a hundred times from every stump in Illinois, that the people of a territory can, by lawful means, exclude slavery from their limits prior to the formation of a state constitution."

Douglas supporters cheered.

"That's what your editor wants to know," Dietrich shouted to Chapel over the noise.

Chapel nodded and chewed his lip.

"Mr. Lincoln knew that I had answered that question over and over again."

"Not to the Southern press," muttered Dietrich to himself.

"It matters not what way the Supreme Court may hereafter decide as to the abstract question of whether slavery may or may not go into a territory under the Constitution; the people have the lawful means to introduce it or exclude it as they please. Slavery cannot exist a day, or an hour, anywhere, unless it is supported by local police regulations established by local legislature. If the people who are opposed to slavery elect representatives to that body who by unfriendly legislation effectually prevent it, then it will not be introduced. If, on the contrary, they are for it, their legislation will favor its extension, no matter what decision the Supreme Court may be on that abstract question. I hope Mr. Lincoln deems my answer satisfactory on that point."

The Douglas partisans cheered and applauded loudly.

"Mr. Lincoln may," said Chapel to Dietrich, "but to my editor and many others who will deem that a restriction on our peculiar institution, that will not be satisfactory."

"The third question which Mr. Lincoln presented is, if the Supreme Court of the United States shall decide that a state of this Union cannot exclude slavery from its own limits, will I submit to it? I am amazed that Lincoln should ask such a question."

From the crowd came a voice, "A schoolboy knows better."

"Yes, a schoolboy does know better. Mr. Lincoln's object is to cast aspersions upon the Supreme Court. Only one man in the entire history of America ever, even for a moment, pretended such a thing. I admit that the Washington Union, in an article published on the 17th of last December, did put forth that doctrine. I denounced the article on the floor of the Senate. Mr. Toombs, of Georgia, immediately got up and lectured me, saying that I ought not have deemed the article worthy of notice. He said that there was not even one man, woman, or child south of the Potomac in any slave state who did not repudiate such absurdity. Mr. Lincoln knows that. He might as well ask me, suppose Mr. Lincoln should steal a horse would I sanction it."

The Douglas supporters laughed.

"He insults the Supreme Court by supposing they would violate the Constitution. I tell him such a thing is not possible. It would be an act of moral treason that no man on the bench could ever descend to. Mr. Lincoln, himself, would never commit such an act.

"The fourth question of Mr. Lincoln is, are you in favor of acquiring additional territory in disregard as to how such acquisition may effect the Union on the slavery question? This question is very ingeniously and cunningly put."

Deacon Boss, Democrat Party leader, could be heard clearly in the background, "Now we've got him."

"The Black Republican creed lays it down expressly, that under no circumstances shall we acquire any more territory unless slavery is first prohibited. I ask Mr. Lincoln whether he is in favor of that proposition."

Turning to face Lincoln, Douglas asked, "Are you in favor or opposed?

"He does not like to answer. He turns, Yankee-fashion, and without answering asks me. I answer that whenever it becomes necessary in our growth and progress to acquire more territory I am in favor of it without reference to the question of slavery. When we have acquired it, I will leave the people free to do as they please, either to make it slave or free territory, as they prefer.

"I trust now that Mr. Lincoln will deem himself answered on his four points. He racked his brain so much in devising these four questions that he has exhausted himself, and had not strength enough to invent others. As soon as he is able to hold a conference with his Abolitionist advisors, Lovejoy, Farnsworth and Frederick Douglass, he will frame and propound others.

"I know that some people in this country think that the famous Negro Abolitionist Frederick Douglass is a very good man. The last time I came here to make a speech, I saw a carriage, and a magnificent one it was, a beautiful young lady was sitting on the box seat atop the carriage whilst Frederick Douglass and her mother reclined inside, and the owner acted as a driver."

Douglas's remarks generated a confused buzzing in the assembly. Some people called out, "Shame on the owner." Others called to Douglas, "What of it?" "What have you to say against it?" The chant of "White, white, white" was taken up.

"All I have to say of it is this, if you Black Republicans think the Negro ought to have social equality with your wives and daughters, you have a perfect right to do so. All of you who believe that the Negro is your equal have a right to entertain those opinions, and, of course will vote for Mr. Lincoln."

Some Douglas admirers shouted out, "Down with the Nigger!" "Keep them away from our women." "The races shall not mix."

"I have a word to say on Mr. Lincoln's answers to the interrogatories which he has pretended to reply to here today. Mr. Lincoln makes a great parade of the fact that I quoted a platform as having been adopted by the Republican Party at Springfield in 1854, which, it turns out, was adopted at another place. Mr. Lincoln loses sight of the thing itself in his ecstasies over the mistake I made. He thinks that that platform was not adopted on the right 'spot.'

"It may be that I was led into an error as to the spot on which the resolutions were proclaimed, but I was not and am not in error as to the fact of there being the creed of the Republican Party. The identical platform, word for word, was published in Mr. Lincoln's own town eleven days after the convention. I had good evidence for believing the resolutions had been passed at Springfield. Mr. Lincoln should have known better, but he said not a word about his ignorance, whilst I am accused of forgery. Mr. Lincoln charges that I did you and him injury by saying that this was the platform of your party. But the very same platform was adopted by nearly all the counties where the Black Republican Party had a majority in 1854. Either Lincoln was pledged to each one of the propositions, or every Black Republican violated his pledge of honor to his constituents. Take either horn of the dilemma you choose. There is no dodging the question. I want Lincoln's answer."

Lincoln then replied for half an hour.

"The long portion of the judge's speech was devoted to the various resolutions and platforms adopted in the different counties which he supposes are at variance with the positions I have stated today. Many of the resolutions are at variance with the positions I have assumed. All I have to ask is that we talk reasonably and rationally about it. I have never tried to conceal my opinions. He may examine all the members of the Republican Party who voted for me, and if he finds any person who says that I made any pledge to any person inconsistent with what I say now, I will resign from the race, and give him no more trouble.

"The plain truth is this: We met together in 1956 from all over the state and we agreed upon a common platform. Now we are bound as a party to that platform. Cannot the judge be satisfied? I'll tell you what he is really afraid of. He is afraid that we will pull together.

"The judge again addressed himself to a speech of mine made at Springfield in June last. I trust that nearly all of you in this intelligent audience have read that speech. I leave it to you to inspect it closely and see whether it contains any of those 'bugaboos' which so frighten Judge Douglas."

Marching bands and party officials escorted the candidates back to the Brewster House. Supporters carried banners and flags, which they waved as they marched. Ladies waved handkerchiefs and called out to friends. Each group competed to see who could make louder cheers for their champion. The cannon commenced firing, and young boys threw firecrackers to add to the din.

Dietrich stayed in the square writing furiously in his notebook, not even noticing the people streamed around him. Chapel walked to the speakers' stand and leaned against it. He shook and flexed the fingers of his right hand. Idly Chapel noticed that a group of four roughly dressed men moved purposefully toward Dietrich. One of the men turned his shoulder and deliberately bumped into Dietrich.

"Watch where you're going," the man blustered.

Dietrich looked up from his writing.

"I'm sorry, I was writing my notes," said Dietrich. He resumed writing.

"See, I told you," the man said to his friends. "He talks like a Dutchman. Why are you writing anyway? Judge Douglas stopped talking some time ago."

Dietrich closed his notebook and put it in his coat pocket. "I am a reporter. I was recording the words of both candidates."

"A foreigner and an Abolitionist," said the man, smiling. "You are just what we are looking for."

Chapel walked toward the men casually.

"There ain't many Niggers around to beat on, but we found us a Nigger-lover. We're going to make you sorry that you ever left the old country."

"Gentlemen," said Chapel, lengthening his Southern drawl, "is there a problem here?"

The man turned and looked at Chapel, who was approaching slowly.

"There is no problem here," answered the man. "In fact, feel free to join us in the coming dance. We aim to teach this wooden-headed foreigner a lesson he won't forget."

Chapel said, "I am sorry to hear that."

"Why?" the man demanded. "Is he a friend of yours?"

"Yes," answered Chapel. "He is. I would appreciate it if you and your friends would leave him alone."

"Why don't you join the fun? We can take two as easily as one man."

"Four against two. Are you so frightened that you need a two-to-one advantage before you are willing to contend?" asked Chapel.

The man's face reddened. "I fear no man. I just did not want to deny my friends the pleasure of contributing to the cause."

"From your accent I'd say you were from Kentucky or Tennessee," said Chapel.

"Kentucky," answered the man.

"I don't know how you settle disputes of honor in Kentucky but where I am from, Virginia, we don't need four men to fight one, or even two. If you are not a coward, we can settle this one on one. I'll give you the choice of weapons."

Realizing that he had been challenged, the man swiveled his head as if looking for an escape.

"I've got no quarrel with you," pleaded the man. "It is this foreign blockhead I was challenging. I'll give him the choice of weapons."

Dietrich clouted the man in the mouth with his fist, knocking him into the mud. He lay on his back groaning as tears filled his eyes and blood dribbled from his lips.

"I choose fists," said Dietrich. He looked at the three men staring at the man on the ground. "Who's next? Step up."

The three men backed away and then turned and ran.

"Don't forget your leader," Chapel called, but there was no one left to hear.

Dietrich reached down and lifted the man up with one hand. "Do you still want to teach me a lesson?"

The man blinked his eyes and then shook his head. Dietrich opened his hand and the man fell back into the mud. Dietrich and Chapel headed toward the train station.

"Know Nothing Party members," said Chapel. "They hate Niggers, Dutchmen, Irishmen, Catholics and mostly anybody they reckon they can scare. Ask them what the party platform is and they said, "I know nothing.""

Dietrich nodded. "At least their party is well named."

In the train station, Dietrich and Chapel began to discuss the debate.

"Mr. Lincoln answered Douglas's inquires and posed some of his own," said Chapel.

"Yes," said Dietrich, flipping the pages of his notebook. "He needed to do that at minimum. He identified the platform Judge Douglas tried to tie him to as not being the Republican Party convention platform."

"But, Mr. Lincoln hesitated to lay the lumber to Judge Douglas. Judge Douglas implies that Mr. Lincoln failed to do his duty in Congress during the Mexican War. Judge Douglas called Mr. Lincoln a drunk, which everybody who knows Mr. Lincoln can swear is not true. Judge Douglas is not hindered by Mr. Lincoln's tender conscience. Mr. Lincoln takes care to avoid laying false charges. It makes Mr. Lincoln appear uncertain compared to the judge's thunder."

"I agree," said Dietrich. "Judge Douglas blisters Mr. Lincoln. Mr. Lincoln will not reply in kind. On the other hand, he did get Judge Douglas to admit to his local legislation trumps the Supreme Court doctrine. That will not be popular among Judge Douglas's Southern supporters."

"I'm not so sure," said Chapel. "It is an idea that appeals to many in Illinois. That might strengthen Judge Douglas's hand. We Southerners cannot vote in Illinois."

CHAPTER EIGHTEEN

August 31, 1858
Springfield, Illinois

Mary Todd Lincoln screamed. Her face was red. Her eyes were narrowed, and tears coursed down her face. She crumpled the newspaper she had been reading and threw it with all her might at Lincoln's face. Lincoln made no move to protect himself. In one hand Lincoln held a rolled-up newspaper.

"Seven!" she shouted. "Judge Douglas so fears you that he agrees to only seven debates over three months, and you waste the first one by letting him get under your skin so badly that you attempt to interrupt him and interfere with his speech. Do you know how that appears to voters? You allow him to make you appear uncivil and rude."

"He lied outrageously," stated Lincoln. "He knows...."

"He lied!" Mary's voice went up an octave. She stamped her foot. "Of course he lied. Did you think he would tell the truth and debate you on the issues? He wants to be re-elected, doesn't he? How would that happen if he told the truth?"

Lincoln opened his mouth. Mary shook her finger at him. Lincoln closed his mouth.

"Judge Douglas fights for his political future. You know how he burns to be president. He has no vision except of himself in the highest office, no concept outside his own skin to use to guide his steps. You use the Declaration of Independence to show that all people were created in the image of God. Black, white, Indian — whatever we are, we are all children of God. Judge Douglas has no answer so he engages in the lowest form of fear-mongering and base mockery. You cannot expect that he would act out of fairness and honesty as you would in his place. You must not make the mistake of thinking that others will act as honorably as you do."

"But..."

Mary looked at Lincoln sharply. Lincoln fell silent.

"You must see that Judge Douglas fears to confront you openly. There is no calumny that he will not accuse you of, knowing it is false. He cannot debate you on even ground any more than he could contend with you in a wrestling match. Why do you think that he agreed to only seven debates, with him having the final say in most of them? He can spout humbug with the best of them. He can solemnly proclaim that we must all support the rulings of the Supreme Court that slavery cannot be excluded from the territories, but at the same time announce that local police law enacted by the representatives of the people in a territory undoes the Supreme Court ruling. Which is it, then? Of all his opponents, you can best show that the Senator from Illinois, like the king in the fable, has no clothes on."

"He fears me, Molly?" Lincoln asked.

"Calling me by the pet name you have for me will not distract me. Father, you are always fond of quoting Robert Burns and saying we cannot see ourselves as others see us. It is plain to all around you that there is no man as well suited to the senate — and even better the presidency — in these troubled times as you are. If you could see yourself without your doubts and foreboding, you would know that for a surety."

Mary's voice lowered to her usual register. Her complexion lightened.

"The Judge is terrified of you. Of all the opponents he could have to face, you are by far the most formidable. In the Senate, his opponents do not dare debate him for fear of being destroyed by his words. He has not faced a man of honor who will not kowtow in fear. He laid his trap by soft words and false respect in hopes that his attack would throw you off stride, just as it did. You speak from the heart, invoking the Declaration of Independence. He speaks for himself. You invoke the ideals of the founders of the nation. He claims to defend the rule of the majority, calling it popular sovereignty, but who is there who threatens to set up an oligarchy or a kingship in the state of Illinois? Why defend that which is not under attack?"

"Oh, Mother, if you could but speak for me, I would vanquish the judge for sure. Still, he is a man of powerful intelligence."

With her head thrown back and her eyes shining, Mary said, "Judge Douglas is a very little 'Little Giant' by the side of my tall

Kentuckian, and intellectually my husband towers above Douglas just as he does physically."

Lincoln looked at Mary admiringly. Mary then noticed the crumpled newspaper at Lincoln's feet and burst into tears.

"What a harridan I have become," said Mary through her tears. "Some people say I am crazed and sometimes I act like a madwoman."

Lincoln pulled her to him and stroked her hair. Mary sobbed. "Father, how can you stand to put up with me? I have no right to throw something at you just because I am angry. Why ever did you marry me?"

Lincoln smiled. "Of all the coterie of young ladies in Springfield, you were the most intelligent, the most interested in politics, and, of course, the prettiest one. Ninian Edwards always said you could make a bishop forget his prayers."

"But now I am fat," said Mary. "I have a wicked temper."

"Back when I was crude and uncivilized," said Lincoln, "I mean even more than I am now, I contracted in a feeble way an engagement with a woman who was far too wise to marry me. When she released me from my promise, I said that I would never marry. I claimed I would have no blockhead who would be willing to marry a blockhead like me."

Mary calmed herself. "That, Father, was before you met me."

"Exactly," answered Lincoln.

For a few moments, they continued to embrace.

"I have here a report of the Freeport debate, which I believe will be more to your liking."

"Where is it?" Mary pulled the newspaper from his hand and began to read intently.

"You answer his interrogatories, good. You pose questions in return, better and better. His quotes of Republican resolutions are from a convention in Springfield that never happened. What cheek! He will deny that it matters, of course and blame others for the misunderstanding."

Mary turned the page. "Ah ha! As I predicted, he blames others for his mistake. He's forced to answer your questions and alleges that the people of a territory can exclude slavery despite the

Supreme Court's 'theoretical' ruling. I swear he would not think it theoretical if he were to find himself a slave. He insults you again with the old false charges. He raises the common disdain for Negroes."

Mary read on. "This time you do not rise to the bait but call him a fearful man. We both know that his real fear is that he will be defeated in the election."

Lincoln looked at Mary. "I know that I have not been at home much lately, and I know it is hard on you when I am gone."

Mary nodded.

"I have come home for a brief time, but we both know that I must soon be on my way again."

"I know, Father, and it is what I want also. I will try to be good. I will try not to act like a hellcat every time you come home."

***

Dietrich sat on the steps of the Myers and Caldwell Boarding House next to his much-traveled carpetbag. Wearily, he started cleaning mud from his boots with a stick. He wondered for the hundredth time why Mrs. Myers was so particular about keeping her front porch clean. As a reporter, he suspected that there was a story connected with it, but he had never worked up the nerve to ask.

"Mr. Dietrich," called a voice. Dietrich looked up to see Tom Edwards striding toward him with a speed surprising for a man with his girth.

"I'm pleased to see that you finally made it back to Springfield," said Edwards. "If you're still of a mind to find out about the Duff Armstrong trial, you should come to the hotel at once. Henry Shaw and Abram Bergen are both in town on legal business before the state Supreme Court."

Dietrich frowned as he tried to remember why the names seemed familiar.

"Mr. Shaw, the man who assisted the prosecution of Duff Armstrong," said Edwards with a touch of impatience. "Mr. Bergen is a young lawyer who observed the entire proceedings. Both of them are friends of Mr. Lincoln."

Dietrich snatched up his carpetbag and headed into the house, leaving the muddy boots outside. "I'll get my notes," Dietrich called over his shoulder. "Can you contact Chapel at Key's Tavern?"

"I'll send young Meyers," answered Edwards to the disappearing Dietrich.

Shaw and Bergen were seated at a table in the hotel lobby, discussing legal papers spread in front of them when Dietrich and Edwards entered. Shaw was a handsome man with wavy brown hair. A thick gold chain with a gold compass for a fob ran from a buttonhole in his vest to one of the vest pockets. Bergen's long blond hair needed a trim. His pant legs were a little too short and the sleeves of his frock coat were a little too long.

Edwards introduced the men to Dietrich and, as they started to talk, Chapel hurried into the hotel lobby to join them.

"You are fortunate that young Bergen and I both had business in front of the Illinois Supreme Court," said Shaw in a rumbling voice. "In fact, we represent opposing sides in a land dispute. We attorneys are a strange breed. We contend vigorously in court. We storm and rage at each other, but before and afterwards, we remain friends and colleagues."

"In the Duff Armstrong murder trial Mr. Shaw was hired to assist the prosecutor by the family of the deceased," said Bergen. "The family knew about Mr. Lincoln's reputation as a staunch defense attorney. Mr. Fullerton, the prosecutor, unlike Mr. Shaw and me, is not an admirer of Mr. Lincoln."

"Is that due to political considerations?" asked Dietrich.

Bergen looked at Shaw. "Mr. Fullerton is a Douglas man and he's been a Democrat since birth, but I think there is more to it than that."

"Mr. Lincoln started with only the clothes on his back and through dogged diligence, the friendship of others, and some astonishingly good fortune, he has become one of the foremost legal practitioners of our generation," said Shaw, rubbing his chin. "Some men think he has risen too fast and come too far. They suspect that Mr. Lincoln had some sort of hidden advantage denied to them, although no such advantage has ever been identified. Others compare their achievements with Mr. Lincoln and feel envy. Some men value family background over personal achievement and believe that Mr. Lincoln is 'common.' I think Mr. Fullerton may hold all of those beliefs. He's a fine lawyer and a good man, but he is not as well liked. He lacks the skill at friendship and the sensitivity for the feelings of others, at which Mr. Lincoln excels."

"Personally, I find it admirable that Mr. Lincoln has achieved all that he has starting with the disadvantages he was saddled with," said Bergen.

Shaw nodded, "So do I. Mr. Lincoln is a ferocious courtroom opponent during a trial and a true friend afterward, win or lose. When Mr. Fullerton heard that our friend would undertake to defend Duff Armstrong, he was not nearly as sanguine about the outcome of cases as he had been before. He readily welcomed my assistance when I offered it."

Chapel glanced at Dietrich. "Did Mr. Fullerton feel unhappy about the outcome of the Duff Armstrong case?"

Shaw said, "Yes, and he has been vocal in his unhappiness. However, if you gentlemen want to learn about the trial, we may be getting ahead of ourselves. Mr. Fullerton asked me to assist him some weeks before the trial was scheduled to start in earnest. I presume you gentlemen know about the first postponement."

Dietrich answered. "We know that Mr. Lincoln used the time to scout the territory in question, to talk with the neighbors and to question Mr. Walker about the Norris trial in particular detail."

"It is said that Mr. Lincoln can try a case he knows nothing about the day he arrives in town. In the court circuit the judge and attorneys would travel together, arrive in a particular jurisdiction, set up court, and deal with all pending cases one after another in the course of a day. Maybe that's where Mr. Lincoln got the reputation of not preparing for cases. He certainly prepares thoroughly now."

"I've heard that when people heard Mr. Lincoln would be arriving in town for circuit court, they would mount horses, race out into the countryside to ask him to represent them, and, of course, to deny his services to their opponents," said Bergen.

Shaw nodded, "That did happen. It was rare but not unheard

of. Practicing the law was a physically demanding profession in those days. Lodging and food were bad. Often roads were nonexistent and streams had to be forded. The practice of law was based more on common sense and on a sense of fairness rather than case law and precedent. Most attorneys had other jobs such as newspaper editor or livery stable owner. They practiced on those few days when court was in session in the region. The rest of the time they worked at their other employment. Mr. Lincoln was one of the few who had no other means of support so he traveled around the circuit when it was on the move with Judge Davis, Mr. Swett and a few others. He learned to get to the heart of a case quickly."

Shaw looked off into space. "In those days, even more than now, people would come to town for the entertainment of listening to the cases. Naturally, the political parties would take advantage of the crowds and put on debates about the issues of public interest. Mr. Lincoln was nearly always chosen to argue the Whig Party position."

"But in this case, he had time to prepare," said Chapel diffidently.

"My apologies, gentlemen," said Shaw. "I was distracted by my memories. No doubt at my age it seems more interesting in retrospect than it actually was at the time."

"I came to watch the case," said Bergen. "It is an education for a young lawyer to watch Mr. Lincoln in action. He has a way of examining witnesses and conducting a defense that you cannot find in books. He is always gracious with his time and patient with questions. I have watched several of his trials in various courts and I did not want to miss this one. When I first spoke to him, he told me that he arrived five days before the start of the trial to go over the Norris trial with Mr. Walker once again and to talk with his witnesses and reassure them."

"In November the prosecution intended to call six witnesses, the most important being Doctor Stephenson and Charles Allen. It was Mr. Allen who was closest to the assault and who was universally respected as an honest man with no ax to grind. This time we subpoenaed a dozen men. Back in November, Mr. Lincoln had planned to call ten men. For this trial he added a few names to the list each day until he had twenty-two in all. Mr. Fullerton and I were mystified by the number of witnesses Mr. Lincoln subpoenaed. Mr. Fullerton asked the judge to insist that Mr. Lincoln tell us at once all the witnesses he would call, but the judge declined to so rule. At the Norris trial, Norris had testified alone on his own behalf. We asked ourselves — why in the world did Mr. Lincoln need so many?

"And there was another mystery, too," Bergen said. "By the fifth of May, all of the witnesses were present and accounted for except one. Charles Allen, the most credible witness to the actual assault and the key to the entire prosecution, had not appeared and could not be located by the sheriff. The Menard County sheriff was ordered to produce him instantly. When he could not, on the sixth a special writ was issued to all the sheriffs in Illinois instructing them to find and convey Allen to the court as soon as possible."

Dietrich frowned. "So Mr. Lincoln won the case due to the absence of a witness against Duff?"

"Is that what the rumors of Mr. Lincoln somehow winning the case unfairly are based upon?" asked Chapel.

The attorneys laughed together.

"No," started Bergen, but he was laughing too hard to continue.

"Not at all," began Shaw, but he had to stop to compose himself.

"I do not see what is so blamed funny about that," came a rough and resentful voice. The men looked up to see Jacob Armstrong looming over them.

"I don't reckon that is funny at all," said Armstrong. "But I can solve what you called a mystery."

"Why don't you join us?" asked Chapel politely. "You appear to have something to add to our conversation. I am anxious to hear it."

Armstrong pulled his hands into fists and stood silently for a moment. Then he relaxed, walked over to another chair and pulled it close to the table where the men were sitting.

"Mr. Shaw, Mr. Bergen," said Dietrich, "I'd like to introduce you to Jacob Armstrong, the younger brother of Duff."

141

Shaw and Bergen nodded. Armstrong scowled, but then stiffly he nodded back.

"I promised Ma that I would find you two," said Armstrong, ignoring the attorneys. "She said to tell you what I should have told you when you came out to the farm."

"If you would like the two of us to depart, we would certainly do so," said Shaw.

Armstrong scowled again and then sat silently as if he could not determine how to politely ask the men to leave.

"You can stay. Me and some of the boys had hand-carried Allen to a hotel in Virginia, Illinois, which was maybe twenty miles away from Beardstown. Somehow, Mr. Lincoln reckoned that we were the ones who had Mr. Allen. Mr. Lincoln took hold of me and my brothers and told us to fetch Allen at once. He asked us if we knew of anything more likely to convince the jury that Duff was guilty than to hide the strongest witness against him. He asked us how long we thought it would take for Sheriff West to find Allen once he commenced to serious looking. I guess we weren't convinced. Then, he asked us how Ma and our families would make out with the lot of us being in prison for interfering with the court. We still held out. Finally, he asked what we thought Ma would say when he told her that it was us who took Allen and who was hiding him."

Armstrong hung his head. "That very day we brung him back, but Ma figured it out anyway. She swears Mr. Lincoln didn't tell her and I reckon she's smart enough to reckon it on her own. She says, since then, we owe Mr. Lincoln for getting Duff out of jail and for keeping the rest of us out of jail. I tell you, there ain't gonna be many Democrat votes out of Menard County if the Armstrong men have anything to say about it. My daddy supported Mr. Lincoln when he first ran for the legislature and he claimed that only two men in all of New Salem dared to vote for Mr. Lincoln's opponent. I reckon we can do nearly as well for him in old Menard."

Armstrong stood up abruptly, knocking the chair back onto the floor. He set the chair upright and without a backward glance strode out of the hotel.

Shaw looked at Bergen. "Well, I didn't know the details, but I knew that Mr. Lincoln said something to one of the Armstrong men just before Allen appeared on the scene. I assumed it was something like that."

"Why would Mr. Lincoln want to be sure the witness likely to be the most damaging to his defense would appear?" asked Chapel in a puzzled tone of voice.

"I believe we are putting the cart before the horse once again," answered Bergen patiently. "With all the witnesses present at last, Mr. Fullerton and I went over our strategy once again and attempted to predict what Mr. Lincoln had up his sleeve. Our conjectures, however, were in vain. The next task was to select a jury from the venire men. We, of course, wanted sober men of reflection and experience. We wanted men past the rough passions of youth."

Shaw looked at Bergen. "Mr. Lincoln and Mr. Walker, on the other hand, wanted to choose men who could see themselves doing what Duff had done and who might someday need a sympathetic jury themselves. Mr. Lincoln wanted younger jurors. He told me once that he favored fat, jolly men who were at ease with life and do not like to judge others."

"For two days we battled over the selection of the jurors," said Shaw. "The result is one I have often enough had with Mr. Lincoln, although on each man I thought I was winning, when I examined the jury as a whole, I discovered that Mr. Lincoln had managed to get a very young group of men whose personal conduct was likely to leave them sympathetic to Duff Armstrong. Then the trial started. Let me set the scene for you."

Shaw's narrative left out no details.

CHAPTER NINETEEN

May 7, 1858
Menard County Courthouse, Beardstown, Illinois

Judge James Harriott, who had presided at the trial of James Norris, looked up from the papers on his desk and stared at Lincoln. The judge was used to seeing Lincoln in his customary rumpled black suit. It was not unusual for Lincoln's suit to show dust or occasionally a rust-colored stain. This morning, for the first time ever, Lincoln wore an immaculate white suit to a trial. Judge Harriott noted that, on closer examination, the sleeves were much too short. Lincoln's wrists and large hands protruded. The suit fit Lincoln as badly as his black suit did, but it did command attention. Lincoln's white suit contrasted with the somber black, grey and brown suits of the other men in court.

Judge Harriott noted that Fullerton and Shaw had arranged a careful tableau at the prosecution table. Press Metzker's young widow was seated in a prominent position next to the attorneys. Dressed in black, her pretty pale face and blue eyes might have drawn the attention and sympathy of the men of the jury seated in the jury box. Judge Harriott noted that Lincoln and Walker had balanced the scene by placing Hannah Armstrong, also dressed in black, next to the defense attorneys. Her sons flanked their mother.

Judge Harriott noticed that Abram Bergen sat leaning forward intently immediately behind the defense table. The courtroom was packed with spectators. A murder trial was of major interest in the community. Seeing Lincoln, who was rumored to be the probable Republican candidate for the United States Senate, as the leading defense attorney was an added attraction. Very few people who could find any excuse to be present were missing.

Bergen was bemused. He had greeted Lincoln when he took his seat and strategically placed himself so he could concentrate on Lincoln's defense of the case. Lincoln, however, had not turned to face Bergen, had not acknowledged his effusive greeting, and had not even been aware of him. Now, Bergen noted, Lincoln sat immobile, his head leaning back on his shoulders and his eyes locked on one spot on the featureless ceiling above. With his weathered skin, his overhanging forehead, and his lack of response and interest in what was happening around him, Lincoln could have been a half-wit or a weary laborer at the end of a very full day of exertion.

The judge cleared his throat. "The court will come to order. Is the prosecution ready?"

Fullerton, a short, tidy man, rose to his feet. "We are, your honor," he answered. Fullerton's clear deep voice carried to all corners of the courtroom.

"Is the defense ready?"

Lincoln slowly unfolded himself and rose. His eyes became alive and his face became animated. "The defense is ready," he replied. Lincoln's high-pitched voice was audible throughout the room.

"Mr. Fullerton, you may make your opening statement."

Lincoln relaxed into his chair as Fullerton walked over to the jury box.

"Gentlemen," said Fullerton, looking at the jurors, "this case fills me with sadness and anger. I regret that I am standing here before you. I regret that you are here to listen and make judgment in this matter. I regret that James Preston Metzker is no longer with us. I regret that his wife is now a widow and that his children are now orphans. Press Metzker was the first to offer help to his neighbors in need. He was a tower of strength to his family. He was a steady provider, a loving husband and father, and a pillar of the community. We shall all miss him."

Metzker's widow could be heard crying quietly in the courtroom.

"Press Metzker, who was as sturdy as one of the tall trees on his farm, will be with us no more. Why? He is gone from this earth because he was cut down in his prime by two godless men. These two brutes, in response to minor annoyances by Press, viciously and cruelly attacked him by ambush and stealth. With cold calculation and wanton immorality, losing sight of the fear of God, two men armed themselves with deadly implements of destruction and committed foul murder. They spilled his lifeblood onto the ground where it cries out to us. They crushed his skull in cowardly and craven actions that robbed him of many years of sweet life. Press will not live to see his children marry and continue his proud name. He will not share years of silver and gold with his beloved wife. His wife, his children and his neighbors were also robbed of many years of basking in the glow of his affections, being comforted in their times of trouble and finding help when it is needed most. Gnawing uncertainty and worry will be the lot of those thus robbed."

Fullerton turned and glared at Duff.

"The prosecution will show that William Armstrong, acting in concert with James Norris, who is already paying for his blasphemous deed of taking a life that belongs to The Almighty, did feloniously and with willful foresight, upon cold-blooded deliberation partake in an ambush using evil weapons which inflicted upon Press Metzker severe, grievous and life-ending wounds. We will prove that while Duff Armstrong distracted Press Metzker from the front, James Norris attacked him from behind. James Norris struck a brutal blow with a wooden club, later identified as a neck yoke from a wagon frame. At the same time or immediately thereafter, Duff struck a vicious blow with a metal substance encased in leather commonly called a "slungshot." You will hear testimony from several witnesses about the identity of the two assailants. There will be no doubt about that. You will also hear medical testimony that each wound, in and of itself, was fatal. Have no doubt about that. Together, the two wounds caused Press Metzker to languish for a time in great pain and distress before finally expiring."

Fullerton turned toward the weeping widow and paused. Then he turned back to the jurors.

"Gentlemen, I am sorrowful when I contemplate the grieving widow and I am filled with wrath when I contemplate the shameless arrogance and wickedness of the men who ignobly decimated the life of a man who gave shelter and support to the civilization that separates men from base beasts. Despite my feelings, I must do my duty, and you, my friends, must do the same. One of the conspirators who schemed to put an end to the life of a man more worthy than both of them combined has been judged and is now safely imprisoned far away from our fair community. The other sits before you. The death of Press Metzker calls for rectification. His very lifeblood calls out from the soil into which it was so wastefully and wantonly spilled. I entreat you to do your duty, and when the evidence is laid out before you it will point toward the only verdict that is possible. That is the verdict of guilty. Thank you for your attention."

Lincoln rose slowly to his feet and walked to the jury box. He stood in silent contemplation for a moment.

"Gentlemen," said Lincoln, "I agree with Mr. Fullerton."

Lincoln paused. "Mr. Fullerton is an excellent attorney, and he understands the law very well. Beyond question, this case is based on a tragedy. We would, all of us, do anything humanly possible to have Mr. Metzker return to us. Sadly, that is not possible. We have to content ourselves with the knowledge that Press Metzker is with Our Savior and beyond the vale of tears that is our life in this world."

Lincoln looked at each member of the jury in turn.

"I hope and trust that you gentlemen paid close attention what Mr. Fullerton said he and the honorable Mr. Shaw will prove to you. If, in fact, they can prove all that he set out to prove, you should and must find Mr. Armstrong guilty. However, let us remember what it is the prosecution has to prove."

Lincoln held up one finger.

"First, the prosecution has to prove that James Norris and Duff Armstrong acted in concert and from a prior plan. They will not be able to do so because, in fact, there was no prior plan. As Mr. Fullerton has already admitted, Duff Armstrong confronted Press Metzker head on. If James Norris took advantage of that for nefarious purposes of his own, that is not the fault or responsibility of Duff Armstrong. He cannot be held accountable for what another person did. If you conclude that James Norris caused the death of Press Metzker, it does not necessarily follow that Duff Armstrong had a role in his senseless murder. Unlike the prosecution, the defense has only the burden of presenting enough information that you conclude there is a reasonable doubt that they acted together."

Lincoln held up a second finger.

147

"Second, the prosecution has to prove that the second injury was the result of Duff Armstrong's actions. If the injury was due to some other cause, or if a reasonable man can conclude that the injury might be due to another cause, that is sufficient reason all by itself for a verdict of not guilty."

Lincoln held up another finger.

"Third, if the injury Duff Armstrong admittedly caused was not serious enough to cause death by itself, or if a man can find a reasonable doubt that it was sufficient by itself alone, then Mr. Armstrong is decidedly not guilty of Mr. Metzker's demise."

Lincoln dropped his hand to his side.

"You have heard the prosecution present a particular theory of the tragic events that ultimately resulted in the meaningless and vicious slaughter of a good man. The prosecution cannot change that theory. They cannot say that a man died due to strangulation and later change that and say that he died from a knife wound. Mr. Fullerton enumerated the elements of the crime. Please keep in mind that he must prove it each and every step along the way. The defense does not have to prove anything at all. That duty and burden is solely the responsibility of the prosecution. Any missed step, any link not fully forged, and the chain comes apart, the charges fail and Duff Armstrong must be found not guilty. Gentlemen, your duty charges you to pay close attention and seek out that flawed, weak link. I thank you for your close attention."

Lincoln walked slowly back to his chair.

"Mr. Fullerton, please call your first witness," announced Judge Harriott from the bench.

CHAPTER TWENTY

August 31, 1858
Springfield, Illinois

Shaw coughed and looked at Bergen, Chapel and Dietrich. "Excuse me, gentlemen, but my throat is getting sore and I could use a libation."

Dietrich hurried off and returned in a few minutes with a glass of lemonade.

Shaw looked at the glass and smiled. "It is not exactly what I had in mind, but it will suffice."

He took a drink and exhaled.

"I need to prepare for tomorrow, and this looks to be a logical stopping place."

"Mayhap I may be of some service," said Bergen. "Please correct me if I am mistaken, Mr. Shaw, but it seemed to me that the first series of witnesses were not, in themselves, remarkable or crucial to the outcome of the case. If I may attempt a summary?"

Shaw nodded and sipped at his drink.

"The prosecution presented ten men who had seen all or part of the altercation. There were, of course, some minor disagreements about details, but in essence all the men said that Duff confronted Press and that Norris came out of nowhere with a vicious and unexpected attack with a club or bludgeon of some sort. On cross-examination, with great politeness, Mr. Lincoln got each one to admit his limitations as a witness. All the men had been drinking. Some were positioned so as to see very little. Others had views that were obscured by trees or leaves. Most were admittedly far away from the action. Very few men claimed to see exactly what weapons were used. Taken singly, each witness's testimony had flaws. Taken together, they tended to back each other up and give the clear impression that Duff, Press and Norris were the ones involved in the struggle."

Bergen looked at Shaw, who nodded again. Bergen continued.

"Mr. Lincoln asked most particularly if any man had seen Duff with Norris before the fight began. Nobody had. They were not seen to have arrived together. They were not seen to have exchanged confidences. There was no evidence of a signal given that the fight was about to begin."

"Mr. Lincoln immediately seized upon a weakness of the prosecution," said Shaw. "Although the timing was suggestive, we could not prove that there was a conspiracy between Norris and Armstrong. It was clearly in our interest to link Armstrong to Norris so that each would share in part responsibility for the actions of the other person. We could not achieve that beyond doubt."

"Mr. Fullerton's opening statement may have over-promised what you could actually show the jury," said Bergen.

"Perhaps so," agreed Shaw. "However, if the jury accepted that, it greatly simplified our case. If we could tie Duff to a man already convicted of a crime, his conviction would drag Duff down with him. We knew that Mr. Lincoln would fight to separate the two men and use Norris as the scapegoat. It is difficult to imply anything in a courtroom so you have to come out and say something directly or yield the matter entirely. We decided to make the charge that Norris and Armstrong conspired against Metzker, even knowing our evidence was weak. The rest of our case was strong. We knew that if the jury accepted the charge, we were well down the road toward a conviction."

"The next witness starts the ball rolling in earnest," said Bergen.

"'Tis true," agreed Shaw. "Unfortunately, with the obligations I have scheduled, I do not know when we may be able to continue this discussion. I need to rest and prepare now. I have to leave Springfield right after court tomorrow and I am engaged for some weeks after."

"Sadly the same can be said for me," said Bergen.

"Would there be another legal matter in which you are both engaged?" asked Chapel hopefully.

"Nothing comes to mind," admitted Shaw. "I rarely have the chance to skin a lawyer as young as Abram here. After I school him tomorrow in court, heaven knows when he will have the courage to face an old lion like me again."

"Come to think of it, Mr. Shaw and I did promise Mr. Lincoln to attend one of the debates," said Bergen. "We both had the time free to attend the debate in Charlestown and we made arrangements to go there. Perhaps we could meet up after the debate."

"Yes," said Shaw, "I forgot. You are reporters and surely you will be covering that. We could meet at the Charlestown Hotel after the festivities are over and converse at some leisure."

CHAPTER TWENTY-ONE

September 15, 1858
Jonesboro, Illinois, Union County Fairgrounds: The Third Debate

"So this is Egypt," said Dietrich without enthusiasm.

"I feel that we have traversed the desert for forty years to get here," said Chapel. "It appears that few Egyptians have bothered to make the journey and those who have appear to be little excited."

"I don't know about that," said Dietrich. "I reckon that there are about twice as many in the audience as live in the town; same as at Ottawa and Freeport. At the hotel they told me the state fair is up and running in Centralia, which is nearby, and many people are there."

"This audience is solidly for Judge Douglas but I do not expect much in the way of demonstrations," said Chapel. "The most excited observers I saw were a team of oxen carrying a banner for Judge Douglas. The banner was hanging bottom upwards."

At the end of Senator Douglas's address, Dietrich looked over at Chapel and grumbled, "I could have stayed in bed had I kept a copy of Judge Douglas's last speech."

"Or if you had a copy of the speech he made before that," said Chapel. "If he should forget what he had planned to say, I believe I could very nearly recite it myself from having heard it so often. Lincoln and Trumbull conspired to abolitionize Whigs and Democrats. Republicans make a platform in favor of abolition and Frederick Douglass supports them. Lincoln invites the states to war with one another. The founding fathers authorized slavery. Lincoln opposes the Dred Scott decision because it does not give perfect equality to Negroes. Let the people decide whether they want slavery or not. If we take over Cuba, parts of Canada or Mexico, people there will decide. States should decide their own business."

Dietrich applauded but stopped when Lincoln stepped forward to speak.

At the end of Lincoln's reply, Dietrich slipped his thumbs

under his suspenders and started to orate, "Judge and I agree that the states should decide themselves about their business, as I told him many times. Where I disagree is that he and his friends, by supporting the ultimate spread of slavery, undo the actions of the founding fathers. They thought slavery was on the way to ultimate extinction. Until the Nebraska Bill, we all thought that. There was no conspiracy with Trumbull. Democrats as well as Republicans oppose slavery and support at least basic rights for Negroes. Popular sovereignty should give the people, not the Supreme Court, the final say on slavery. My principles are known and are the same everywhere. When the judge claimed I was so upset at the last debate that I had to be carried off, he must have been crazy to mistake being carried in triumph for being carried due to need."

Chapel stooped and pretended to be ready to carry Dietrich on his back. When Douglas started to speak, both men straightened and took out their notebooks. However, at the end of the speech, neither man had written much.

"Maybe Charlestown will be different," said Chapel.

"I've heard the judge talk about Mr. Trumbull tricking Mr. Lincoln out of a seat in the Senate so often that I wonder what the story is," said Dietrich, shutting his notebook.

"I heard about it from one of Mr. Lincoln's backers," explained Chapel. "In 1855, there was an election for senator in the Illinois legislature. Current Senator James Shields, who was a strong backer of Judge Douglas, was up for re-election as his term had expired. Due to the Nebraska Bill, there was strong opposition to the National Democratic Party and to Judge Douglas in particular. On the first ballot Mr. Lincoln polled forty-five votes out of the fifty needed for election. Mr. Trumbull, then an anti-Nebraska Bill Democrat, had five. Senator Shields had forty-one. You would expect that the five legislators would yield to the forty-five. However, that did not happen.

"Mr. Trumbull would not release his voters to go for Mr. Lincoln. The Douglas Democrats decided to change candidates, dropping Senator Shields in hopes of gathering enough votes to keep Illinois with two pro-Douglas Democratic senators. They knew that Joel Matteson, who was the Democratic governor, was popular with the legislators of all parties. He could attract votes if the balloting continued round after round. The anti-Nebraska legislators who were Democrats found it hard to vote for Mr. Lincoln, who was, after all, a member of the opposition Whig Party. After the ninth ballot, Mr. Lincoln saw that, if things continued as they were going, Governor Matteson would become the next senator. Mr. Lincoln told his forty-five voters to join Mr. Trumbull's five. Mr. Lincoln's supporters were not anxious to jump ship and support Mr. Trumbull, who was, back then, still a Democrat. Mr. Lincoln had to persuade them. He practically had to beg his most loyal backers to go with Mr. Trumbull. In the end, Mr. Lincoln's forty-five voters went over to Mr. Trumbull. Mr. Trumbull won the contest, and the Douglas supporters lost. So Mr. Trumbull was willing to risk losing the election to further his personal ambitions, and Mr. Lincoln was willing to lose the contest for the eventual betterment of what would later become the Republican Party.

"Judge Douglas takes advantage of the opportunity to present Mr. Lincoln as something of a buffoon and Mr. Trumbull as an untrustworthy turncoat," said Chapel. "He uses the story to assail both Mr. Lincoln and Mr. Trumbull at the same time."

"But now Mr. Trumbull is energetically campaigning for Mr. Lincoln all over the state. Why would he do that if he and Mr. Lincoln were competitors?"

"Judge Douglas implies that Mr. Trumbull is indebted to Mr. Lincoln," said Chapel. "If you asked him away from the debates and in confidence, he might tell you that Mr. Trumbull would rather have Mr. Lincoln contending for Judge Douglas's Senate seat than contending for his own."

"There is probably just enough truth in that way of answering that it is difficult to disprove," said Dietrich. I'll wager that Mr. Trumbull does not want Mr. Lincoln to set his sight on his Senate seat."

"I would not want him to set his mind on my job," said Chapel.

"I reckon you need have no worries on that account."

"It is easier to discount the charge that the Whig Party was 'Abolitionized,'" said Chapel. "The Whig Party lost its heart and its brain when Henry Clay and Daniel Webster both died in a short period of time. They welded the Whig Party together between the northern and southern sections of the country. Whether you agreed with them or not, they were giants in the governance of the United States. The lesser men who replaced them could not continue what the two statesmen had held together by sheer will."

"I do not doubt that Senator Douglas truly misses their wisdom even if they were in opposition to his party," said Dietrich. "We will need all the abilities of all good men in Congress to keep the fraying Union together."

Chapel nodded and spoke. "Do you believe Mr. Lincoln's argument that there is a conspiracy to extend slavery to every state and territory?"

"A conspiracy?" Dietrich shook his head. "Not if you mean did the men meet and plan in secret and set a written plan of action based on formal agreement among them to accomplish goals they purposefully hid from the public. Judge Douglas has convinced me that did not happen. But if you mean that the Southern Supreme Court judges, the president and others intend to forcibly defend and even extend slavery, yes, that I believe. I believe also that Judge Douglas, by his willingness to treat slaves like farm animals, whiskey or crop production, and his 'don't care if slavery is voted up or down' is aiding their goals, although he may not be backing slavery itself, as such."

"May God help the United States," said Chapel.

"May God help us all," replied Dietrich.

CHAPTER TWENTY-TWO

September 18, 1858
Charlestown, Illinois, Coles County Fairgrounds: The Fourth Debate

"This, I take it, is Lincoln country," said Chapel, pointing to one of the many banners hanging from the windows in town.

"Really?" asked Dietrich smiling. "From what evidence do you draw that conclusion?"

"I was undecided until I detected a banner that must have been eighty feet in length with a portrait of young Lincoln driving his ox team into the area," said Chapel.

"It is keen observations like that which must have propelled you into the field of journalism."

"That and the lack of skills to succeed in any honorable field of endeavor," said Chapel. "I presume it was similar with you."

"In my case the presence of an available position and the promise of actual cash money proved irresistible," said Dietrich. "Alas, I did not adequately consider the difference between the promise of money and the actual presence of money."

Chapel smiled.

"With the dust from the candidates' parades, I can hardly make out the banners," said Chapel.

"And the candidates are so covered with dust that they look like farmers after a day of plowing," said Dietrich.

Lincoln stepped forward to speak at a quarter to three. He was greeted by cheers and applause. After a moment, he said, "While I was at the hotel today, an elderly gentleman called upon me to find out whether I was really in favor of producing a perfect equality between Negroes and white people.

"While I had not proposed on this occasion to say much on that subject, yet as the question was asked me, I thought I would answer it. I will say that I am not, nor ever have been, in favor of bringing about in any way the social and political equality of the white and black races.

"I am not, nor ever have I been, in favor of making voters or jurors of Negroes, nor of qualifying them to hold office, nor to intermarry with white people; and I will say in addition to this that there is a physical difference between the white and black races which, I believe, will forever forbid the two races living together on terms of social and political equality. I, as much as any other man, am in favor of having the superior position assigned to the white race. I say upon this occasion, as I have on many others, I do not perceive that, because the white is to have the superior position, the Negro should be denied everything.

"I do not understand that, because I do not want a Negro woman for a slave, I must necessarily want her for a wife. My understanding is that I can just let her alone. I am now in my fiftieth year, and I certainly never have had a black woman for either a slave or a wife. So it seems to me quite possible for us to get along without making either slaves or wives of Negroes. I will add to this that I have never known a man, woman or child who was in favor of perfect equality, social and political, between Negroes and white men — with the possible exception of Judge Douglas's old friend, Colonel Richard M. Johnson."

Lincoln's supporters whooped, laughed and applauded. Dietrich looked at Chapel with a puzzled look on his face. "Colonel Johnson," Chapel shouted over the noise of the crowd, "was vice president of the United States for one term fifteen years ago or so. He never married, but he had two daughters by a mulatto slave he received as part of his father's estate."

Dietrich nodded and redirected his attention to Lincoln, who was saying, "… add to the remarks I have made that I have never had the least apprehension that I or my friends would marry Negroes if there was no law to keep them from it, but Judge Douglas and his friends seem to be in great apprehension that they might if there was no law to keep them from it."

The crowd roared with laughter.

"I give him the most solemn pledge that I will to the very last stand by the law of this state, which forbids the marrying of white people with Negroes. There is no place where an alteration of the social and political relations of the Negro and the white man can be made except in the state legislature, and as Judge Douglas seems to be in constant horror that some such danger is rapidly approaching, I propose that the judge be kept at home and placed in the state legislature to fight against the danger he fears.

"When Senator Trumbull returned to Illinois in August, he made a speech in Chicago in which he made a charge against Judge Douglas, which I understand proved to be very offensive to the judge. I personally knew nothing, and sought to say nothing, about it. I said only that I know Judge Trumbull and believe him to be a man of veracity. Judge Douglas then said he should hold me responsible for the slanders. I will hand out to the reporters portions of Judge Trumbull's speech and of Judge Douglas's speech."

Lincoln devoted the rest of his time to the charges and counter-charges between Trumbull and Douglas.

When Douglas stood to speak, his voice showed the strain the campaign had put on it.

"Ladies and gentlemen, I had supposed that we were assembled here today for the purpose of a joint discussion between Mr. Lincoln and myself upon the political questions that now agitate the whole country. Let me ask you what questions of public policy relating to the welfare of this state or the Union has Mr. Lincoln discussed before you?"

Shouts came from the audience, "None. None." The shouts were followed by loud applause.

"I am glad that I have at last succeeded in getting an answer out of him upon this question of Negro citizenship and eligibility for office, for I have been trying to bring him to the point on it ever since this canvass commenced. I will now call your attention to the question which Mr. Lincoln has occupied his entire time in discussing. He spent his whole hour in retailing a charge made by Senator Trumbull against me."

Douglas spent the rest of the speech recounting the differences between him and Trumbull.

After the applause for Douglas died away, Lincoln spoke again.

"Fellow citizens, Judge Douglas has said to you that he has not been able to get from me an answer to the question whether I am in favor of Negro citizenship. So far as I know, the judge never asked me the question before. He shall have no occasion to ever ask it again, for I tell him very frankly that I am not in favor of Negro citizenship. I mentioned in a speech of mine that the Supreme Court had decided that a Negro could not possibly be made a citizen, and without saying what was my ground of complaint in regard to that, or whether I had any ground of complaint, Judge Douglas has from that manufactured nearly every thing that he ever says about my disposition to produce an equality between the Negro and the white people. Judge Douglas tells people what my objection was when I did not tell them myself."

Lincoln's admirers responded with loud laughter and applause. Members of the audience called out, "Good. Good."

"Judge Douglas has told me that he heard my speeches north and my speeches south and there was a very different cast of sentiment in the speeches I made at the different points. I call upon every fair-minded man to read them and I dare Judge Douglas to point out any difference between my printed speeches north and south."

At the end of the speeches, the partisans of each candidate formed a parade. With bands playing and a brass cannon firing, each candidate was escorted from the speaking platform to his hotel. Chapel and Dietrich climbed up and sat upon the speakers' stand as each man scribbled in a notebook. As usual, Chapel finished first. He looked out into the dwindling crowd while Dietrich continued to write. Finally, Dietrich put his notebook down and started to shake out his writing hand.

"Well, it was not like Jonesboro," said Dietrich. "I had to take notes this time. Maybe Mr. Lincoln and Judge Douglas overheard our remarks. There was new material. Still, all together, I'd say this was the dullest of the debates thus far."

Chapel shook his head.

"I hope that I will be able to read what I wrote later on," said Dietrich.

Chapel sighed.

"Are you sad again?" asked Dietrich. "Did your editor send you another commendation?"

"No," answered Chapel. "I had no such missive."

"When I hear from my editor, he is usually questioning my expenses or complaining about my spelling. My paper is still considering whether to support Mr. Lincoln. I suspect that, in the end, the editor will give him a milk-and-water recommendation. What does your editor say about supporting Judge Douglas?"

"My editor concluded that Judge Douglas's statements about citizens of a territory being able to cast over the ruling of the Supreme Court by police regulations make him a fair-weather friend to slaveholders and a knave at heart."

"I'm sorry," said Dietrich. "That's just what you feared would happen."

"The longer I am away from Virginia, the more foolish it appears to talk of disunion, but I know when I get home I will be swept up in the tide. Like many men, I do not want my state to quit the Union, but I am a Virginian. What the citizens of Virginia do is what I will do."

"Surely it will not come to that," insisted Dietrich. "Surely there is a way to keep the Union intact. There are those men who would throw away the history of our great country for their particular interest, be it slavery or Abolitionism, but there are only a few of them."

Chapel shook his head.

"I have learned from you," said Dietrich earnestly. "I hope you have learned from me. I have never known a Negro personally. You know many such. I have come to see that, if they are freed, we must somehow make plans for that and not leave them adrift. You taught me that. I can see that it might be better for the nation as a whole to have gradual emancipation and compensation for slaveholders."

"Yet I have not convinced you that in the South slave territory must grow or our civilization must falter. If I cannot convince even you, how can the men in the South and the North come to a peaceful resolution of our differences?"

Dietrich sighed. "I still cannot countenance the extension of slavery. I believe it must, at the least, wither away. But I believe that men of good faith working together can ease the change that must come, both North and South."

"My editor wrote an editorial expressing the idea that if we Southerners had our own nation we could annex Cuba and at least part of Mexico to keep expanding to the South. He supports the current adventure in Nicaragua, albeit I have no doubt it will come to nothing in the end."

Dietrich's eyes went wide. "That would mean three wars in succession. Forgive me, but it sounds like lunacy. I have seen battle in Europe and, believe me, it is to be avoided if at all possible. War cost me my home. My youth ended forever on the battlefield. You cannot possibly imagine the horror of war."

Chapel said, "My editor and the people of Virginia cannot imagine it. And we are much more peaceful than the hotheads in South Carolina and elsewhere. It pains me to think that the lunatics may yet end up running the asylum."

Chapel shuddered.

"Perhaps I am gathering moonbeams, and I will awake to find my fears vanish with the dawn. So, what do you think of the candidates so far?"

Dietrich answered, "I would say that they are not so completely far apart in their thinking. I do not believe that Judge Douglas is in any way a supporter of slavery. If he had his way, I suspect he would end the practice. Mr. Lincoln is not an immediate Abolitionist. The difference, it appears to me, is that the senator wants to remain agnostic and to allow the people to decide whether they want slavery. Mr. Lincoln accuses him of acting like slaves are farm crops, whiskey or manufactured boots. Mr. Lincoln grants to slaves the standing of people, children of Providence, but he denies their right to vote, to sit on juries or serve in the legislature. Judge Douglas accuses him of having no plan or idea for what happens after the slaves are freed. Each man's accusation of the other is correct, as far as I can see."

"A good analysis," said Chapel. "I think they are both good men who would represent Illinois well in the senate, though neither man appears to recognize how fervently the South supports the expansion of slavery. Mr. Lincoln has surprised me by being able to stand up to the senator so well. Judge Douglas wore him out in the first debate, but since then Mr. Lincoln has come up to scratch each time."

"I did not find the dissertation on Trumbull versus Douglas to be of interest," said Dietrich, "but Mr. Lincoln has learned to respond to Judge Douglas's challenges without fail. He has become a puncher as well as a counter-puncher. I warrant that he felt he could not allow the charges to go unanswered lest the Democratic newspaper chide him for being afraid to answer."

"Let us head back to the hotel," said Chapel. "We both have an article to write and mail off. Tomorrow we will meet with Mr. Bergen and Mr. Shaw to resume learning about the Armstrong trial."

***

Bergen and Shaw appeared shortly after breakfast the next morning in the parlor of the Charlestown Hotel. They shook hands with Chapel and Dietrich.

"It was a masterful performance," said Shaw as he sat down. "The debate, I mean. The performance of both men gives me pride in the men that represent this great state. As much as I admire Mr. Lincoln and as many times as he has outwitted me in court, I still expected Judge Douglas to hammer him like a blacksmith hammers heated iron. Judge Douglas has debated on the national stage with the very greatest men of our age. He is, himself, more prominent than even our president. Members of the Senate sometimes give in to his desires simply to avoid crossing swords with the man. I did not expect a thrashing, but I did expect that he would rule the day. That did not happen. Both of them went at it hammer and tongs, and the sparks lit up the heavens."

"Mr. Lincoln did not appear to give as good as he got in the first two debates, but he did appear to answer every salvo with a salvo of his own," said Chapel. "He seems to be finding his footing against his formidable opponent."

Dietrich agreed. "As a contest it was well fought, and the candidates did not just repeat their earlier remarks, but I, frankly, heard little of national interest, unlike the earlier debates."

"I envy the two of you," said Bergen. "You have seen every debate. I believe the future of the country is being shaped before our eyes. I think we will tell our grandchildren that we saw the Douglas-Lincoln debates."

"Knowing the future is something that Divine Providence has seen fit to deny us," said Chapel.

"Probably in his wisdom The Almighty decided it was merciful that we do not know the pain and trouble that awaits us in this vale of tears," said Dietrich. "Could we live with pleasure the life before us if we knew how it would end and how many disappointments were in store for us?"

"You two are a gloomy lot this day," said Bergen, smiling.

"You see, gentlemen, how feckless youth reacts to age and wisdom," said Shaw.

"How went the Illinois Supreme Court dispute between the two of you?" asked Dietrich.

Shaw and Bergen laughed.

"I learned that, to become an old lion, one must develop strength and savvy well beyond the common run," said Bergen. "In short, I had my tail tied in knots from which I am still disentangling myself."

"I warned you, young lion," said Shaw. "In truth, young Bergen did himself proud. You must remember, gentlemen, that a contest of law is not like a game of horseshoes. We do not start with an even opportunity on an even field of competition, taking turns so that the skill or luck of one of the contestants determines the eventual outcome. Before the Supreme Court, Mr. Bergen had the much weaker side of the argument, and fewer similar cases had been ruled in favor of his side of the argument. Despite his disadvantages, he made an excellent argument using the tools at his command, and the outcome was far closer than an unbiased reading of the matters would have led a learned person to expect. The young lion gave proof that the lord of the pack had better watch out for the new contender for his throne."

"In the Duff Armstrong trial it would have been accorded a victory if Mr. Lincoln persuaded the jury to bring back a conviction of manslaughter or felonious assault," said Chapel. "However, he did what many deemed impossible and got a verdict of not guilty."

163

Shaw grimaced. "If you want to talk about seeing an old lion stalking, killing and disemboweling his prey, you should talk about what Mr. Lincoln did to Mr. Fullerton and me at that trial. Shall we recommence with those events, gentlemen? As I recall, we were about to call our medical expert witness to the stand. Let me begin at that point."

CHAPTER TWENTY-THREE

May 7, 1858
Menard County Courthouse, Beardstown, Illinois

"Mr. Fullerton, you may call your next witness."

"Thank you, your honor," Fullerton said. "The prosecution calls Doctor B.F. Stephenson."

As Lincoln folded himself back into his chair, Doctor Stephenson walked to the witness stand. Doctor Stephenson was an older man with a snowy white beard and neatly combed white hair.

"Your honor, if we need to, we can establish Doctor Stephenson's expertise."

"I reckon we'll agree that the good doctor is a good doctor," said Lincoln.

The audience tittered, and the judge looked around him sharply. Judge Harriott banged his gavel once. "You may proceed, counselor."

"Thank you, your honor," said Fullerton, nodding once at the judge. Fullerton turned and approached the witness.

"Doctor Stephenson, did you attend to the medical care of the late James Preston Metzker, known as Press Metzker of Cass County in our fair state of Illinois?"

"I did," answered Stephenson.

"Did you attend him on August 31 and September 1 in the year of Our Lord 1857?" asked Fullerton.

"That I did," answered Stephenson.

"What was the reason, doctor, that you ceased your medical attentions to Press Metzker on the first of September?"

"On that date Mr. Metzker died," said Stephenson bleakly.

Fullerton walked over to the defense table and ostentatiously looked at some papers.

Walker leaned over and whispered to Lincoln, "That's a good trick. He leaves the jury thinking about the death of Press Metzker. Will that hurt our case?"

Lincoln leaned toward Walker and whispered, "It does leave

an impression with the jury, but it will not hurt us unless we argue that Press is still alive."

"Why don't you object to his obvious playacting?"

Lincoln smiled. "Fullerton is calling the tune I intended to dance to. Once the judge allows this, he will allow me to do my play-acting. Mr. Fullerton will not be in any position to object."

Fullerton held up a paper triumphantly and marched back over to the doctor.

"Doctor Stephenson, in your duties as a physician, did you determine what caused the untimely and unwarranted death of Press Metzker?"

Stephenson nodded, "I did."

"Would you please describe for the court the cause of death?" asked Fullerton. "Please tell us why Mr. Metzker came to meet such a cruel death at such a young age as to leave his widow and children bereft of his loving care."

Walker looked over at Lincoln, who was looking off into space.

"Mr. Metzker sustained two serious injuries," said Stephenson, "either of which could have been fatal. One was a skull fracture in the middle of the lower back portion of the skull."

Stephenson placed his hand on his head to indicate the location. "It was a deep fracture and the bone was pressed in against the surface of the brain. In addition, there was a second skull fracture at the top near corner of the right eye socket."

Stephenson touched his face and traced the location of the second fracture with his finger.

"You tell us, Doctor, that either wound by itself could be sufficient to result in the death of even a hale and hearty young man?"

"That is correct," said Stephenson.

"Did you speak to Mr. Metzker about how he came by the injuries?"

Stephenson paused, looking at Lincoln.

"Mr. Lincoln," called out the judge, "do you want to make an objection of hearsay?"

"Your honor, I reckon the jury should hear what Mr. Metzker said to the doctor and since he is, sadly, no longer on this earth,

Doctor Stephenson is the only person who can tell us what he said."

"Very well," said Judge Harriott. "Since there is no objection from the defense, I will allow the doctor to respond to the question."

Fullerton was not able to hide an expression of surprise.

"Mr. Metzker told me that he was attacked by James Norris and Duff Armstrong," said the witness. "He said Norris hit him with a club and Armstrong hit him with something. He did not know what it was. Norris jumped him from behind without warning, and Armstrong came at him from the front. He said he had a terrible headache and the fight was over in seconds. He said he pulled himself upon his horse and immediately headed home."

Stephenson continued. "Mr. Metzker said he became so dizzy that he fell off his horse a couple of times on the way home. He said that he did not remember how many times he fell off. It was certainly more than once and could have been four or five times."

Fullerton frowned briefly. Stephenson started again.

"His headache grew worse on the way back home. He said he was barely able to dismount, and he staggered inside his house. Mrs. Metzker put him to bed and sent their son to me at daybreak. I came as soon as I could, but upon examination I knew that there was nothing I could do for him. Mr. Metzker got weaker as the day went on. He took a little water, but he would not eat. He lost the ability to speak and slipped into a coma. In the afternoon he perished."

"Are you absolutely certain, Doctor, that the injuries Press sustained in the fight caused his death?" asked the prosecutor.

"I am certain. I attended Press Metzker and his family for years. He was a strong, healthy young man who would probably have lived to a ripe old age except for the vicious attacks upon his person."

"Thank you, doctor," said Fullerton, shaking his head sadly. "Your witness, Mr. Lincoln."

Lincoln rose and walked calmly toward the witness stand.

"Doctor Stephenson, have you been in practice in this area for a long time?"

"Yes," said Stephenson.

"And you have known the Metzker family for many years?"

"Yes," Stephenson answered.

"Then the events of the year past must have been a tragedy for you personally as well as for the Metzker family, correct?" asked Lincoln.

"It was a needless tragedy."

"Completely senseless," agreed Lincoln. "The mixture of heedlessness and alcohol often leads to disaster, doesn't it?"

"Don't I know it," said Stephenson.

"If I might ask you for some clarification," said Lincoln. Stephenson nodded.

"You mentioned that either wound could have been fatal," said Lincoln.

"Yes, sir," answered Stephenson.

"Which wound was the more severe, doctor?" asked Lincoln.

"The wound to the back of the head," answered Stephenson immediately.

"Could you explain why that wound, and not the wound to the front of the skull, was more serious?" Lincoln asked.

"Yes, the wound to the back of the skull was delivered with terrible force. It smashed in the skull," Stephenson explained. "The club had to be wielded with full strength. Pieces of skull lacerated the brain. It was a grievous, grievous injury."

"You testified about that injury during the Norris trial. Did you not?"

"I did," responded Stephenson.

"So you studied on that injury at some length?"

"Yes, I did," said Stephenson.

"In that earlier trial, did you testify that the injury to the back of the head alone, the injury caused by Norris smashing Mr. Metzker's skull with terrible force using a club, would have caused his death?"

Stephenson frowned and closed his eyes. "I don't know if I was asked that but that wound alone would have been fatal."

"I must object, your honor," said Fullerton. "Mr. Lincoln is

168

leading the witness, and the matter covered is irrelevant."

"Mr. Fullerton objects that the matter is irrelevant?" asked Lincoln. "It does not matter to him that Press Metzker was a dying man immediately after his encounter with Norris?"

"Mr. Lincoln, save your arguments for your closing summary at the end of the trial," said Judge Harriott sharply.

"Yes, your honor," said Lincoln contritely.

"Doctor Stephenson, you have listened to both trials. Have you heard anyone say that Duff Armstrong struck Mr. Metzker before Norris did? Wasn't Mr. Metzker already dying before Duff struck him?"

Shaw popped to his feet. "Objection, hearsay."

"The prosecution does not want you to answer, Doctor," said Lincoln. "I will withdraw the question."

Lincoln walked back to the defense table and looked through some papers.

Walker whispered to Lincoln, "Legally, the order of the injuries does not matter if both were fatal bruises."

"The jurors might think that it matters," replied Lincoln in a whisper. "In my experience very few jurors practice law."

Lincoln headed back toward the witness stand and stopped a few feet away.

"Doctor Stephenson, we have spoken about the skull fracture at the back of Mr. Metzker's head. I propose, now, to talk about the fracture that originated at the right eye socket. Do you understand?"

"Of course," said Stephenson.

"I'm certain that you do, sir," said Lincoln smiling. "I just want to be certain that everyone in the courtroom is with us."

"I understand, sir," replied Stephenson. He glanced at the jury.

"Thank you, sir," said Lincoln. "You testified that the injury that caused the fracture to the back of Mr. Metzker's skull was the result of a terrible blow. In order to cause a fracture of the eye socket, like the one Mr. Metzker suffered, how much force is needed?"

"It would take much less force than the other injury."

"Much less force," repeated Lincoln, looking over at the jury. "You also testified that Mr. Metzker could not have survived the fatal bruise to the back of his skull. Have you had patients other than Mr. Metzker who had a fractured eye socket?"

"Yes, I have."

"Have you also in your professional reading or consultations read about or heard of other patients who had fractured eye sockets and no other serious injuries?"

"Yes."

"Did any of these patients, yours or that you read about, survive their injury?"

"Most of them did," answered Stephenson. "I can recall patients of mine who survived that injury. Especially young strong patients with a will to survive are likely to recover completely."

Lincoln stepped closer to Stephenson. "Would you describe Mr. Metzker as a young strong man with ample reason to live?"

Stephenson answered, "I would."

"I'm curious," said Lincoln. "Do you recall how the fractures of the eye socket you saw, read about or consulted about occurred?"

Stephenson was silent for a moment. Then he replied. "Some injuries occurred in fights, some from being kicked in the face by a horse or a mule, some from having something fall upon them from a height, some from the patient falling and one, as best I can recall, from a buggy overturning. There could have been other causes in addition."

"Thank you, doctor," said Lincoln. "I have no more questions."

CHAPTER TWENTY-FOUR

September 19, 1858
Charlestown, Illinois

"Mr. Lincoln did not ask Doctor Stephenson whether Mr. Metzker would have survived had the eye socket fracture been his only injury," said Dietrich.

"Precisely," answered Bergen. "Mr. Lincoln did not know how the doctor would answer that question. Therefore, he did not ask. He led the jury to think that it was probable without having to ask the potentially fatal question."

"Mr. Fullerton and I debated briefly if we wanted to ask that particular question and we decided not to ask either," said Shaw. "We had his testimony that either of Mr. Metzker's injuries could have been fatal. We decided, wisely I believe, to leave it at that."

Bergen said, "Thinking about it now, I do not know if even Doctor Stephenson himself knew how he would answer. Such a question could be fatal for either side."

"I do not understand what a 'fatal question' is," said Chapel.

"You brought it up," said Shaw to Bergen. "You explain it to our esteemed journalistic friends."

"There is an old story that lawyers tell to illustrate the truism that one of the most dangerous things that an attorney can do is to ask a question to which he does not know the answer. No doubt the teachers of the Code of Hammurabi used it with their students. It happened that a young attorney found himself cross-examining the only witness who averred that his client was the one who bit off the ear of the man he was fighting during a tavern brawl. The attorney got the witness to admit that the room was dark. He got the witness to admit that he had been drinking. He got the witness to admit that he was at some distance from the melee. Finally, the attorney got the witness to admit that, in the confusion and darkness, the witness could not swear he had seen the attorney's client bite off the man's ear. However, instead of stopping, the attorney went on to ask one question more.

"If you did not see my client bite off the man's ear," asked the attorney, "why did you testify that he did?"

"Well," the witness answered, "I did see him spit it out."

Shaw and Bergen laughed until there were tears in their eyes. Chapel and Dietrich joined in the laughter also.

"So, if Mr. Lincoln asked Doctor Stephenson about patients who had fractured eye sockets, Mr. Lincoln probably knew that the doctor had treated patients with that sort of injury and that the patients survived," said Dietrich.

"Almost a certainty," Bergen piped in. "He must have questioned people in the community about Doctor Stephenson's medical practice. I would wager that, if Doctor Stephenson had not remembered, Mr. Lincoln would have been ready with names and dates of treatment."

"Had we done the same we would have been prepared to ask the doctor about differences between the injury or injuries his patients suffered and the injury to Press Metzker," said Shaw. "However, we did not. Mr. Lincoln out-worked us on the matter and we did not anticipate his line of questioning."

"Let us return to the trial," said Shaw, settling back into his chair. "The prosecution had only one witness remaining, and that was Charles Allen. He was the one witness who was not a partisan. He was close to the scene, not impaired by spirits, and, of all the witnesses, he was the only one whose testimony could not be challenged or gainsaid. We decided to put him on as the last witness and to separate him from the other witnesses to the assault for a number of reasons. First, he presented himself better than the other witnesses. Second, his testimony had been absolutely crucial to Norris's conviction. Third, we wanted his testimony to stand out to the jurors. The other witnesses were a mixed group and some had limited credibility. We did not want possible doubts about them to taint Mr. Allen's testimony."

Shaw's tone became focused as he recalled the events in the courthouse on May 7, 1858.

***

Shaw and Fullerton conversed quietly at the prosecution table for a few moments.

"Your honor, the prosecution would like to call Mr. Charles

Allen to the stand."

Charles Allen stood and walked calmly to the witness stand. He was a robust man with short curly gray hair and alert brown eyes. Allen's face was tanned and weathered.

"Do you swear to tell the truth, the whole truth and nothing but the truth, so help you God?"

With his hand placed firmly on the Bible, Allen answered, "I do, so help me God."

Fullerton strode across the courtroom and stopped in front of the witness.

"Would you please identify yourself to the court?"

"My name is Charles Allen. I reside on my farm located in Menard County, not far from the town of Havana."

"Can you tell the jury, please, where you were on the night of August twenty-ninth of the year last?"

"I was at Walker's Grove from the afternoon of August twenty-eighth until the early morning hours of August twenty-ninth. After that I went home."

"While at Walker's Grove did you witness an assault upon the person of one Press Metzker?"

"I did, sir," said Allen.

"Before telling us about the assault, let me ask questions about other matters. Had you been drinking?"

"Yes, sir," answered Allen. "I had taken some whiskey, but it is not my custom to drink to excess. I was still sober when I witnessed the assault."

"Were you located at a distance from the assault?"

"I was, mayhap, twenty yards or so away and seated so as to look directly at the events."

"Were there any obstructions between you and the defendant and Mr. Metzker that obstructed your observations of the events in question?"

"No, sir."

"We have been told that the assault occurred late at night, at or around eleven. Is that consistent with your memory of events?"

"Yes, sir," said Allen. "I did not look at my watch immediately before or after the assaults, but my best estimate is that that would have occurred right at or very close to 11 p.m."

"Tell me, sir," said Fullerton, "how could you see clearly from a distance of twenty yards at that time of night?'

"The moonlight was bright," replied Allen. "It was not a full moon, but it was nearly full, and the moon was high in the sky, just past being overhead. It shone down upon the scene and illuminated it with clarity."

"Were you tired?" asked Fullerton. "Had you been sleeping?"

"I was fully awake," answered Allen. "I had been talking with friends about the horse races that day. I was fortunate enough to win a little hard cash and I went a little apart. I was reckoning on what would be the best thing to do with my winnings when the assault occurred."

"That answers my preliminary questions," said Fullerton. "Now, sir, would you describe that assault for the jury, please?"

Charles Allen paused for a moment and then he started to speak, looking off over the heads of those seated in the chamber.

"I was sitting on the hillside, as I said, perhaps twenty yards or so from where there is a flat place between hills. Below me, I noted that Press Metzker was walking unsteadily in my general direction on the flat. A man I recognized as Duff Armstrong confronted him and started to talk loudly to him. Then, I saw James Norris flash in behind Press and clout him with all his strength on the back of Press's head. Norris had a wooden club in his hand and made a vicious strike, rising up on his toes to get more height and leverage. I saw Norris bring the club down with all his might.

"I heard the blow," said Allen. "It was a sickening sound, like smashing a rock into a watermelon."

Fullerton winced.

"Did you also see Duff Armstrong attack Press Metzker?"

"I did," answered Allen. "After the strike by Norris, Duff Armstrong swung from his shoulder and struck Press on the forehead just above the right eye and close to his nose. I did not hear that blow, but I saw it quite clearly."

"Did Armstrong use his fist or did he have a weapon?"

"He had a weapon," said Allen. "It looked to me to be a metal ball encased in leather and hung from a rope that is called a

174

slungshot."

Fullerton moved deliberately to the prosecution table and returned with the slungshot that had been entered into evidence at the start of the trial. Standing where the jurors and the witness could see, Fullerton held the slungshot by the end of the rope and allowed the leather-covered metal ball to rotate in little circles. Even the whispers in the courtroom stilled as everyone stared at the lethal-looking weapon. Fullerton allowed the silence to grow for several moments. When he spoke, several members of the jury and the audience flinched.

"Mr. Allen, do you recognize this grievous devil-inspired device?"

"It looks like the weapon Duff Armstrong used to assault Press Metzker. It is at least the same type of implement."

"Were you aware, before you gave any testimony about the crime in any trial, Mr. Allen, that the Menard County Deputy recovered this very weapon from the ground close to where Press Metzker was brutally assaulted and murdered?" said Fullerton, still allowing the weapon to dangle.

"I was not, sir," answered Allen.

Fullerton jerked the rope. The slung shot jumped and people in the courtroom gasped. Slowly, Fullerton wrapped the rope around the leather cover.

"Mr. Allen, would you please demonstrate for the jury the fatal blow Duff Armstrong struck on poor Press Metzker? Mr. Shaw, would you join us and take the part of the deceased?"

As Shaw walked across the courtroom, Walker looked at Lincoln to see if he would object. Lincoln sat unmoving and appeared disinterested in what was taking place in front of him.

"Would you please position yourself as Duff Armstrong and tell Mr. Shaw how to stand as the victim?" asked the prosecutor.

Lincoln remained quiet and immobile as Allen told Shaw where to stand. Allen moved to stand directly in front of Shaw.

"Will you please use the slungshot to show the court how Duff Armstrong attacked Press Metzker?"

"No, sir!" said Allen, showing emotion for the first time. "That is a dangerous weapon and I would be likely to injure Mr.

Shaw even using it very slowly."

"You're right," said Fullerton, feigning shock. "I did not consider how deadly the hellacious weapon really is. Please forgive me."

"Perhaps Mr. Allen could show us with his open hand," suggested Shaw.

"That is an excellent idea," said Fullerton. "Mr. Allen, could you show us how the blow was struck?"

"Armstrong raised his hand above his shoulder to about eye level," said Allen, demonstrating as he talked. "He brought it down hard like a man cracking a whip."

Allen brought his arm down slowly.

"Could you show us at the speed Armstrong used."

Allen took a full step back and repeated the motion, this time quickly.

"Did Armstrong use his full strength?" asked Fullerton.

"It seemed to me like he did."

"Can you show us on Mr. Shaw where the blow to Press Metzker landed?"

Allen took a step forward.

"It landed about here," said Allen, using his finger to trace a short line on Shaw's forehead from the brow above Shaw's right eye into the eyebrow. "I could not be certain if it continued on the eye itself or not."

"Can you show us again at full speed?"

Allen stepped back and demonstrated the movement again.

"One more time, please."

Again Allen demonstrated.

"Thank you, Mr. Allen," said Fullerton. "I have no more questions for you."

"Mr. Lincoln, would you like to cross-examine the witness?" asked the judge.

Lincoln rose to a standing position.

"Your honor, I'd like to reserve my cross-examination of this witness for a later time."

"Very well," said Judge Harriott. "I believe the prosecution has completed calling its witnesses."

"We have, your honor," said Fullerton.

"Then I declare a recess until one o'clock for dinner. Jurors will refrain from discussing this case with anyone, including other jurors." Judge Harriott banged his gavel. "We will resume at one. Court is dismissed."

People filed out of the courtroom, talking excitedly about the course of the trial and arguing about what the verdict would be. Local restaurants and boarding houses began to fill up with people wanting to eat. Lincoln escorted Hannah Armstrong from the courtroom and walked with her along the street. Hannah kept a firm grip on Lincoln's arm.

"I don't think I can go back in there," said Hannah in a shaky voice. "I cannot listen to any more men accuse Duff of murder."

"You don't need to," replied Lincoln.

"How much longer will it take?" asked Hannah.

"We will finish today, I expect," answered Lincoln, steering Hannah around some muddy ground.

"I cannot stand to hear them talk so about Duff," said Hannah with tears in her eyes.

"I'm afraid you'll have to," said Lincoln. "People will gossip. Even after Duff is likely acquitted, some will say that he got away with murder."

Hannah froze and stared up at Lincoln.

"Duff will be a marked man," said Lincoln, looking down at Hannah. "He will need to walk very carefully around the law, and the Metzker family, too. I'll talk to him, and you need to talk to him, too. Tell him that he cannot run wild or take chances after this. He will have to be as law-abiding and proper as a preacher's wife in a parish full of spinsters."

Hannah attempted to speak and finally forced out the word, "Acquitted?"

"I will do everything in my power to make it so," answered Lincoln. "I hope and expect he will return home with you tonight."

Tears began to run down her face as Hannah stood silently and looked up at Lincoln. She reached out and patted him on the arm.

"I'll be back in the courtroom then."

Then she turned and walked away.

Lincoln strolled down the street, smiling and nodding toward the people he passed. Noticing Bergen approaching, Lincoln's face lit up and he smiled broadly.

"Abram," said Lincoln, "have you come to observe the trial? I reckon that it may prove instructive. I wish that you had arrived in time to see the prosecution case, though. They had a most interesting approach that may not be apparent if you only observe the defense."

Lincoln reached out his hand and shook hands with Bergen.

"I heard the prosecution," answered Bergen. "In fact, I was sitting right behind you."

"Did you slip in just before the case began?" asked Lincoln. "Because I swear that I never saw you."

"No, sir," answered Bergen. "I greeted you and wished you good fortune. Don't you remember?"

"I certainly would have remembered that," answered Lincoln. "Are you making a joke? If so, you need to practice your delivery."

"No, sir," answered Bergen. "I willingly yield that arena to you. I suspect that you were mentally fully engaged in the upcoming contest, and that you did not allow yourself to be distracted."

"I have been accused of that before," admitted Lincoln. "I suppose that it might be so. Come tell me what you think are the areas that I should attack during the defense argument. I must tell you that it is my firm hope and intention before the day is out to have Duff Armstrong acquitted."

***

Upon hearing the word "acquitted," Dietrich turned his head abruptly toward Bergen and spoke. "Acquitted? How could that be? Charles Allen's testimony was damning all by itself. The weight of the testimony of the other witnesses backed him up in every particular. Mr. Lincoln's questioning of the doctor — Stephenson, was it? — was very well done, but it could not erase that the wound caused by Armstrong could have been fatal. The jurors were not likely to convict Armstrong of murder, but I don't see how they could acquit him of manslaughter, or at least a serious assault charge. How could that be?"

"Nevertheless, we know that Duff was acquitted. We knew that when we started to follow this path. What we need to discover is how," said Chapel.

"Keep in mind that you have only heard the prosecution case," said Bergen. "Mr. Fullerton and Mr. Shaw are excellent attorneys. At this point in the case, the jury would very likely be thinking the same thoughts you just expressed, Mr. Dietrich. As an attorney, I could see chinks in the prosecution armor that Mr. Lincoln would probably attack, but observers not trained in the law would agree that things look grim for Armstrong at this point."

"At the risk of sounding like a character from Edgar Allen Poe, I suspect that resolution of that mystery will have to be postponed," said Shaw, pulling his pocket watch out of his vest pocket and opening the case. "I regret, gentlemen, that my available time here has nearly expired."

Dietrich and Chapel looked at Bergen.

"Alas, gentlemen, I had hoped to have more time available, but duty calls," Bergen said.

Shaw snapped the watchcase closed. "I'll tell you what I can do. I enjoyed listening to the debate and I would like to hear another. The next debate is in Galesburg and nearly a month away. Given that much time, I can arrange my schedule so as to have enough time the day after the debate to devote to you gentlemen so that we may complete the defense side of the trial. Would it be possible, Mr. Bergen, for you to join us at that time?"

"I could," said Bergen. "It may even be possible to have Mr. Lincoln's co-counsel, Mr. Walker, join us at that time. I will write and inquire. He is heavily involved in the campaign. He may intend to attend the debate in Galesburg. If so, I believe he would be willing to join us. I regret the delay, but it is doubtful that Mr. Shaw and I can work out a common free time and place before then."

"I will certainly be there," said Dietrich. "I presume Mr. Chapel will."

"I will," said Chapel. "Let us resolve to meet then."

CHAPTER TWENTY-FIVE

October 7, 1858
Galesburg, Illinois, Old Main of Knox College: The Fifth Debate

The weather at Galesburg on October 7 gave evidence that summer was over and the election was not far off. Although the freezing rain of the past day and evening stopped, there was still frost on the ground. The intermittent whistling wind made it impossible at times to hear the candidates — except for those few people who managed to occupy the area immediately in front of the speakers' stand. In spite of the weather, the audience was the largest for any of the debates so far; thousands of people had arrived at the college to hear Douglas and Lincoln speak.

Chapel and Dietrich arrived far earlier than the two-thirty starting time. They took up positions directly in front of the speakers' stand.

"It is infernally cold," said Chapel, stomping his feet.

"You have never been to Pennsylvania in the winter," said Dietrich.

"It could not be colder than this," said Chapel, shivering.

"I dislike to disagree but I must. I overheard Mr. Lincoln tell some of his supporters that he had occasion to visit Philadelphia during the winter. He said he saw and admired the famous statue of William Penn in the main square. Mr. Lincoln said he observed one especially cold morning that Mr. Penn had slipped his hands inside his pockets."

Dietrich chuckled, and Chapel smiled. A banner torn from one of the windows skittered along the ground as the wind pushed it along. It wrapped itself around Chapel's legs.

Dietrich laughed. "You see, if you wait long enough, the flags and banners will throw themselves about you and keep you warm. It is cold, but the sun is shining brightly and the heated contentions of the debaters may yet raise the temperature to a commodious level."

Douglas addressed the crowd with a hoarse voice that did not carry as well as it had earlier in the campaign. Dietrich chewed on the end of his pencil and Chapel looked bored while Douglas again described popular sovereignty and repeated his other arguments. The reporters perked up when Douglas charged the Democratic Buchanan administration with supporting Lincoln.

"You know that the axe of decapitation is suspended over every man in office in Illinois, and the terror of proscription is threatening every Democrat by the present administration unless he supports the Republican ticket in preference to my Democratic associates and myself. I could find an instance, in the postmaster in the city of Galesburg, and in every other postmaster in the vicinity, all of whom have been stricken down simply because they discharged their duties honestly and supported the regular Democratic ticket.

"The Republican Party is unlike all other political organizations. It is a sectional party that appeals to northern pride, northern ambition and northern prejudices, against southern people, southern states and southern institutions. The leaders hope to unite the northern states in one great sectional party, and as the North is the strongest section, they will be enabled to out-vote, conquer, govern and control the South.

"Is there a Republican residing in Galesburg who can travel into Kentucky and carry his principles with him across the Ohio River? This Republican Party is unable to proclaim its principles in the north and in the south. It cannot even proclaim them in all parts of the same state. My friend Lincoln in the extreme northern part of Illinois can proclaim bold and radical Abolitionism like Giddings, Lovejoy or Garrison, but when he gets a little further south he claims he is a disciple of Henry Clay and has nothing at all to do with Abolitionism, Negro equality or Negro citizenship.

"At Charlestown he defied me to show that there was any difference between his speeches in the north and in the south. In a speech in Chicago in July last, Mr. Lincoln took the ground that the Negro race is included in the Declaration of Independence as the equal of the white race, and there should be no such thing as a distinction making one superior and the other inferior."

Someone in the audience called out, "That's right!"

"Yes," snapped Douglas, nodding vigorously. "I have no

181

doubt that you think it is right, but the Lincoln men down in Coles, Tazewell and Sangamon counties do not think it is right." Many in the audience cheered and applauded. Someone in the audience yelled, "Good."

"Well, you say good," said Douglas, pointing at the man who yelled. "You are going to vote for Mr. Lincoln because he holds that doctrine. I will not blame you, but I will show you in immediate contrast to that doctrine what Mr. Lincoln said down in Egypt in order to get votes there." Douglas repeated what Lincoln about the differences between the races.

"Good for Mr. Lincoln," came from the audience.

"Fellow citizens," bellowed Douglas, straining his voice to be heard, "here you find men hurrahing for Mr. Lincoln and saying that he did right, when in one part of the state he stood up for Negro equality, and in another part, for political effect, discarded the doctrine and declared that here always must be a superior and inferior race. Now, how can you reconcile those two positions? He is to be voted for in the south as a pro-slavery man, and he is to be voted for in the north as an Abolitionist."

Laughter came from a small group of Douglas's adherents in the audience.

"When I was down in Monroe County a few weeks ago, I saw handbills posted announcing that Mr. Trumbull was going to speak on behalf of Lincoln, and what do you think the name of his party was there? Why, the 'Free Democracy.' Monroe County has always been an old fashioned Democratic county, and hence it was necessary to make the people believe that they were Democrats fighting for Lincoln. Come up to Springfield and you will find that the convention of his party dare not adopt the name of Republican, but assembled under the title of 'all opposed to the Democracy.' Thus you find that Mr. Lincoln's creed cannot travel through even half of the counties of this state, but that it changes hue and becomes lighter and lighter as it travels from the extreme north, until it is nearly white when it reaches the extreme south end of the state.

"I tell you that this Chicago doctrine of Lincoln's — declaring that the Negro and the white man are made equal by the Declaration of Independence and by Divine Providence — is a monstrous heresy. The signers of the Declaration of Independence never dreamed of the Negro when they were writing that document. When Thomas Jefferson wrote that document he was the owner, and so continued to his death, of a large number of slaves. Did he intend to say in the Declaration that his Negro slaves, which he held and treated as property, were created his equals by Divine Law, and that he was violating the law of God every day of his life by holding them as slaves? Every man who signed that instrument represented a slaveholding constituency. Not one of them emancipated his slaves after he signed the Declaration."

Members of the audience applauded politely.

"Mr. Lincoln insists that the Dred Scott decision would carry slavery into the free states, that the Supreme Court would violate our constitution and laws."

A voice from the audience rang out, "They already did with the Dred Scott decision."

Douglas ignored the voice and hurried on. Nine cheers for Douglas followed his speech.

Then Lincoln stood up and walked to the front of the stand. After the cheering and applause died down, he began to speak.

"My fellow citizens, a very large portion of the speech which Judge Douglas has addressed to you has previously been delivered and put in print."

A ripple of laughter passed through the crowd. Dietrich smiled at Chapel and nodded vigorously.

"I do not mean that for a hit upon the Judge at all."

Louder laughter followed.

"The Judge has alluded to the Declaration of Independence and insisted that Negroes are not included in that declaration; and that it is a slander upon the framers of that instrument to suppose that Negroes were meant therein. He asks you: Is it possible that Mr. Jefferson, who penned the immortal paper, could have supposed himself applying the language of that instrument to the Negro race and yet hold a portion of that race in slavery? Would he not at once have freed them? I have only to remark that I believe the entire records of the world, from the date of the Declaration of Independence up to within three years ago, may be searched in vain for one single statement, from one single man, that the Negro was not included. I defy Judge Douglas to show that he ever said so, that Washington ever said so, that any president, any member of Congress, or that any man living upon the whole earth ever said so, until the necessities of the present policy of the Democratic Party, in regard to slavery, had to invent that affirmation.

"And I will remind Judge Douglas and this audience, that, while Mr. Jefferson was the owner of slaves, in speaking upon this very subject, he used strong language. He said 'I tremble for my country when I remember that God is just.'

"The next thing to which I will ask your attention is the Judge's comments upon the fact, as he assumes it to be, that we cannot call our public meetings Republican meetings. He instances Tazewell County as the 'Friends of Lincoln' and Monroe County as the 'Free Democracy.' I have the honor to inform Judge Douglas that he spoke in the very county of Tazewell last Saturday, and when he spoke he did not venture to use the word 'Democrat.'"

Lincoln turned to Douglas and asked, "What do you think of this?"

The audience erupted into laughter and cheering.

"In the contest of 1856 his party delighted to call themselves together the 'National Democracy,' but now, if there should be a notice put up anywhere for a meeting of the National Democracy, Judge Douglas and his friends would not come. They would not suppose themselves invited. They would understand that it was a call for those hateful postmasters appointed by the present Democratic administration whom the Judge talks about."

Many in the crowd laughed.

"Now a few words in regard to those extracts from speeches of mine, which Judge Douglas has read to you, and which he supposes are in very great contrast to each other. Those speeches have been before the public for a considerable time, and if there is any conflict in them, the public has been able to detect it.

"When he says I make speeches of one sort for the people of the northern end of the state and of a different sort for the southern

184

end of the state, he assumes I do not understand that my speeches will be put in print and read north and south."

Someone close to the speakers' stand called out, "Give it to him, Abe."

"Perhaps by taking two parts of the same speech made in either part of the state he could have got up as much of a conflict as he found between my speech in Chicago and my speech in Charlestown. I have all the while maintained that perfect social and political equality between the black race and the white race was an impossibility, and with it, I have all the while said that in their right to 'life, liberty and the pursuit of happiness,' as proclaimed in that old Declaration, the inferior races are our equals.

"What has been the evidence that the Judge brought forward to prove that the Republican Party is a sectional party? The main one was that in the southern portion of the Union the people did not let the Republicans proclaim their doctrine amongst them. I ask his attention also to the fact that by the rule of nationality he is himself fast becoming sectional. His speeches now would not go as far south of the Ohio River as they have formerly gone. He tells us today that all the Democrats of the free states are agreeing with him, while he omits to tell us that the Democrats of any slave states agree with him. Whatever may be the result of this ephemeral contest between Judge Douglas and myself, I see the day rapidly approaching when his pill of sectionalism, which he has been thrusting down the throats of Republicans for years, will be crowded down his own throat."

Tremendous applause came from many parts of the audience. Dietrich spoke to Chapel, whose head was bowed over his notebook: "Southerners object to what they now call the Freeport Doctrine based on what Judge Douglas said in Freeport. He spoke about unfriendly police regulations that make slavery impossible in the territories and nullify in effect the Dred Scott ruling."

Chapel replied, "To be fair, that has always been the Judge's position."

"Yes," answered Dietrich, "but it was a position he did not espouse openly in the southern states. With newspaper reports, he cannot manage what he accuses Mr. Lincoln of having one set of principles in the north and another set of principles in the south."

Lincoln continued. "In order to fix the charge of extreme Abolitionism upon me, Judge Douglas read a set of resolutions which he declared had been passed by a Republican state convention, in October of 1854, at Springfield, Illinois, and he declared I had taken part in that convention. It turned out that, although a few men calling themselves an Anti-Nebraska state convention had sat at Springfield at that time, I did not take any part in it, nor did it pass the resolutions as Judge Douglas read.

"Seven days later at Freeport, Judge Douglas declared that he had been misled by Charles H. Lanphier, editor of the Illinois State Register, and Thomas L. Harris, member of Congress in that district. He promised in that speech that when he went to Springfield he would investigate the matter. Since then, Judge Douglas has been to Springfield, and I presume has made the investigation, but a month has passed since he has been there and he has made no report of that investigation. I have waited sufficient time for the report of that investigation and I have some curiosity to see and hear it. A fraud, an absolute forgery was committed, and the perpetration of it was traced to the three —Lanphier, Harris and Douglas. Whether it can be narrowed in any way so as to exonerate any one of them is what Judge Douglas's report would probably show."

Lincoln's partisans applauded.

"It is true that the set of resolutions read by Judge Douglas was published in the Illinois State Register on the sixteenth of October, 1854, as being the resolutions of an Anti-Nebraska convention. But it is also true that the publication was a forgery then. The idea that it was done by mistake is absurd. The article contains part of the real proceedings, showing that the writer had the real proceedings before him and purposefully threw out the genuine resolutions and fraudulently substituted the others. Lanphier then, as now, was the editor of the Illinois State Register, so that there seems to be little room for his escape. But Lanphier had less interest in forgery than the other two. The main object at that time was to beat Yates and elect Harris to Congress, and that object was known to be very dear to Judge Douglas. Harris and Douglas were both in Springfield when the convention was in session; they both left before the fraud appeared in the paper."

From the audience came a call, "Who done it, Judge?"

Lincoln waved his hands to quiet the crowd. "The fraud having been apparently successful upon the occasion, both Harris and Douglas have more than once since then been attempting to put it to new uses. Like the fisherman's wife, whose drowned husband was brought home with his body full of eels, said when she was asked, 'What is to be done with him?' — 'Take the eels out and set him in the water again as bait.' On the ninth of July, 1856, Douglas attempted it again upon Norton in the House of Representatives. On the twenty-first of August last, all three re-attempted it upon me at Ottawa. Douglas makes no complaint of Lanphier, who must have known it to be a fraud from the beginning. He, Lanphier and Harris are just as cozy now and just as active in the concoction of new schemes as they were before the general discovery of this fraud. I hope to be pardoned if I now insist that the mere fact of Judge Douglas making charges against Trumbull and myself is not quite sufficient evidence to establish them!"

Many in the crowd shouted and cheered. "Hit him again," was heard from many quarters.

"There he made an argument worth of a court summation," said Chapel.

"At Freeport I asked the Judge, if the Supreme Court of the United States shall decide that the states cannot exclude slavery from their limits, are you in favor of following such a decision, as a rule of political action? Judge Douglas made no answer. He contended himself with sneering at the thought that it was possible for the Supreme Court ever to make such a decision. However, the essence of the Dred Scott case ruling is compressed into the single sentence: 'Now as we have already said in an earlier part of this opinion, upon a different point, the right of property in a slave is distinctly and expressly affirmed in the constitution.' Affirmed means the Supreme Court ruled it cannot be separated from the constitution without breaking the Constitution. Judges in every state shall be bound by it. Nothing in the Constitution or laws of any state can destroy a right distinctly and expressly affirmed in the Constitution of the United States.

187

"Judge Douglas says we must yield to the Supreme Court, but he himself was one of the most active instruments at one time in breaking down the Supreme Court of the state of Illinois, because it made a decision distasteful to him — a struggle ending in the remarkable circumstance of his sitting down as one of the new judges who were to oversee that decision, getting his title of judge that very way."

Again the Lincoln supporters rallied and cheered him with enthusiasm. Lincoln retired as three great cheers rang from the entire audience.

Judge Douglas rose to complete his time. "The first criticism that Mr. Lincoln makes on my speech is that it is in substance what I have said everywhere in the state when I have addressed the people. I wish I could say the same of him."

The Douglas supporters laughed.

"I cannot hold him to a common standard in the different portions of the state. He did not pretend — no other man will — that I have one set of standards for Galesburg and another for Charlestown. I have proved that he has a different set of principles for each locality."

From the audience came cries of, "That's not so. You did no such thing."

"Silence, if you please. All I could ask of him was to have delivered the speech he made today in Coles County instead of old Knox. Here I understand him to re-affirm the doctrine of equality — that by the Declaration of Independence, the Negro is declared the equal to the white man. He tells you today that the Negro was included in the Declaration of Independence."

A voice called from the assembled, "We believe it."

"You believe it very well," Douglas echoed.

At this point catcalls, groans and shouts went up.

"Gentlemen, I ask you to remember that Mr. Lincoln was listened to respectfully and I have the right to insist that I shall not be interrupted in my reply."

Lincoln stood up and lifted his long arms to the heavens, imploring silence. Then Lincoln spoke while looking at the most disruptive men in the audience. "I hope that silence will be preserved," said Lincoln. Lincoln nodded toward Douglas, who returned the nod.

"Mr. Lincoln devoted considerable time to the circumstances of my having read at Ottawa a series of resolutions as having been adopted at Springfield. He has used hard names — has dared to talk about fraud and forgery and insinuated there was a conspiracy between Mr. Lanphier, Mr. Harris, and myself to perpetuate a forgery. He did not deny those resolutions were adopted by a majority of many counties in the north, and this became the platform of the party in the majority of counties upon which he relies for support. He didn't deny the truthfulness of the resolutions but takes exception to the spot where they were adopted; just as he thought the Mexican War unjust because it was not begun on the right spot."

The Douglas supporters laughed.

"Now I never before believed that Abraham Lincoln would have been guilty of what he has done this day in regard to those resolutions. The moment it was intimated to me that the resolutions were adopted at Bloomington, and then at Aurora, and then at Rockford, instead of Springfield, I did not wait for him to call my attention to it but led off and explained in advance what the mistake was and how it was made — frankly, as an honest man would. I explained the authority on which I made the statement: having seen these transcripts quoted by Major Harris in Congress as having been adopted by the first Republican convention in Illinois, I wrote to Major Harris asking for the authority as to place and time. Harris being extremely ill, Charles H. Lanphier called at his sickbed, received his answer and wrote to me that it was adopted at Springfield on the fifth of October, 1854, and sent me a copy of the newspaper containing them. I do not believe there is an honest man in Illinois who did not believe that it was an error I was led into innocently. I do not believe there is an honest man on the face of this state who doesn't abhor with disgust Lincoln's insinuation of my complicity with that forgery as he calls it."

The Douglas partisans applauded.

"Does he want to push these things to the point of personal difficulties here? I began this contest treating him with courtesy and spoke of him with words of respect. He seems now to try to divert the public attention from the enormity of his revolutionary principles by getting into personal quarrels, impeaching my sincerity and integrity.

"Now I have a few words to say on the Dred Scott case which has troubled the brains of Lincoln so much. He insists that decision would carry slavery into the free states, notwithstanding that the decision itself says the contrary. He would change the government from one of laws to one of mobs. The strong arm of power and violence will be substituted for decisions of the court of justice. I stand by the laws of the land. I stand by the Constitution and resist mob law and violence."

The few Douglas partisans applauded loudly and the Lincoln supporters clapped politely.

CHAPTER TWENTY-SIX

October 8, 1858
Galesburg, Illinois

The next morning Chapel and Dietrich met Shaw and Bergen in the dining room of the Galesburg House.

"Would you gentlemen care to join us for breakfast?" asked Bergen.

Dietrich and Chapel seated themselves at the table and ordered for themselves.

"Young Mr. Walker said that he is able to attend to us a little later this morning," said Shaw after the waiter left. "He, Judd, and Anthony are doing a post-mortem analysis of the speeches with Mr. Lincoln this morning. I must say that I was even more impressed with Mr. Lincoln on this occasion than I was when I heard him before. Mr. Douglas had little new to say, though, beyond his statement that Mr. Orr of South Carolina and other southern congressmen support the exclusion of slavery when the people of a territory do not want it there."

"I don't believe that his statement is correct," said Dietrich.

"Nor do I," said Shaw. "I did not say it was correct. I only said that it was new. I doubt that many South Carolina Gamecocks would agree with Judge Douglas."

"I believe that Mr. Lincoln has gone from a trot to a canter," said Chapel. "It is getting later in the contest, but Mr. Lincoln has finally caught his rhythm. Judge Douglas is becoming weary."

"I had not heard before the part about Judge Douglas using the supposed Republican resolutions to attack his opponents in Congress before he trotted them out against Mr. Lincoln," said Bergen. "It appears that, by trying to tie them around Lincoln's neck, he may end up with them tied around his own."

"As I know from my own experience, Mr. Lincoln will not stand pat but seeks ever to improve his position," said Shaw. "I reckon that he and his friends have been investigating those resolutions from the moment when they first heard of them. It's like when he asked Bergen what he thought of the Duff Armstrong prosecution. I know that he had his own plan in his mind, but he was willing to listen to another person to see if there was anything additional that he could make use of."

"I had not heard before some of the details about Judge Douglas and his disagreements with the state Supreme Court," said Dietrich. "That puts his reverence for the United States Supreme Court decision in a different light."

"Most of us lawyers wait for state and local courts to affirm the Supreme Court ruling before we accept them," said Bergen.

"Mr. Lincoln might have benefited from having the strong support of the crowd," said Chapel. "He will not be the favorite of the listeners in the final two contests."

"Mr. Lincoln improves at anything he assays by practice and by hard labor," said Shaw. "In the first debate he nearly interrupted Judge Douglas when assailed by his false charges. Here at Galesburg, when the judge accused him falsely and the crowd reacted, he stood up and asked that they allow Judge Douglas to be heard. I trust he will not be swayed by any attack beyond this juncture."

Walker walked into the dining room and over to the table.

"Gentlemen," said Walker, "I am at your disposal."

A waiter came to the table, and Walker ordered coffee.

"You are most welcome, Mr. Walker," said Bergen. "We were about to start to discuss Mr. Lincoln's defense of Duff Armstrong. With you, Mr. Shaw and myself present, I believe we will be able to provide an accurate account for our friends in the press."

The waiter returned and poured coffee for all the men.

"It was Mr. Lincoln's defense of Duff that gave me an inkling of how truly remarkable a man Mr. Lincoln is," said Walker. "He still amazes me, even now. Just this morning a man asked him about a rumor that the crowd around the speaking stand at Knox College was so thick that the candidates had to enter the college building from the west side and thereafter go through a window on the east side to reach the stand for the debate. Very solemnly Mr. Lincoln agreed that it was so and stated that he was pleased it was so. The man asked him why and Mr. Lincoln explained that after the journey he could finally claim that he had been through college."

The men laughed.

"I enjoyed reading about the earlier debate," said Shaw. "When Judge Douglas took opposition to the notion that a house divided cannot endure, Mr. Lincoln warned him that he was dealing with a loftier authority than himself."

The men nodded and chuckled.

"I met a woman in Freeport who told me that after Judge Douglas spoke she felt sorry for Mr. Lincoln, but after Mr. Lincoln spoke she felt sorry for Judge Douglas," said Dietrich.

Again the men laughed.

"Traveling south for a debate we were ensconced in the caboose of a freight train with the brakeman and a few friends when the train was sidetracked to let the special Douglas election train with his luxurious personal car rush by. There was a brass band on Douglas's train playing 'Hail to the Chief,' and a cannon fired whenever the train went through a town. Mr. Lincoln saw them fly by and laughed. He said, 'Boys, the gentlemen in that car evidently smelled no royalty in our carriage.'"

The men hooted with laughter.

"You may recall that at Charlestown Judge Douglas claimed that Mr. Lincoln had been lax in his support of the American troops during the Mexican War, which he opposed," said Chapel. "Mr. Lincoln espied O.B. Finklin, a Douglas Democrat, who had been in Congress with him at the time and he seized upon the opportunity to point him out, saying Finklin could confirm that Douglas was twisting the facts. At the end of the debate, I overheard Finklin telling friends, 'Mr. Lincoln damn near shook all the Democracy out of me today.'"

Then a waiter arrived with food and the men abandoned their conversation for the business of eating.

At the end of the meal, Shaw pushed his plate back and spoke, "We are assembled here for the purpose of recounting the events of the Duff Armstrong murder trial for our journalistic friends. Walker has told them part of the events. Bergen and I have told them another part of the events. I believe together we will be able to reconstruct the rest of the trial. Where did we stop?"

"I believe that when we left off, Mr. Lincoln had just announced to me that he expected an acquittal before the day was out and he asked for my opinion about where the prosecution's case could be assailed," said Bergen.

Walker continued the story. "Mr. Lincoln has a way of listening and attending to young attorneys that makes us feel that we are making a real contribution to a case, even though it may not be so. Before the dinner recess was over, he met with Mr. Bergen and me in concert and asked our opinions, even though I feel certain that he had his defense strategy already firmly in mind. Not, mind you, that he let on about it to me. What happened next was as unexpected to me as to anyone in the courtroom. He started the defense slowly with a parade of witnesses who claimed that they had seen the fight and that they did not see Duff use any weapon save his fist. Mr. Lincoln was careful with each man to have him state his relationship with the Armstrong family and with the Metzker family. Nearly all of the witnesses were related to the Armstrong family. He also had them describe the time of the assault (near 11 p.m.), how far they were from the assault, and how much they drank that night. Personally, I thought it was a waste of time. None had been as close as Charles Allen. All had drunk more. I was afraid Mr. Lincoln was about to lose the interest of the jury. When he called Nelson Watkins, I expected more of the same."

"So did I," said Bergen. "Remember that Nelson's brother had testified just a little while before."

The story unfolded as Walker spoke.

***

Like a lot of the men who had testified before him, Nelson Watkins looked uneasy and nervous on the witness stand. He was a compact young man of plain appearance, brown hair and eyes. His clothing and callused hands suggested that he was a farmer. Lincoln walked over toward him slowly and addressed him in a soothing voice.

"Your name is Nelson Watkins?"

"Yes, sir, it is."

"You attended the horse races on August 29 at Walker's

Grove along with your brother?"

"Yes, sir, I did."

Lincoln strolled to the exhibit table and picked up the slung-shot. Then he moved close to the witness stand. The audience and the jurors stirred.

"Do you recognize this, sir?" asked Lincoln, the slungshot hanging from his hand.

"Yes, sir. That's mine. I made it at my home and carried it to Walker's Grove."

People in the courtroom audience and in the jury box whis-pered to one another and leaned forward.

"How do you know it's the one you made?" asked Lincoln.

"Because I recognize the leather as what I sewed and the rope as what I used," said Watkins.

"Can you tell us what is inside the leather casing?" asked Lin-coln.

"There is a metal ball," answered Watkins, wiping sweat from his forehead.

"Can you tell us what sort of metal the ball is made of?"

"It's copper with a thin lead coating," said Watkins.

"How did you get such an unusual metal ball?"

"I cast it myself. I had the metal to hand and just decided that's how I wanted it done."

Lincoln put the slungshot on the defense table and pulled a knife out of his pocket. He opened the blade.

"With the court's permission and with Mr. Watkins's permis-sion also I would like to cut open the slungshot so the jury can ex-amine the metal ball inside," said Lincoln, gesturing toward the slungshot.

"Go ahead," said Judge Harriott, leaning forward.

"Mr. Watkins?"

Watkins nodded.

Lincoln cut open the leather casing and removed the metal ball. He scratched the surface of the metal ball with his knife, which revealed the copper underneath. Lincoln gave the ball to the judge to examine and then handed it to the jurors. Each juror in turn examined it.

"Mr. Watkins, did you have the slungshot with you on the night of August 29?"

"I did."

"Did you loan it to anyone?"

"No, sir."

"Did anyone take it from you?'

"No."

"Did you misplace it at any time?"

"I did not."

"Was it out of your possession at any time on the night of Mr. Metzker's death?"

"No sir."

"Not even for a moment?"

"Never, sir."

"Did the accused, Duff Armstrong, ever have the slungshot at any period of time, however brief, on the night of August twenty ninth?"

"He did not, sir."

"You are certain of that?"

Watkins nodded.

"Would you please answer the question with words so there can be no doubt about what you say?"

"I am certain for a fact, Duff never touched it."

Lincoln paused and looked over at the jurors.

"Several days later that slungshot was found near the scuffle ground. Can you tell us how that might have happened?" asked Lincoln.

"When I went to sleep under a wagon," said Watkins, blinking, "I set the slungshot and other things I had on me on the underside of the wagon frame. In the morning I got the other things but forgot about the slungshot. I suppose, I'm guessing, that when the wagon moved it fell off close to the scuffle ground."

"Could someone have retrieved it during the night?" asked Lincoln.

"Not without waking me," said Watkins. "I was not disturbed during the night."

"Are you a light sleeper?"

"I wake up real easy."

"Even when you've been drinking?"

"It don't matter. And I had not drunk much. If anybody had been poking around the wagon, I would have woken up for a certainty. I can never sleep if there are people moving about. I sought out a wagon far away from everybody else and I was undisturbed during the whole night."

Watkins stuck out his jaw, as if daring anyone to challenge his statement.

"Did anyone else sleep under the wagon that night?"

"No, sir."

"Where were you when you first spied the slungshot after you left it on the wagon at Walker's Grove?"

"I was in the sheriff's office in Havana."

"Was that at the time of the trial of Jimmy Norris?"

"It was."

"You are quite certain that this slungshot is the one that you constructed, and no other?"

"I am certain."

"Thank you, Mr. Watkins. I have no further questions."

"Mr. Fullerton," said Judge Harriott, "do you have any questions for this witness?"

Fullerton and Shaw engaged in a brief whispered conversation at the prosecution table.

"Yes, your honor," said Fullerton.

Fullerton approached the witness stand. "Mr. Watkins, would you have us believe that, there was no way under heaven that anyone could have taken your slungshot from under the wagon where you slept?"

"That's right," said Watkins, crossing his arms.

"Even when you were sound asleep? Even though you had been drinking? Even though in the morning you forgot about the weapon?"

Watkins looked confused.

"Objection, your honor," said Lincoln rising. "Mr. Fullerton is pelting the witness with questions so fast that he has no time to respond."

"Objection sustained," said the judge. "Mr. Watkins, you do not need to respond to those questions. Mr. Fullerton, ask your questions one at a time and allow the witness sufficient time to respond."

"I apologize, your honor," said Fullerton. "I further withdraw those questions. Mr. Watkins, can you swear with total certainty that upon waking in the morning you are absolutely and definitely certain that you never saw the slungshot at all?"

Watkins frowned.

"Let me rephrase the question," said Fullerton, stepping closer to the witness. "You testified that when you went under the wagon to go to sleep, you put the slungshot on part of the wagon close to where you slept. You testified that when you left Walker's Grove, you forgot about the weapon. I'm interested in the time between when you awoke and when you left Walker's Grove. Can you swear to this court under oath that, during that period of time, you never saw the slungshot at all?"

Watkins began to sweat.

"I don't think I saw it," Watkins said uncertainly. "I would have taken it with me."

"Thinking is not sufficient for a court of law," thundered Fullerton. "Are you absolutely certain? Did you see it then and forget it later?"

"I cannot say that I am wholly certain," admitted Watkins.

"No further questions," snapped Fullerton.

Lincoln climbed to his feet slowly and moved deliberately over to the witness.

"Mr. Watkins," said Lincoln, "do you know what time it was when you went to the wagon to go to sleep?"

"Well," said Watkins, frowning, "I know it was so dark that I had trouble finding my way. I don't know the exact hour, but it had to be at least two hours after midnight."

"Thank you," said Lincoln. "I have no other questions for you."

***

"If you are keeping score," said Shaw with a wry smile, "you can now add misidentification of the weapon to the prosecution's

198

failure to prove a conspiracy between Norris and Armstrong. The prosecution theory of the crime is rapidly unraveling before your very eyes. Mr. Allen, you may recall, was much more cautious about the weapon that we prosecutors were."

Shaw shook his head.

"We decided that the longer Watkins was on the stand the bigger impression he would make on the jury so the cross-examination was very brief. Any hope we had of mitigating the testimony was destroyed by Mr. Lincoln's single question on re-direct examination. Watkins testified he had the weapon in his possession while the crime against Metzker was being committed. He lost or forgot it after that. The reason for Mr. Lincoln naming so many witnesses was then altogether too clear to us. He did not want us to question Watkins and to learn about the slungshot. To our discredit, we assumed Watkins was just another weak witness to the assault. All we could do was to wait for the next unexpected blow. It came close on the heels of this one."

"Tactically, Mr. Lincoln set up a line of witnesses that he virtually cross-examined himself," said Walker. "When he finished, there were no reasonable questions left to ask. His approach helped the jurors see him as an honest man, willing to admit the weaknesses of his own witnesses. It also lulled the prosecution into passivity and allowed Mr. Lincoln to set his own rhythm of the proceedings. When he brought forth a witness to destroy a piece of the prosecution's case, the prosecution was out of the habit of questioning and discounting testimony."

"Not to mention that he had out-worked the prosecution once again and tracked down a damaging piece of information that Mr. Fullerton and our friend, Mr. Shaw, did not even know of," said Bergen.

"Speaking in my own defense, I was not hired by the Metzker family until shortly before the trial started, and I had limited time to prepare," said Shaw. "My role was that of a courtroom advisor, not an investigator."

"Do you think that you would have questioned the bona fides of the slungshot if you had been retained earlier?" asked Chapel.

"Are you joking?" asked Shaw. "Had I been retained sooner,

I would have taken the finding of a weapon at the crime scene as a gift from the gods and done nothing more, just as Mr. Fullerton did."

The men laughed.

"I think we should adjourn to the lobby so I can show you in more congenial surroundings the next step Mr. Lincoln took to disembowel the prosecution," said Shaw.

CHAPTER TWENTY-SEVEN

May 7, 1858
Menard County Courthouse, Beardstown, Illinois

"I call Doctor Charles Parker," said Lincoln.

A ripple of noise went through the audience as Doctor Parker walked to the stand carrying a human skull. Parker was a distinguished looking man well past middle age with gray hair and blue eyes. He moved easily and vigorously for a man of his age. After Doctor Parker was sworn in, Lincoln approached the witness stand. In short order he established the doctor's credentials and reviewed his experience.

"So would it be fair to say that you are unusually experienced with human bone structure in general and with the human skull in particular?" asked Lincoln.

"Yes, sir."

"May I?" asked Lincoln as he picked up the skull. "Most folks think of the skull as one bone, but that is not correct, is it?"

"No, sir."

"Could you please explain?"

"There are two major classes of bones associated with the skull. One class is named the cranial bones, which act as a sort of internal helmet to protect the brain. They surround the entire brain with thick bone."

"Sort of like how a bucket holds water?" asked Lincoln.

"I suppose so. Actually, come to think of it, that is a good description," said Parker, nodding. "Then there are the facial bones, which run from under the forehead down on each side."

"Does that include the mandible, commonly called the jaw?" asked Lincoln, tracing an oval shape on the front of the skull with his finger so that the jurors could see which areas were being described.

"It does. These bones have anchors for muscles that allow for things like talking, chewing, widening and narrowing of the eyes as well as facial expressions. They are much thinner than the bones of the cranium."

"Are the bones of the skull absolutely solid or are there small openings at various points in the skull?"

"In addition to the obvious openings for the mouth, the eyes, and the ear canals, there are also small openings that we call foramina. They are small holes or notches that allow nerves and blood vessels to reach various parts of the brain and the skull."

"Returning to the cranium," said Lincoln, turning the skull so that the back faced the jurors, "would a circle roughly this size…" Lincoln traced his finger around the exterior of the skull, "…approximate the occipital bone?"

"It would."

"And would that part of the skull be very thick and durable?"

"It would."

"Part of that helmet you described as protection for the brain inside?"

"Exactly."

"Would this area approximate the parietal bone?" asked Lincoln, tracing an oval around the top of the skull.

"It would."

"And would this area approximate the frontal bone?" asked Lincoln. He turned the skull so that the front faced the jurors and traced an uneven line along the top half of the eye sockets across the top of the nose cavity and roughly a third of the way back along the top of the skull.

"Yes, sir," answered Doctor Parker.

"Are there in addition," asked Lincoln, turning the skull so that the side faced the jury and pointing at various spots, "paired bones on each side of the face consisting of the temporal and sphenoid bones?"

"There are," answered Doctor Parker.

"And is there also a bone that forms part of the internal eye socket," asked Lincoln, "referred to as the ethmoid bone?"

"Yes, sir," answered Doctor Parker. "All those bones together make up the cranium."

"Are there also a series of bones that are referred to as facial bones?"

"There are fourteen of those."

"We will spare this jury that particular anatomy lesson. Returning once again to the cranium, are there joints that hold the individual bones together like mortar holds together bricks in a wall?"

"There are. The joints are called sutures."

"Why are there so many different cranial bones?"

"While a person is an infant or a child and still growing, the internal organs, including the brain, are growing just like the bones and the rest of the body is growing. The individual cranial bones grow along with the growing brain, allowing the bones to provide some protection and also allowing for increasing space for the growing brain."

"Is it accurate to say that by the time a person reaches full adulthood, like Press Metzker had, that the skull has become one solid construction, albeit the jaw is hinged?"

"That is correct."

"So the sutures become as rigid as the bones themselves?"

"Yes, sir."

"Lincoln handed the skull back to the witness. "Did you hear the testimony presented in this trial?"

"I did."

"Did you hear Doctor Stephenson testify that the severe wound Mr. Metzker received at the back of the skull – would that be upon the occipital bone?"

"It would indeed."

"Did Doctor Stephenson testify that such a grievous wound would inevitably be fatal?"

"He did," answered Parker.

"Would you agree with his testimony?"

"Absolutely. In all my experience and in all my reading as well, I have never come across anyone who survived an injury as grievous as that described in the testimony to that particular part of the skull."

"Did you also hear Doctor Stephenson testify that persons with the injury Mr. Metzker received to the front of the face, and no other injury, were able to survive?"

"I did."

"Do you concur?"

"I do. In my personal medical practice and in my reading, I have encountered a number of persons who recovered their health after suffering such an injury."

"Did you also hear Doctor Stephenson testify that the blow that crushed Press Metzker's occipital bone — crushed the thick cranial bone designed to protect the brain — had to have been given with extraordinary force?"

"I did," answered Parker. "I concur that it had to have been an incredibly vicious strike to cause the amount of damage that resulted."

"Considering, doctor, the extreme force of the blow and that the skull is a solid object, could a blow to the back of the skull cause a break in the area of the corner of the right eye socket?"

The jurors leaned forward in rapt attention.

"Depending on the direction of the blow and the force, a single blow could easily cause damage at more than one place on the skull, particularly at a spot thinner and opposite to the location of the blow. A rigid structure, like a skull, could show multiple injuries from a single strike. I have seen it in my practice."

"Doctor, would you please show the jury how that might happen?"

Parker drew a line with his finger from the back of the skull to the eye socket.

"Would it be like stepping on ice on a pond that is not quite sufficiently frozen to hold a man's weight? Sometimes cracks run out from the footprint, sometimes the ice under the foot holds together and cracks occur at weak places not immediately under the foot, and sometimes both the ice under the foot and ice further off both show cracks?"

"Exactly," said Parker. "The force from the weight of the man may cause a direct effect both under the foot and, in addition, at some distant point which was only indirectly influenced by the force so long as the ice is one rigid piece. Other pieces of ice on the pond not connected with the rigid piece would not be affected."

"Thank you, sir. In listening to other testimony, did you notice any other possible causes for the injury Press Metzker received in his right eye socket not related to the fight with Duff Armstrong?"

"I did."

"Would you please share with us what those possible causes were?"

"Doctor Stephenson mentioned falls as one possible source of that injury. He also said that Press Metzker told him he fell off his horse on the way home. As best I recall, it was more than once, but Mr. Metzker could not say how many times he fell. Any one of the falls might have caused the injury. Then, too, it could be that his horse was spooked by the unexpected behavior of its rider falling off. A horse might, without meaning to, kick his rider in the face. Doctor Stephenson mentioned that possibility also."

"Thank you, Doctor Parker. I have no further questions."

"Mr. Fullerton," said Judge Harriott, "do you have any questions for this witness?"

"Yes, your honor," said Fullerton.

Fullerton walked across the courtroom slowly.

"Doctor Parker, is it your testimony that Doctor Stephenson told this court that Mr. Metzker might have come by the injury to his right eye socket by falling from his horse or by being kicked by his horse?"

"No, sir," answered Parker.

"That accords with my memory also," said Fullerton. "Wasn't Doctor Stephenson speaking hypothetically?"

"I believe so," answered Parker.

"So would it be correct to say that Doctor Stephenson did not offer the opinion that Mr. Metzker's injury could have been caused by a fall from his horse or by a kick from his horse?"

"To the best of my recollection it would," agreed Parker after a momentary hesitation.

"Could the injury to Mr. Metzker have occurred from Duff Armstrong assaulting him with a weapon, as Charles Allen testified?"

"It could."

"No further questions."

"Mr. Lincoln, do you have any additional questions for this

witness?" asked the Judge.

"Only a few, your honor," said Lincoln, rising.

"Doctor Parker, is it your recollection that Doctor Stephenson was speaking hypothetically about the type of injury Mr. Metzker received?"

"Yes, sir."

"So he did not offer the opinion that Mr. Metzker's injury specifically could not have occurred from falling from his horse or being kicked by his horse. Equally he did not offer the opinion that the injury could so occur. He did not say yea or nay about the specific injury at all. Correct?"

"Yes, sir. As best I recall, he was not specifically asked about those possible causes of Mr. Metzker's injuries at all."

"So then, Doctor Stephenson did not have the opportunity to express an opinion about whether or not those possible causes we just discussed could have resulted in Mr. Metzker's injury to his eye socket?"

"I believe that is correct."

"Thank you, Doctor," said Lincoln. "I have no additional questions."

"Mr. Fullerton," asked Judge Harriott, "do you have any more questions for Doctor Parker?"

Fullerton shook his head.

"Doctor Parker, you are excused," said Judge Harriott. "Mr. Lincoln, please call your next witness."

***

Shaw looked around the table at Dietrich, Chapel, Bergen and Walker and then shook his head and sighed.

"There you have it, gentlemen. Mr. Lincoln first removed the weapon from the prosecution, and then he offered a plausible alternative for the wound Mr. Metzker received. The good news is that we in the prosecution have now finally stopped dismantling our own case. The bad news is that at this juncture, Mr. Lincoln has taken over that duty and is performing it admirably."

"I talked with Judge Harriott after the trial," said Bergen. "He told me that he found Mr. Lincoln to be wholly convincing while Doctor Parker testified. He said in his opinion, this was the point at which Mr. Lincoln won an acquittal. I myself thought that Mr. Lincoln sounded much better informed than many physicians."

"How did he acquire such knowledge?" asked Dietrich.

"One of the essential weapons of an attorney is the ability to study an area of interest in a case narrowly but intensively," said Shaw. "A good attorney can become an expert in an area, for the purposes of a trial without learning any extraneous information. I would not, for example, trust Mr. Lincoln to perform an operation on my brain, albeit I would trust him to defend a surgeon accused of malpractice who performed such an operation. In this case, I would venture that Doctor Parker schooled Mr. Lincoln, who is a ferocious student in areas of necessity. Mr. Lincoln also has the virtue of translating complicated ideas into common parlance so that the least informed juror feels that he understands.

"Have you any other questions? At this juncture we of the prosecution have but one string on our bow. We still have Charles Allen who gave convincing testimony that Duff Armstrong did in fact strike Press Metzker with a weapon. It is to Mr. Allen, our last best hope, that Mr. Lincoln next puts his attention."

Shaw returned the focus to the courtroom scene.

***

"The defense re-calls Charles Allen."

There was an audible buzz from the audience as Allen was called to the stand and sworn in.

Lincoln rose and stepped toward him. "Mr. Allen, can we refresh the memories of the jurors about your earlier testimony?"

"Yes, sir," said Allen calmly.

"Would you please state for the court your name and your residence?"

"My name is Charles Allen. I live on a farm in Menard County, close by the town of Havana."

"Thank you, sir," said Lincoln. "Do you own the farm?"

"I do."

"Were you acquainted with Press Metzker and Duff Armstrong?"

"I was."

"Were you friends with both men?"

207

"I was."

"You had no quarrel or bad feeling with either man?"

"I did not," said Allen. "I liked both men and considered them both friends."

"So you have no reason to tilt your testimony here one way or the other? There is no personal advantage to you in favoring one man over the other?"

"That's right."

"Very well," said Lincoln. "Would you please remind the jury of when you went to Walker's Grove?"

"I arrived after chores on the afternoon of August 28 of the year past. I stayed there until early in the morning of the next day."

"What was the reason for your being there?"

"I came to see the horse races."

"Yes," said Lincoln. "I believe you said you were successful in your wagering?"

"Yes, sir," said Allen, smiling for the first time since he took the stand. "I was fortunate enough to win a little money."

"Fortunate, I have no doubt," said Lincoln, returning the smile. "However, it is also my experience that the knowledgeable bettor has above average luck."

Allen ducked his head briefly but did not respond.

"Had you been at Walker's Grove before?"

"Many times."

"For the horse racing?"

"Yes, sir."

"With some success in the past?"

"Yes, sir, but never like this," said Allen.

Lincoln nodded. He straightened his posture and the expression on his face changed to one of sadness.

"Unfortunately, Mr. Allen, it is not a happy event that brings us here today, but a tragic one. There was a death in the moonlight that calls out for explanation. Sadly, that is why we are here."

Lincoln paused. Allen had a grave expression on his face.

"If I could, Mr. Allen, I would like to bring the circumstances of your testimony back to the memory of the jurors."

"Yes, sir."

"I believe that in your earlier testimony you said that the event took place — well, when did they take place?"

"As close as I can call it was just about 11 p.m.," said Allen.

"I know that you heard other men testify as to the time. Is 11 p.m. your personal recollection, or is it what you have heard other men say?"

"My personal recollection independent of what others said is that the events took place very close to eleven o'clock at night."

"Wasn't it dark at that time of night?"

"No, sir," answered Allen. "The moonlight was more than sufficient for me to see what happened."

"What was the phase of the moon?"

"It was not full, but it was nearly so."

"Would you please estimate how full it was?"

Allen sat silently for a moment.

"Perhaps three quarters full."

"If the moon were low in the sky even though nearly full, wouldn't the trees block out much of the light?"

"It would have if the moon had been low in the sky, but the moon was almost overhead."

"Are you certain the moon was almost overhead?"

"Absolutely," said Shaw.

"If the sun was at the same spot during the day, what time would it be?"

Again, Allen sat for a few moments in silence.

"It was not directly overhead. By my estimate it was where the sun is at about one o'clock in the afternoon."

"Do you mean just beginning its descent toward the horizon and very much closer to the midpoint than to setting?"

"Exactly."

"You have no doubt of that?" asked Lincoln.

"I am quite certain."

"In all three of these statements," asked Lincoln, "the degree of certainty that you have about them is?"

"Beyond all doubt," said Allen. "I am wholly certain."

Lincoln nodded.

"Are you equally certain about the phase of the moon, the time and the position of the moon in the sky?"

"I am."

"Since you are certain in all particulars, let us continue. Can you describe where you were located in relation to the scuffle ground?"

"I was on the side of a hill and the combatants were below me," said Allen, gesturing with his hands.

"Sort of like being on the side of a bowl?"

"Yes, sir," agreed Allen. "I was on the side of the bowl. Duff, Press and Jimmy were on the bottom of the bowl."

"Weren't there trees in the way?"

"No, sir. Not where I was sitting they weren't."

"Weren't you too far away to see clearly?"

"No sir. I was twenty yards away maybe."

"Did you pace it off?"

"No, sir, but I am a good judge of distance," said Allen. "My best estimate would be neigh to sixty feet."

"How were the men standing in relation to where you were?" asked Lincoln.

"Press was standing facing Duff head on. Jimmy came out of nowhere behind Press and, quick as a wink, he used some sort of club to strike him on the back of his head."

"Could you see all three men at the same time?"

"Yes, sir. They were a little bit sideways to the hillside. Press couldn't see Jimmy behind him. He was facing Duff."

"And could Duff see Jimmy through Press, or did Press block his sight?"

"I never thought of that," said Allen, sounding surprised. "Duff could not have seen Jimmy. Press was right in the way."

"I believe you testified that Jimmy Norris struck first," said Lincoln. "And that the blow made a terrible sound?"

"Yes, sir," said Allen. "It was awful. Almost immediately after, Duff struck Press with an overhand blow that landed on or near his eye. Duff struck him with something that resembled a slungshot."

"You could see that clearly?" asked Lincoln. "You were sixty or so feet away with no trees cutting off your vision because the moon was just past directly overhead and nearly full?"

"Yes, sir," said Allen. "It was not a thing I wanted to see, nor a thing I wish to see ever again. But it is what I did see."

"You said you heard the blow from Norris," said Lincoln. "Did you also hear the blow from Armstrong?"

"Not as I remember," answered Allen.

"From that distance would you expect to hear the sound of a fist hitting a face?"

"Not likely," answered Allen.

"But you testified, didn't you, that you saw something in Duff's hand that you thought had the shape of a slungshot?"

"I did."

"Wasn't the moon much lower in the sky so that the light was much dimmer and so that you can not be certain of what exactly that you saw from sixty feet away?"

"No, sir. The moon was high in the sky albeit not exactly overhead and the moonlight was bright enough for me to see all that I have said."

Lincoln turned and walked to the defense table. He moved aside a stack of papers and from underneath the papers he picked up a thin paper pamphlet. Lincoln walked to the prosecution table and showed the pamphlet to Fullerton and Shaw. Then he walked to the judge's bench and handed it to Judge Harriott.

"Your honor, I wish to enter this into evidence as a defense exhibit. As you can see, this is a Jayne's Almanac for 1857. If you would be so good, sir, as to turn to the page for the month of August. There it is. Thank you, your honor. If you would be good enough to read down the last column for the time stated on the twenty-ninth. If you could, please note the time. Thank you."

Lincoln retrieved the almanac from the judge and walked to the witness stand, carrying the almanac in his hand.

"You are no doubt acquainted with the term sunset?"

"Yes, sir," said Allen.

"It is, of course, that moment at which the upper edge of the sun passes below the horizon. Is that how you understand it?"

"Yes, sir."

"There is a less common term, which is moonset. Do you know what that means?"

"I guess it would be the moment that the upper edge of the moon passes below the horizon."

"You are correct, sir," said Lincoln. "That's just what it means. What I have here is a copy of Jayne's Almanac for last year. This page is for August of that year and this last column gives the times for moonset. Times are figured from Philadelphia, but there is little enough variation in the time from the east to the west that we use the times herein throughout the United States. Would you please be good enough to read the time of moonset for August ninth to the jury?"

Allen read the page and blinked. He said in a shaky voice, "12:03 a.m."

"Yes, Mr. Allen at three minutes after midnight the entire moon had disappeared beneath the horizon. However, you told us that at 11:00 p.m. just one hour earlier, the moon was just past the midpoint of the sky. Isn't it true that at 11:00 p.m. the moon had to be at the very edge of the sky, sitting on the horizon and ready to set?"

Some people in the audience began to talk. The noise level in the courtroom rose quickly. Judge Harriott pounded his gavel on his bench for silence. Lincoln retrieved the almanac, walked to the jury box and handed the almanac to the first juror. He read it, grinned and passed it to the man next to him.

Shaw jumped to his feet and ran from the courtroom. Fullerton waited until the jurors had all seen the almanac. Then he walked to the jury box and looked at it for himself. After several minutes, Shaw returned with an Ayer's Almanac, which gave the time of moonset based on New York as 12:06 a.m. and a Gordy's Almanac, which gave the time of moonset based on Boston as 12:05 a.m.

Lincoln requested that all three almanacs be entered as evidence and without a further word he took his seat.

***

"The trial was over at that point," said Shaw with a grimace, "even though it did not end formally for some time after that. I questioned Mr. Allen. On re-direct, I got Mr. Allen to say that, wherever the moon was in the sky, it gave sufficient light for him to see. He declined to withdraw his testimony that Duff Armstrong struck Press Metzker with a weapon shaped like a slungshot. He had not identified the weapon constructed by Nelson Watkins, but had said only that the weapon used resembled that of Watkins'. But 'twas of no avail. Mr. Lincoln relieved the prosecution first of the weapon, second of the wound, and third of the key witness."

"But really, of what importance was the position of the moon?" asked Dietrich. "If Mr. Allen could see clearly, he could see what happened. If he glanced up earlier and noted the position of the moon, why would he bother to ascertain its position later on?"

"Would that you had been on the jury," said Shaw. "You are correct, of course. However, jurors are routinely told that, finding a witness less than credible on one matter, they may question his credibility on other matters. By this time in the trial, with the mistakes we had already made, our entire case stood solely on this one witness. If the jurors believed him implicitly, we some slight chance of prevailing. With the witness impeached, we had no chance at all."

"I think that you may be neglecting the role of Mr. Lincoln's closing argument," said Bergen.

Shaw shook his head. "No, I give Mr. Lincoln credit for an excellent closing argument. Mr. Fullerton did his very best. He recounted the witness statements that had convicted Jimmy Norris. He described a number of circumstances that could have resulted in Duff Armstrong having access to the slungshot. He challenged Doctor Parker's testimony with Doctor Stephenson's statements about two separate fatal bruises. He argued that Norris and Armstrong had acted in concert. He argued that the almanacs actually confirmed that there was a three-quarters full moon out, which would have given ample light for Mr. Allen to see what he steadfastly testified to. It was a good argument. It was, also, not enough."

"Mr. Lincoln started by taking off his coat," said Bergen. "He unbuttoned his vest and removed that also. Then he pulled off his tie, took off his old-fashioned starched collar and rolled up his sleeves. He looked like a man preparing for work, which, I suppose, he was. He was wearing home-made knitted yarn suspenders and during his argument one of them slipped off his shoulder."

"Like a careful craftsman, Mr. Lincoln began with a careful review of the duties of each side of the case," said Walker. "He reminded the jury that the defense was not obligated to prove anything. The prosecution had to prove every link in the chain of argument and that a single weak link would cause the chain to fail. He re-introduced the idea of reasonable doubt. Then he reviewed the prosecution theory of the crime. Was there a conspiracy between Norris and Armstrong? No witness had said so. No physical evidence had been produced. Not a single shred of evidence of any kind had been produced. The prosecution simply claimed that, since three men had been at one spot at the same time, two of them must have conspired against the third. Was that true? Mr. Lincoln said that he had noticed three jurors leaving the courthouse together. Were two of them necessarily conspiring against the third? Had the prosecution proved anything?"

Shaw picked up the story: "Mr. Lincoln reminded the jurors that the prosecution had presented them with a slungshot that they claimed had been the murder weapon. The defense had produced the weapon's maker and he claimed the weapon had been in his personal control for the entire night. Mr. Lincoln said that the defense had then been reduced to speculations of a fantastical nature about how the weapon might have been unobtrusively procured from its maker and equally unobtrusively returned to him. Mr. Lincoln described that as highly entertaining speculation, and wondered if Mr. Fullerton had a history as a magician, but was it proof of anything more than an active imagination?"

Shaw smiled.

"After that, Mr. Lincoln spent time on a detailed review of the medical testimony. He found no discrepancy between the testimonies of Doctor Stephenson and Doctor Parker. He carefully reviewed their areas of agreement and argued that Doctor Stephenson did not even have the opportunity to offer an opinion about multiple injuries resulting from a vicious blow upon a human skull. He reminded the jurors that Metzker had fallen from his horse a number of times, which might have caused the injury to the front of Metzker's face. Once again, he said the prosecution had not proved that the injury described was inflicted by Duff Armstrong."

"Mr. Lincoln was quite circumspect about Mr. Allen's testimony," said Walker. "He said nothing that could be, even remotely, interpreted as an accusation of lying, but only said if Mr. Allen was so badly mistaken about the position of the moon, he might be mistaken about other aspects of his testimony. During the last ten minutes or so he spoke of personal feelings."

Walker looked at Shaw and nodded.

"Mr. Lincoln talked about how he had come to the area a poor and friendless boy with little more than the clothes upon his back," said Shaw. "He told how Jack and Hannah Armstrong took him into their home. They gave him food, clothing and a place to sleep when he had naught. They had no expectations in return. He had no prospects to speak of. There were honest tears in Mr. Lincoln's eyes, and more than one juror's eyes glistened. Mr. Lincoln talked about bouncing the infant Duff upon his knee and being treated as a member of the Armstrong family."

Shaw took a deep breath.

"Mr. Lincoln said that he hoped that, now, he was in the position of finally being able to repay a small part of the kindness he received in such abundance, by helping the recently widowed Hannah and honoring Jack's dying request to return Duff to his mother. Hannah could be seen and heard sobbing at the defense table. He took the jury by storm. Mr. Lincoln's tears were genuine. His sympathies were totally enlisted in the favor of the young man, and his terrible sincerity could not but arouse the same passion in the jury. There was nothing about the actual trial in this part of the summary, but his inspired speech was incited by his gratitude to the young man's father and mother. The jurors sat entranced, barely daring to breathe. At the end of the speech several jurors burst into tears. Men and women throughout the audience were similarly affected. In all the years I have known Mr. Lincoln, I aver that I have never seen him so affected. I believe the strength of that speech alone could have saved a proven criminal from the gallows."

For a few moments none of the men spoke.

"Mr. Lincoln did one thing more," said Walker. "He had concerns about the standard jury instructions that allowed for conviction on the lesser charge of manslaughter. After all, Norris was not convicted of first-degree murder, but he was convicted of manslaughter. Mr. Lincoln asked the judge to include in the jury instructions two additional paragraphs that Mr. Lincoln wrote. I have a copy of them here for you."

Walker handed the page to Chapel, who read it and then passed it to Dietrich. It read: The court instructs the jury that if they have any reasonable doubt as to whether Metzker came to his death by the blow on the eye or the blow on the back of the head, they are to find the defendant not guilty, unless they further believe from the evidence, beyond all reasonable doubt, that Armstrong and Norris acted in concert against Metzker, and that Norris struck the blow on the back of the head.

That if they believe from the evidence that Norris killed Metzker, they are to acquit Armstrong unless they also believe from the evidence, beyond a reasonable doubt, that Armstrong acted in concert with Norris in the killing or purpose to kill or hurt Metzker.

Walker pulled a pocket watch out of his vest pocket and opened the case.

"I for one must depart quickly. If you gentlemen have questions after reflecting upon the trial, I will attend the two remaining debates, and you may find me after either or both."

CHAPTER TWENTY-EIGHT

October 13, 1858
Quincy, Illinois, Washington Park: The Sixth Debate

Douglas arrived at nine-thirty the night before on a special train provided by the Chicago and Quincy Railroad. He had a personal, lavishly appointed special railroad car generously provided by the railroad. Douglas was greeted by an enormous bonfire that had been built in his honor. Enthusiastic supporters turned out in the hundreds. A torchlight procession escorted him to the Quincy House, and all along the route men held up transparencies with patriotic and democratic messages.

Lincoln arrived in the morning at nine thirty on a train from Macomb. He rode in a regular passenger car. Lincoln was greeted by a long procession of supporters and in the procession was a model ship on four wheels pulled by four horses and labeled "Constitution." Men dressed as sailors rode on the ship, and a live raccoon was at the helm. The raccoon was the symbol of the old Whig Party. In the Douglas procession there was a wagon labeled "Dred Scott," which prominently displayed a dead raccoon hanging from its tail.

"This is much better weather than in Galesburg," said Chapel.

"Yes," said Dietrich. "The rains have stopped, and although the roads are still muddy, it is a clear and cool day."

"Many people came by boat," said Chapel. "I've seen delegations from Missouri and Iowa that came across the Mississippi. Interest in the Douglas-Lincoln contest is growing all around the country."

"This is one of the most hotly contested counties," said Dietrich. "This part of Illinois is a bit more for the Democracy than for the Republican Party, but parties want to open their arms to embrace additional men."

"At the same time neither party wants to ignore their committed voters, so they cannot stray too far from the policies that attracted their solid base of support. The danger is not so much that a committed voter would go over to the opposition party as that he will get disgusted with his own party and refrain from voting at all," said Chapel.

"The Democrats have won the battle of the banners here. The Republican offerings are less numerous and less impressive," Dietrich observed.

"The Democrats have more money and a better organized party structure. They should have. The party has been in existence a lot longer. Remember that Mr. Lincoln at the start followed Judge Douglas around in hopes of scaring up a crowd big enough to talk to."

"Mr. Lincoln has come a long way since then," said Dietrich.

"Yes," agreed Chapel, "but the question is — has he come far enough?"

Shortly before the speakers were to arrive, part of the railing around the stand collapsed, spilling twelve or fifteen people backwards to the ground along with a heavy wooden bench. Three persons were severely bruised, but no one was seriously injured. A bench reserved for ladies also collapsed, but only the women's dignity was wounded. Still, a number of women appeared to be dazed and had to be escorted away from the speakers' stand that had been erected in the square.

At about two-thirty Lincoln, looking fresh and rested, began his speech. He reviewed the familiar arguments and then took a new tack.

"I was aware, when it was first agreed to have these seven joint discussions, that they were the successive acts of a drama to be enacted not merely in the face of audiences like this, but in the face of the nation, and to some extent, due to Judge Douglas, in the face of the world. I am anxious they should be conducted with dignity and in good temper. But Judge Douglas implicated my truthfulness and my honor when he said I was doing one thing and pretending another, and because he does this, I do not understand that I am bound, if I see a truthful ground for it, to keep my hands off him. Now I say I will not be the first to cry, 'Hold!' I think it originated with the judge, and when he quits, I probably will, too.

"He asks me if I wish to push this matter to the point of personal difficulty. I tell him no. He did not make a mistake in one of his early speeches when he called me an 'amiable' man, though perhaps he did when he called me an 'intelligent' man."

People throughout the crowd laughed.

"It really hurts me very much to suppose that I have wronged anybody on the earth. I again tell him no! I very much prefer, when this canvass shall be over, however it may result, that we at least part without any bitter recollections of personal difficulties. I say to the judge and to this audience now that I will again state our principles as well as I hastily can in all their enormity, and if the judge hereafter chooses to confine himself to a war upon these principles, he will probably not find me departing from the same course."

Someone in the audience called out, "Well spoken."

When Douglas stepped forward to speak, the applause of his supporters matched that which Lincoln had received. In a hoarse voice he implored the audience to be silent so that he might speak.

"It will not do to charge a forgery on Charles H. Lanphier or Thomas L. Harris. No man on earth who knows them and knows Lincoln would take his oath against their word."

The Douglas supporters cheered. Douglas continued with his familiar oration. Toward the end of his speech Douglas commented, "There are many points touched by Mr. Lincoln that I have not been able to take up for the want of time. I have hurried over each subject that I have discussed as rapidly as possible so as to omit but few, but one hour and a half is not sufficient for a man to discuss at length one half of the great questions that trouble the public mind."

When Lincoln stepped up to speak, his supporters raised their voices and created so much noise that people on the platform could not hear each other speaking. When the noise died down, Lincoln again spoke.

"My friends, since Judge Douglas has said to you in his conclusion that he had not time in an hour and a half to answer all I had said in an hour, it follows of course that I will not be able to answer in half an hour all that he said in an hour and a half."

Many people throughout the audience applauded and laughed.

"I wish to return Judge Douglas my profound thanks for his

public annunciation here today to be put on record that his system of policy in regard to the institution of slavery contemplates that it shall last forever. The judge informed me and this audience that the Democratic newspaper, the Washington Union, is laboring for my election to the Senate. That is news to me — not very ungrateful news either. I hope Mr. W. H. Carlin here will be elected to the state senate as a Democrat and that he will then vote for me for senator."

Carlin, seated on the platform, nearly fell out of his chair. Then he shook his head in firm denial. The audience laughed.

"Carlin doesn't fall in, I perceive, and I suppose he will not do much for me."

Even Douglas laughed at that.

"Judge Douglas says that the territorial legislature may withhold necessary laws or bypass unfriendly laws against slavery. The truth of the matter is this: His Supreme Court, cooperating with him, has squatted his squatter sovereignty out. He has at last invented this sort of do-nothing sovereignty that the people may exclude slavery by a sort of sovereignty that is exercised by doing nothing at all. Is that not running his popular sovereignty down awfully? Has it not got down as thin as the homoeopathic soup that was made by boiling the shadow of a pigeon that had starved to death?"

The Lincoln supporters laughed and cheered.

"He says that my oath would not be taken against the bare word of Charles H. Lanphier or Thomas L. Harris. Well, that is altogether a matter of opinion."

Lincoln supporters laughed and cheered. At the end of Lincoln's speech his supporters cheered and clapped with great enthusiasm for several minutes.

As the audience streamed away, Dietrich and Chapel made their way over to the speakers' stand. They sat on the steps, still writing in their notebooks. Neither man noticed when a man sidled up to the step below them.

Then he spoke: "Ain't it a shame that Old Abe has to engage in such personal insults, lies and name calling in hopes that his Abolitionist doctrines won't get shown in the light of day."

Dietrich and Chapel looked up, surprised.

"Adam Houston, as I live and breathe," drawled Chapel. "Have you decided to try to cover the debates by actually attending one outside of Chicago?"

"Perhaps he has run all the Negroes out of Chicago and so he has come in hopes of beating one here."

"I wasn't going to beat on even that one," insisted Houston.

"That's right," said Chapel. "Now, I remember. You just thought it would be great fun to watch."

Houston frowned. Dietrich said, "As to lies and insults, I seem to remember that Judge Douglas accused Mr. Lincoln of being a drunkard as a youth, although Mr. Lincoln does not drink and never did. Douglas also accused Mr. Lincoln of serving whiskey in his store."

"I've heard rumors that Mr. Lincoln had to plead guilty to the latter since, after all, Douglas was certain of that charge, having been Mr. Lincoln's biggest customer," said Chapel.

"I've no doubt that the Douglas supporters regret that Mr. Lincoln has started to give as good as he gets."

"At least Senator Douglas is consistent in his doctrines from debate to debate, unlike that baboon, Lincoln."

"He's consistent in his words, too," said Chapel. "If you hear one Douglas speech, you've heard all Douglas speeches."

"But I do admire your careful logic and reasoned analysis of the issues, as shown by you calling Mr. Lincoln a baboon," said Dietrich. "What was it you accused Mr. Lincoln of? Engaging in personal insults for want of anything meaningful to say?"

"Now you've heard an actual speech," said Chapel. "Now you have Mr. Lincoln's actual words to lie and re-lie on."

Dietrich laughed.

"As pleasant as this is," said Chapel with an exaggerated drawl, "and I cannot tell you how pleasant — really I cannot — was there some reason for you to come calling?"

"My editor wanted me to find out if you had learned anything about the Duff Armstrong murder trial."

"Actually, we've learned quite a lot," said Dietrich. "We've talked with several of the people involved and we know the course of the trial. We just haven't come up with anything that reflects adversely on Mr. Lincoln."

"Mr. Woodward has two questions and one suggestion. He wants to know why Mr. Walker agreed to assist Lincoln for no recompense. He wants to know if the rumors that Lincoln fraudulently altered an almanac are true. He suggests that there is more than meets the eye with the testimony of Nelson Watkins."

"I had wondered that about Mr. Walker. What do you think, August?"

"I think that editors of newspapers supporting the Democracy and forgery fit together hand in glove. We have come thus far. Why don't we continue to the end? Houston, you can tell Mr. Woodward that it is likely that Mr. Walker will be working with Mr. Lincoln on his Alton speech tonight, but we will endeavor to track him down after the next debate."

"The other we will investigate when we may."

Chapel and Dietrich then started to converse with each other, ignoring Houston.

"So, August, did you think Mr. Lincoln did well?"

"Yes, Thaddeus. I did. He pointed out that Douglas would allow slavery to last forever and stated the difference between the Democracy men who will not say slavery is wrong and the Republicans who insist it is a moral wrong, but one they will not hinder where it now exists."

Houston slunk away.

After the debate, both Lincoln and Douglas stayed in Quincy that evening. The next day both men, with a few friends, embarked on the steamboat City of Louisiana, which steamed 115 miles down the Mississippi River and arrived in Alton at five o'-clock in the morning on Friday, October fifteenth.

CHAPTER TWENTY-NINE

October 15, 1858
Alton, Illinois: The Seventh Debate

Douglas looked weary and bloated as he disembarked from the steamboat. He was greeted by a band of musicians playing patriotic songs and a line of men carrying torches who escorted him to his hotel. A small brass cannon thundered its welcome and filled the air with the stench of black powder.

Lincoln looked weary and dispirited when he stepped off the steamboat a little later. His face lit up when he saw Mary Todd Lincoln and Robert Lincoln waiting for him. Robert was dressed in his uniform, demonstrating his status as the fourth corporal in the Springfield Cadets. Robert saluted his father, who returned the salute. Lincoln scooped up Robert and carried him on his shoulder up from the quay. Robert chattered excitedly about the special train that came all the way from Springfield with the entire corps of the Springfield Cadets. Mary reported the latest political news from Springfield and complained about the garbled coverage of his speeches in the State Register. Lincoln checked his pace to match Mary's, smiled and did not say a word.

Later, in the hotel, Robert, being too excited to sleep and having the permission of his parents, ran off with the hotel owner's son to investigate reports of newborn kittens.

Lincoln allowed Mary to hang and brush his suit as she wanted. He sprawled over a small couch. Then he said, "Mother, we need to talk."

Uneasily Mary sat in a chair facing him.

"This canvass," said Lincoln, looking intently at Mary, "will soon be over. It may well be that I will lose."

"I have a count of legislators, district by district, that I can show you," she told him.

"I would like to see that," said Lincoln. "Right now I want you to tell me that you can steel yourself to the possibility that I will lose, without having a fit or becoming devastated."

"You can't quit yet!"

"I have no intention of doing so," said Lincoln. "I will contend to the bitter end, but I would rest easier if you could tell me that you will try to control your feelings if this canvass ends bitterly."

Mary spoke with great intensity. "I want this, Father. I want it so badly that I can taste it."

"I know. I know that you want it even more than I do. It makes you a wonderful help to me, but I worry about your health and well being should we lose."

"That is a bitter, bitter thought. I would feel that something had been taken away from me, and so much has been taken already," she said with a hint of irritation.

"I know," said Lincoln. "More than anything you would be the first lady of the land, since the men would not countenance that a woman could be president herself. I do not want you to react as you did when Trumbull became senator in my stead. I know you had your hopes pinned to that event and, when it did not happen, your hopes crashed down with great force."

Mary looked down and nodded.

"I know you had the invitations written for the victory party," said Lincoln. "I reckon you had your dress sewn, the band of music reserved, and the menu written out."

Mary was silent.

"I do not want you to do anything like that on this occasion," said Lincoln. "I do not want the outcome to leave you desperately unhappy again. Our boys need you to be healthy and, if not happy, at least not desperately unhappy."

"I have not made the dress yet," said Mary.

"Good. I don't mind if you have bought the material and the fripperies. I hope it is blue. You look good in blue and there will be occasions yet to wear it. Just, mayhap, not this one." Lincoln sat and looked thoughtfully at his wife. After a moment, he spoke. "I do wish, Mother, that you could find it in your heart to forgive Julia Trumbull. She had nothing to do with Lyman winning the senate seat and now he travels the state for me canvassing as hard as I do."

"He stole that election, not yielding his five to your forty-five voters."

"They were Democrats," said Lincoln. "They were not inclined to vote for a Whig like me, even if they opposed Judge Douglas. From my yielding, I gained a solid political friend who is working hard now for our mutual party, the Republicans."

"Working hard because he does not want you to run against him for his senate seat. Now that both of you are Republicans, he cannot count that men of the party will deny you in favor of him."

"No doubt that is true, in part," agreed Lincoln. "But poor Julia had no role in his doings. She is as uninvolved in his political life as you are involved in mine. She is an innocent. The two of you were the best of friends before you both married. You and Julia Jayne were as close as any two sisters."

"I know," admitted Mary. "I have tried, truly I have. I have even spoken to Doctor Smith at church about it. My heart will not forgive a betrayal, and my heart feels as though Julia betrayed me, even though my head tells me otherwise."

"Please try again," said Lincoln. "I know you miss her friendship, and I truly believe that she misses yours as well."

"I will try again," said Mary. "But you know what I am like. In our family I am the one who goes to church and you are the one who forgives. But then, as our Savior said, 'The healthy have no need of a physician.' You have a natural sense of religion which continues to elude me."

Tears came to Mary's eyes.

"Oh, Father, how can you put up with an unforgiving wretch like me? Why not divorce me and find a true Christian woman? Perhaps I will die and you will have the chance to marry again."

"I do not want to divorce," said Lincoln. "It is much more likely that I will die long ere you do. Mayhap you will marry a man who will eat off of the plates I paid for in the house that I bought. He will probably be a real gentleman who will wear matching socks all the time and keep his feet off the furniture."

Early on the morning of October fifteenth, Dietrich and Chapel left their hotel and walked through the streets of Alton.

"I hate this town," said Dietrich.

"Why?" asked Chapel, looking around him. "It looks to be an

225

enterprising place and pretty enough in its way. Besides, it is a beautiful day and we are nearing the end of our quest. After this, we will not be forced to sleep in flea-infested shanties that pass for hotels in the small towns of this state."

Dietrich shook his head. "It's not about where we sleep. In this town, Elijah Parish Lovejoy was murdered about twenty years ago for the terrible crime of attempting to express his opinion that slavery is wrong. Do you know about this?"

Chapel shook his head.

Dietrich continued. "He was a Presbyterian minister who came to believe that slavery was wrong and eventually argued for immediate abolition in his newspaper. He saw Francis McIntosh, a slave who had killed peace officers, get broken out of jail and then burned at the stake by a mob. Then he heard the authorities try to justify the mob taking the law into its own hands. After that, his editorials caused such a commotion that he feared for the safety of his family. He moved from the slave state of Missouri to the free state of Illinois and settled here. He continued to print editorials that inflamed pro-slavery men to such heights that they wrecked his printing presses three times."

Dietrich paused to take a breath.

"He arranged for a steamboat to bring another press and for it to arrive at three o'clock in the morning. With maybe twenty friends, he moved it to a warehouse, but his enemies discovered his plan and surrounded the building. Men in the mob started throwing stones. Lovejoy and his friends found earthenware pots inside the building, which they threw back."

Dietrich took a deep breath that was half a sob.

"Someone in the mob started shooting. The mayor tried to persuade Lovejoy and his friends to abandon the press, but they refused. Torches were thrown at the building. Someone put a ladder up to the wooden roof and carried up fire to burn the building. Lovejoy and a friend managed to tip the ladder over and the men inside the building endeavored to put out the fire started by the torches. A second time men in the mob placed the ladder against the side of the building and, when Lovejoy attempted a second time to dislodge it, the men in the mob were ready. A double barrel shotgun blast caught Lovejoy in the breast, and he died in the arms of a friend. The mob threatened to kill his friends as well, but in the end Lovejoy's friends laid down their arms and were permitted to leave. The press was smashed and thrown into the river in pieces. Lovejoy's body was not recovered until the following day for fear of additional mob violence. He was buried on his thirty-fifth birthday in an unmarked grave so his mortal remains would not be molested. As his funeral wagon was driven slowly toward the graveyard, many men who had been part of the mob mocked and taunted him."

"Was nothing done?" asked Chapel.

"Few officials dared to even mention the incident. Thomas Hart Benton, a prominent man from a prominent family, opined that the freedom of speech did not include the right to say that slavery was wrong. However, there was one young man in the Illinois House of Representatives who said: 'Let every man remember that to violate the law is to trample on the blood of his father, and to tear the charter of his own, and his children's liberty. Let reverence for the laws be breathed by every American mother. In short, let it become the political religion of the nation.'"

"That sounds familiar somehow," said Chapel.

"Yes," said Dietrich. "It is not hard to recognize the distinctive words of Lincoln. So far as I am aware, Judge Douglas has never spoken of the tragedy, if tragedy is what he thinks it was. Now, of course, Judge Douglas throws the charge at Mr. Lincoln that he is conspiring with Elijah's brother Owen to abolish slavery immediately and to put the Negro on the basis of a total equality. Judge Douglas chooses this town for the final debate. I cannot read his heart. I cannot say with total certainty that in so choosing he is giving a message to Mr. Lincoln about what may happen to those who oppose slavery. I can only know what I believe to be so."

Several feet away, in the lobby of one of the hotels, a woman screamed, "How dare you speak to my husband in that way!"

They turned to see what the commotion was.

The tall, well-dressed man who had taunted Lincoln as he came through the hotel lobby stepped back in surprise.

"Are you blind, sir?" asked Mary Todd Lincoln. "Did you not see that he was accompanied by a woman and a child?"

"I beg your pardon," said the man, stiffening. "I did not think…"

"Clearly, sir, you did not think," said Mary. "Do you have a wife and child, or lacking those, as you so clearly lack manners, do you have a mother or a sister?"

"I- I do."

"And do those words commend themselves to your lips when you address someone in their presence?"

The man shook his head.

"The silence you favor now, sir, would have done you credit before," said Mary. "So if you spare your family such language, do you think that entitles you to inflict it then upon complete strangers?"

"No, Ma'am. Again, I apologize."

"From your accent, I take it you are not from these parts. Where are you from?"

"Arkansas, Ma'am."

"I did not realize that such words were considered polite conversation in Arkansas," said Mary. "Is it then true what they say about the citizens of Arkansas?"

The man looked confused.

"I have heard that the citizens of the Kansas territory consented to the name of the territory only after being assured that it would be pronounced differently from the same letters in Arkansas. Apparently they did not want to be associated with people whose learning and elocution was demonstrated by the way they pronounce k-a-n-s-a-s as 'kin saw.'"

The man's face reddened.

"Perhaps, you are thinking that, if I were a man, you might challenge me for the insult," said Mary. "However, if you were a real man, you would have the vocabulary to indicate that you disagree with someone without having to use vulgarity."

The man looked around him, seeking a way to escape.

"You are, I take it, a Douglas supporter."

The man nodded.

"I thought so," said Mary. "You have the unmistakable eloquence of that species of political minion. Don't you know that it is better to hold your silence and be considered a fool than to open your mouth and remove all doubt about the matter? You have, at least, heard the phrase, 'seen and not heard'?"

"Yes, ma'am."

"Let that become your new motto. Well? Haven't you wasted enough of my time? Go away."

The man fairly flew from the room.

Mary turned to Lincoln, who had watched in silence.

"I lost my temper with that blasphemous brute," said Mary. "I'm sorry."

"I'm sorry, too," said Lincoln. "I'm sorry that it is me and not you who will face Judge Douglas today. You are in fine fettle and I believe you would tie a tin can to his tail and set him to flight."

Chapel and Dietrich stood silently on the sidewalk.

The seventh debate took place at Broadway and Market streets. Looking haggard and care-worn, Douglas walked to the front of the speakers' stand and waited for the half-hearted applause to subside. When he spoke, his voice came out roughly in weak tones that few in the crowd could hear clearly.

Dietrich looked up from the page he was writing on, "The judge is back to the same speech."

Chapel smiled. "Not only are his principles the same everywhere, his very words are the same."

"You will find in a speech delivered by that able and eloquent statesman, the Honorable Jefferson Davis, at Bangor, Maine, that he took the same view as Mr. Orr of South Carolina, former speaker of the Congress, and Alexander H. Stevens, the great intellect of the South. The whole South is rallying to the doctrine, that if a people want slavery they have a right to have it; and if they don't, no power on earth shall force it upon them."

The Douglas supporters applauded politely.

Dietrich nodded toward Chapel, "Popular sovereignty, Lincoln's Abolitionism, Lecompton Constitution, Buchanan's opposition, white basis for the government."

Chapel interrupted, "Don't forget Lincoln will set the North against the South, but Douglas will allow each state and territory to set its own laws if they don't contradict the Constitution. Lincoln will have mob rule, but Douglas will respect the decisions of the Supreme Court."

The reporters listened to the rest of Douglas's speech in silence.

Lincoln stepped forward and acknowledged the scattered applause from the small number of Lincoln supporters in the crowd. His high-pitched voice carried so that all in the audience could hear him.

"Ladies and gentlemen, I have been somewhat in my own mind complimented by a large portion of Judge Douglas's speech — I mean that portion which he devotes to the controversy between himself and the present administration.

"This is the seventh time Judge Douglas and I have met in these joint discussions, and he has been gradually improving in regard to his war with the Democratic administration. At Quincy the day before yesterday, he was a little more severe upon the administration than upon any former occasion. I took pains to compliment him for it. I then told him to, 'give it to them with all the power he had.' And as some of them were present, I told them I would be very much obliged if they would 'give it to the Judge' in the same way."

People in the audience laughed. The few Lincoln partisans present applauded.

"I flatter myself that he has really taken my advice on this subject. All I can say now is to recommend to him and to them what I then commended to prosecute the war against one another in the most vigorous manner. This calls to mind the farmer's wife who came upon her husband in deadly combat against a bear. Due to poor relations with her husband and her fear of wild animals she became worried about what the victor might choose to do to her. Unable to fully back either combatant, she said words I now repeat: 'Go it, husband! Go it, bear!'"

The audience cheered and laughed.

"In reference to that part of the Judge's remarks where he undertakes to involve Mr. Buchanan in an inconsistency, I would only remind the judge while he is very valiantly fighting for the Nebraska Bill and the repeal of the Missouri Compromise, it has been but a little while since he was the valiant advocate of the Missouri Compromise. I want to know if Buchanan has as much right to be inconsistent as Douglas has.

"So far as Judge Douglas addressed his speech to me, I have heard the judge state two or three times that in a speech in Springfield I had especially complained that the Supreme Court in the Dred Scott case had decided that a Negro could never be a citizen of the United States. I have omitted by some accident heretofore to analyze this statement. In point of fact it is untrue.

"At Galesburg the other day I said that three years ago there had never been a man who said that the Declaration of Independence did not include Negroes in the term 'all men.' Do not let me be misunderstood. I know that more than three years ago there were men, who, finding this assertion constantly in the way of their schemes to bring about the ascendancy and perpetuation of slavery, denied the truth of it. I know that Mr. Calhoun and all the politicians of his school denied the truth of the declaration. I know of that shameless, though rather forcible, declaration of Petit of Indiana upon the floor of the United States Senate. He said that the Declaration of Independence was 'a self-evident lie' rather than a self-evident truth. But I say that three years ago there never had lived a man who ventured to assail it in the sneaking way of pretending to believe it and then asserting it did not include the Negro."

Lincoln supporters cheered.

"In answer to my proposition at Galesburg last week, I see that some man in Chicago has got up a letter addressed to the Chicago Times to show as he professes that somebody had said so before and he signs himself 'An Old Line Whig.' In the first place I would say he was not an Old Line Whig. I was with the Old Line Whigs from the origin to the end of that party; I became pretty well acquainted with them, and I know they always had some sense, whatever else you could ascribe to them."

Members of both parties laughed.

231

"I know that the fraudulent 'Old Line Whig' attempts to use for his argument part of a speech from Henry Clay — the part of the speech of Henry Clay which I used to prove precisely the contrary.

"We are surrounded today by the friends of Mr. Clay and they will be glad to hear anything from that authority. While Mr. Clay was in Indiana, a man presented him a petition to liberate his Negroes, and Mr. Clay made a speech in answer to it, which he caused to be published. Hear what Mr. Clay said in full:

And what is the foundation of the appeal to me in Indiana, to liberate the slaves under my care in Kentucky? It is a general declaration in the act announcing to the world the independence of the thirteen American colonies, that all men are created equal. Now as an abstract principle, there is no doubt of the truth of that declaration; and it is desirable in the original construction of society and in organized societies to keep it in view as a great fundamental principle. But, then, I apprehend that in no society that ever did exist, or ever shall be formed, was or can the equality asserted among the members of the human race be practically enforced and carried out. There are portions, large portions, women, minors, insane, culprits, transient sojourners, that will always probably remain subject to the government of another portion of the community.

The declaration, whatever may be the extent of its import, was made by the delegations of the thirteen states. In most of them slavery existed, and had long existed, and was established by law. It was introduced and forced upon the colonies by the paramount law of England. Do you believe that in making that declaration the states concurred in it intended that it should be tortured into a virtual emancipation of all the slaves within their respective limits? Would Virginia and other southern states have ever united in a declaration which was to be interpreted into an abolition of slavery among them? Did any one of the thirteen colonies entertain such a design or expectation? To impute such a secret and unavowed purpose would be to charge a political fraud upon the noblest band of patriots that ever assembled in council; a fraud upon the confederacy of the revolution; a fraud upon the union of those states whose constitution not only recognized the lawfulness of slavery, but permitted the importation of slaves from Africa until the year 1808.

I desire no concealment of my opinions in regard to the institution of slavery. I look upon it as a great evil; and deeply lament that we have derived it from the parental government; and from our ancestors. I wish every slave in the United States was in the country of his ancestors. But here they are and the question is how can they be best dealt with? If a state of nature existed and we were about to lay the foundations of society, no man would be more strongly opposed than I should be, to incorporating the institution of slavery among its elements.

"I am vilified today for using Henry Clay's great principles of free government. Judge Douglas has again referred to a Springfield speech in which I said, 'a house divided against itself cannot stand.' The sentiments have been extremely offensive to Judge Douglas; he has warred upon them as Satan does the Bible.

"You may say and Judge Douglas has intimated that all this difficulty in regard to the institution of slavery is the mere agitation of office seekers and ambitious northern politicians. He thinks we want to get 'his place,' I suppose."

Lincoln adherents cheered and laughed.

"I agree that there are office seekers amongst us. The Bible says somewhere that we are desperately selfish. I think we would have discovered that fact without the Bible. I do not claim that I am any less so than the average of men, but I do claim that I am not more selfish than Judge Douglas."

Renewed laughter came from the audience.

"But is it true that all the difficulty and agitation springs from office seeking? There never was a party in this country and there probably never will be one of sufficient strength of disturb the general peace of this country. Does not this question of slavery make

a disturbance outside political circles? What divided the great
Methodist Church into two parts? What has raised this constant
disturbance in every Presbyterian General Assembly that meets?
What disturbed the Unitarian Church in this very city two years
ago? What has jarred and shaken the great American Tract Society
recently? Is it not this same mighty, deep-seated power that somehow operates on minds of men, exciting them and stirring them up
in every avenue of society — in politics, in religion, in literature,
in morals, in all the manifold relations of life?

"Yet the policy that Douglas is advocating is that we are to
care nothing about it! He undertakes to build a policy upon caring
nothing about the very thing that everybody does care the most
about.

"What I insist upon is that the new territories shall be kept
clear of slavery while in the territorial condition. Judge Douglas
assumes we have no interest. If you go to the territory opposed to
slavery and another man comes with his slave, he has the right all
the way and you have no part of it your way. How many Democrats are there about here…"

Someone shouted, "One thousand."

"…who have left slave states and come into the free state of
Illinois to get rid of the institution of slavery?"

Another person shouted, "One thousand and one."

"I reckon there are about one thousand and one," Lincoln acknowledged.

Listeners from both sides laughed.

"This is the eternal struggle between the two principles —
right and wrong — throughout the world. They have stood face to
face from the beginning of time and will ever continue to struggle.
The one is the common right of humanity and the other the divine
right of kings. Whatever shape it develops itself, it is the same
spirit that says, 'You work and toil and earn bread, and I'll eat it.'
No matter whether it comes from the mouth of a king who seeks to
bestride the people of his nation, or from one race of men as an
apology for enslaving another race, it is the same tyrannical principle.

"Judge Douglas constantly said slavery was a question for the court to decide. But after the court made the decision he virtually says it is not a question for the court but for the people. How can they exclude slavery? He says it needs 'police regulation' and 'friendly legislation' to survive. The first thing a territorial legislator does is swear an oath to the Constitution. If it is established by the Constitution that a man may take and hold a slave in a territory, how may a legislator deny him legislation that he needs to enjoy that constitutional right without violating his oath? Why, this is monstrous talk!"

The Lincoln supporters cheered wildly.

"There has never been as outlandish or lawless a doctrine from the mouth of any respectable man on earth! I defy any man to make any argument that will justify unfriendly legislation to deprive a shareholder of his right to hold his slave in a territory, that will not equally, in all its length, breadth and thickness furnish an argument for nullifying the fugitive slave law. Why, there is not such an Abolitionist in the nation as Douglas, after all."

The small group of Lincoln adherents in the crowd created a surprising amount of noise by cheering and clapping.

Douglas's voice became stronger during his response to Lincoln.

"Mr. Lincoln has concluded his remarks by saying that there is not such an Abolitionist as I am in all America. If he could make the Abolitionists in Illinois believe that, he would not have much chance to win the canvass.

"His first criticism upon me is his expression of hope that the war of the administration will be prosecuted against me and the Democratic Party of this state with vigor. It is the first war I ever knew him to be in favor of prosecuting. It is the first war I ever knew him to believe to be just or constitutional. When the Mexican War was being waged, and the American army was surrounded by the enemy in Mexico, he thought that war was unconstitutional, unnecessary and unjust."

Someone called out, "Lincoln's a traitor."

"That a man who takes sides with the common enemy against his own country in time of war should rejoice in a war being made on me now is very natural."

"Mr. Lincoln has told you a great deal today about his being an old line Clay Whig. In 1847, when the Whig state convention was in session, Lincoln made a speech in favor of throwing Clay overboard and taking up Zachary Taylor in his place. He gave the reason that if the Whigs don't take up Taylor, the Democrats would.

"At the Philadelphia convention, Lincoln was then the bitter, deadly enemy of Clay. Singleton testified that Lincoln rejoiced when he found the mangled remains of the murdered Whig statesman lying cold before him. Now he tells you he is an Old Line Clay Whig."

The Douglas partisans cheered and clapped.

"Our fathers made this government divided into free and slave states. They did not establish slavery in any of the states or abolish it, but they agreed to form a government uniting them together and to guarantee forever each state the right to do as it pleased on the slavery question. Lincoln looks forward to a time when slavery shall be abolished everywhere. I look forward to a time when each state shall be allowed to do as it pleases. If it chooses to keep slavery forever, it is its business and not ours. If it chooses to abolish, very good, it is its business and not mine. I care more for the right of self-government, the right of the people to rule, than I do for all the Niggers in Christendom."

Douglas supporters applauded.

"Mr. Lincoln says that our fathers, when they made the government, didn't look forward of this state of things that now exist. He quotes Brooks of South Carolina to prove our fathers then thought that before this time each state acting for itself would abolish slavery. Suppose they did. Suppose they didn't foresee what would happen. Does that change the principles of government? They didn't foresee the telegraph that transmits intelligence by lightning. They didn't foresee the railroads that are the bonds of union between the different states. They did not foresee a thousand other inventions of benefit to mankind throughout the world, but do these facts change the principles of government? They made the government on the principle I state — the right of people to do as they pleased, and then let the people of each state apply it

236

to each change of condition, to each improvement, as they may arise in all time to come."

Someone shouted, "Hurrah for Douglas."

"My friends, if we will only live up to that great fundamental principle there will be peace between the North and the South. The only remedy and safety is that we shall stand by the constitution as other fathers made it, obey the laws as they are passed, and sustain the decisions of the Supreme Court and the constituted authorities."

The Douglas supporters applauded with some enthusiasm.

When Chapel looked over at Dietrich, he noticed that Dietrich was red-faced and shaking.

"Even for Douglas," said Dietrich through clenched teeth, "that was a foul speech. To blame agitators for making trouble about slavery, to call Lincoln a traitor, and to call a political decision abandoning Clay a 'murder' here in the city where Lovejoy was actually murdered, is almost blasphemous."

"It seemed to go over well with the audience," offered Chapel.

"This audience will go for Judge Douglas in great numbers," acknowledged Dietrich. "Mr. Lincoln has learned that, through the newspapers, he is addressing voters throughout the state and people throughout the whole nation."

"We will see how people in the South react to Mr. Lincoln's statement that if people in one locality can undo a Supreme Court ruling to exclude slavery from a territory, people in another locality can undo fugitive slave laws," said Chapel. "I warrant that will raise some eyebrows."

With an almost visible physical effort, Dietrich got his temper under control.

"I did notice that Judge Douglas said Jefferson Davis made a speech in Bangor, Maine, saying citizens could exclude slavery from a territory. I wonder if Mr. Davis would say the same thing in Mississippi. I wonder if Mr. Orr or Mr. Stevens would support excluding slavery in speeches they make to their voters. I suspect they would not."

Dietrich nodded. His breathing began to slow and his color

began to fade toward its normal hue.

"Let's see if we can find Mr. Walker," said Chapel, putting his hand on Dietrich's arm.

They found Walker sitting in the parlor of the Alton House. His carpetbag was at his feet. Walker's clothes were wrinkled and he looked disheveled but happy.

"Mr. Lincoln is with his family," said Walker. "The debates are over, and my political duties are finished. I have a ride arranged to the nearest station and a train ticket for Havana later tonight, but at the moment I am at loose ends. Take a seat, please. Now, how may I be of service to you gentlemen?"

"We still have a question or two about the Duff Armstrong trial," said Chapel, sitting down in a chair close by. "We hope it would not be too big an imposition if we could ask them."

"Fire away," said Walker, sitting back in his chair.

"You told us, sir, that Mr. Lincoln refused to take any fee from his old friend, Hannah Armstrong, because he felt he was re-paying a debt. You also mentioned that you did not present a bill," said Chapel.

"Ah," said Walker. "I wondered when you would ask me why I would put in so much time and labor for no fee. I got no money, but I was more than amply rewarded."

"You mean by doing a good deed?" asked Dietrich.

"That, too, of course," said Walker. "I mean that I derived substantial benefit from the trial. Just working with Mr. Lincoln was a priceless education in lawyering. More than that, ever since the trial I have been known locally as the partner of Abraham Lincoln and one of the attorneys who got Duff Armstrong acquitted. Ere the trial I was one of two young attorneys sharing an office and a practice that was slowly starving to death on whatever legal picking the established lawyers did not want to bother with. Since then, people assume, quite erroneously I assure you, that I actually have some legal acumen that interested Mr. Lincoln sufficiently that he had me join him in a very important case. I now have all the business I can handle. I have enough that my partner, Mr. Lacey, is flourishing on what I have no time to handle. You know that it is all an illusion. In every new case I have to reckon what is required. I suppose I am, now, learning to be a lawyer and I may eventually be a good one. But all I really did was lose the trial of Jimmy Norris. Do you know what the strangest thing of all is?"

Chapel and Dietrich shook their heads.

"When I tell my clients how little I actually did for Mr. Lincoln, they think I am being modest. I have acquired a reputation as both a skilled lawyer and a modest man, which I did nothing to earn. I agreed to help Mr. Lincoln because I thought he would teach me about being a lawyer and I hoped to gain from his reputation."

Walker shook his head.

"You alerted Mr. Lincoln about Allen's testimony on the position of the moon," said Dietrich.

"Which I had not the wit to know that I even knew," answered Walker. "Mr. Lincoln discovered the significance of that."

"You listened and took notes that allowed Mr. Lincoln to discover the rest," said Chapel.

Walker nodded.

"That one thing I did. I am now learning to do more. So, my help to Mr. Lincoln has returned great benefit to me, as I expected. And I find myself oddly troubled by having a reputation for benevolence, which I scarcely deserve."

"Perhaps you will grow into deserving it as you are growing into being considered a good lawyer," said Dietrich. "Then you will have both the reputation and the actuality."

"I may be forced to do so. Did you two also have another question?"

"It has been rumored that Mr. Lincoln altered the almanac he used to impeach Mr. Allen," said Dietrich. "Do you know anything about that?"

"Walker rummaged through his carpetbag. "I have a remembrance for each of you."

Walker handed Dietrich an Old Farmer's Almanac for 1857. He handed Chapel another.

"You can look up moonset on August twenty ninth for yourself. I keep a collection of almanacs for such occasions. I first state that I know of no other man as honest as Mr. Lincoln, nor of any other who has such a profound respect for the law.

"Putting that aside for the moment, think about it. If there was a forgery all the judge or the prosecution had to do was to send to see a different copy. You know from Mr. Shaw that the prosecution found two other almanacs. Of course the judge and the prosecutor would verify the claim. Who would not? Had there been a fraud, Mr. Lincoln would have thrown away the reputation that he has spent his entire professional life building. In addition, the case would have been lost and Duff Armstrong would very likely have been hanged. If Mr. Lincoln even wanted to falsify evidence, which I will never believe, would he choose a fraud so badly constructed and so obviously easy to disprove?"

"Why is the rumor so common?" asked Chapel.

"There are people who would do anything they could to stain Mr. Lincoln's reputation," said Walker. "I could not say why. It worries me."

"Why should it worry you when it is so easy to disprove?" asked Dietrich.

"It is at this time but as time passes and these flimsy little pamphlets disappear, it may appear more valid in the future. Mr. Shaw told me that he did not find any almanacs for last year in the stores. Someone in the courthouse happened to have two. When I started a small collection, I was surprised at how few there were and how difficult they were to locate. I believe the slander will persist, for I truly believe that future ages will remember the Douglas-Lincoln debates. The issues discussed will not be forgotten."

Walker sank back in his chair, suddenly looking drained.

"Thank you, Mr. Walker," said Chapel. "You have been abundantly generous with your time and attention."

After shaking hands with Walker, Chapel and Dietrich departed.

"Let us write and send off our articles from here," said Chapel. "Then we can make our way back to Springfield for the end of the canvass. After that, we will pursue Watkins."

"I agree," said Dietrich. "I need to shake the dust of this town from my feet as soon as possible."

CHAPTER THIRTY

November 15, 1858
Havana, Illinois

As he had promised in his letter in response to the missive from Dietrich and Chapel, Nelson Watkins met the reporters at noon in the dining room of the Havana House.

"I don't know about the wisdom of this," said Watkins. "I know that the election is over, but I worry that the questions you might ask might harm Mr. Lincoln in the future. Maybe you should not ask me anything."

Dietrich exchanged a glance with Chapel.

"Will you answer the questions we ask in a wholly honest way?" asked Dietrich.

Watkins's face showed anger, worry and then resignation in the space of a few seconds.

"I repeat that I am not at all certain this is a good idea. However, upon my honor, I will answer all questions as fully and honestly as I can."

"What is it that so worries you?" asked Chapel.

"The conversation that I had with Mr. Lincoln before the trial. I would not want that to be generally known."

"Tell us about it, please," said Dietrich, taking out his notebook.

Watkins cleared his throat. "When word got around about the deputy had found a slungshot at Walker's Grove, it put me in mind that I had lost the one that I made. I thought I had probably lost it that morning at Walker's Grove, so I went to town and saw the thing during Norris's trial. Sure enough, it was the one I lost. I didn't know what to do. I talked to some neighbors and I reckon that word got around from that."

Chapel nodded encouragingly.

"Next thing I know I got a letter from Mr. Lincoln asking me to come to his office in Springfield. I did that and he asked me about the slungshot."

"What did you tell him?" asked Dietrich.

"I told him he did not want to ask," said Watkins, frowning. "I told him I knew things about that night that would do Duff Armstrong no good. I told him to release me, but he asked me to stay."

"What did Mr. Lincoln do then?" asked Chapel.

"He told me I should not talk to him about anything except the slungshot. He said he did not even want to hear about the other. I told him I had seen the thing and it was mine. He asked in great particular as to how I knew it was mine and how it was made."

Watkins paused.

"He asked me where it was during the night that Press Metzker was killed, and I told him I had it with me the whole night. He kept pressing me, asking about all sorts of ways that I might have let it out of my sight. I kept insisting that nobody could have got it off me.

"He asked me where I put for the night, what time I went to bed and when I first noticed that I had lost it. Then he asked a boatload more questions. I don't remember them all. Finally, he asked me how the slungshot got from where I left in on the underside of the wagon bed, to where it was found by the scuffle ground. He regarded me closely when I answered. I had to say, of course, that I did not know for sure. Then he asked me to speculate and I said it could have stayed on the wagon bed until it fell off near to the scuffle ground."

Watkins stopped and took a sip of coffee.

"Mr. Lincoln asked me if everything I told him was true and warned me that I could not even shade the truth. I said it was."

Watkins paused.

"It was strange. For some time afterward, Mr. Lincoln just looked at me without saying a word. It was like he was looking at my very soul."

"I know what you mean," said Chapel.

"Then he asked me if I would testify about the slungshot. I told him again that I was worried about what I had seen that night. Mr. Lincoln asked me if the sheriff and the deputy talked to me and knew what I saw. I told him they did. He asked if they had called upon me to testify at Jimmy Norris's trial and I said they did not.

Mr. Lincoln said I would not have to testify about what else I knew."

Watkins paused.

"How could he promise me that?"

"I don't know," answered Dietrich. "But at the trial nobody asked if you saw the fight."

"I know," said Watkins. "How did Mr. Lincoln manage that?"

"If I may ask, what did you see that Mr. Lincoln did not want to know about?" said Chapel.

"I saw Duff Armstrong hit Press Metzker in the face with a weapon. It was not a slungshot. I think it was a wagon hammer. I wasn't as close as Mr. Allen, but that's what I saw. I wasn't drunk and the moonlight was enough to see in. I am quite certain about it."

"Did you tell Sheriff West and Deputy Starks what you saw?" asked Chapel.

"I already said that I did," snapped Watkins. "I've answered your questions, although I had my doubts about doing so. If you have no more for me, I have work to do."

"Thank you, sir," said Dietrich.

"Very much obliged," said Chapel.

***

A week later, when Chapel and Dietrich opened the door to the Lincoln and Herndon law office in Springfield, they heard Lincoln reading aloud an article from a newspaper. From the resigned look on Herndon's face, it was obvious that this was a frequent event. The reporters carried newspapers under their arms.

"Gentlemen, I am surprised to see you," said Lincoln as he folded up the newspaper and removed his bare feet from the top of his desk. "The election returns are in and it is definite that the current senator from Illinois is secure in his job. Pull up some chairs. Shouldn't you be interviewing Judge Douglas?"

"If you don't mind, we have a few more questions for you," said Dietrich.

"I don't mind," said Lincoln.

"Should I withdraw?" asked Herndon. "Are these legal matters for which you want privacy?"

"They are not legal matters exactly," said Chapel. "They are somewhat personal and you may wish for discretion."

"I have found that Mr. Herndon is the soul of discretion. I often think out loud in front of him and there is no question or answer that I am unwilling for him to hear. Please, ask away," Lincoln said, smiling.

"Let me, first express my admiration for your labors in the recent canvass," said Dietrich. "I hope the outcome was not too discouraging."

"I feel like the boy who stubbed his toe. I'm too old to cry, but it hurts too much to laugh. My dear wife was more affected than I was. But she has resigned herself to the result. Our lives were not uncomfortable before, and I do not despair to return to obscurity."

"I believe, sir, that such an outcome is not even conceivable now," said Chapel.

"I told you that you are a national figure now," Herndon said firmly. "Judge Douglas was a formidable opponent."

Lincoln nodded in agreement and said, "Yes, it was impossible to get the advantage of him. Even when he was bested, he bore himself as if he won, so the people were bewildered and uncertain of who had the best of it. He presented the humbug of people in the territories being able to overrule the Supreme Court and exclude slavery by 'police regulations,' as if it were actually so. I also own that he was better at the fizzlegigs and fireworks of the canvass than I could ever hope to be."

Lincoln shook his head.

"I could not beat a man who never let the logic of principle displace the logic of success," said Lincoln. "It may be that I should have done better had I taken my wife's suggestion and stopped his mouth with a corn cob."

"In truth we have questions about another matter," said Chapel.

"What would you like to know about the Duff Armstrong murder trial?"

Chapel and Dietrich looked stunned.

Herndon laughed.

"Did you really think my friends would not tell me when your inquiries started? You would have done well to come to me long ere this, and it would have saved me considerable labor. Do you have any idea how many letters it took to persuade Hannah and Watkins in particular that they should cooperate with you in every detail?"

"You told them to answer our questions?" asked Chapel.

"Did you think Mr. Shaw was willingly confessing the weaknesses of the prosecution he assisted to gentlemen of the press?"

Lincoln threw back his head and laughed uproariously. Soon Herndon, Chapel and Dietrich were laughing with him. After some moments, Lincoln regained control.

"I am indebted to you gentlemen," said Lincoln, wiping his eyes. "I have not laughed like that since the election and I sorely needed to."

"I should have wondered why so many people were willing to talk with us so honestly. May we ask our questions?" asked Chapel.

"Of course," said Lincoln.

"How were you able to tell Hannah Armstrong at dinner recess that you knew Duff would be acquitted?" asked Dietrich.

"Objection," said Lincoln in his best courtroom voice, "assumes facts not in evidence. I did not tell her that I knew Duff would be acquitted. She may remember it differently now, but I only indicated that I expected he would be acquitted. Upon hearing Mr. Allen testify, I knew that he was an honest man and that the jury would see him as such. Knowing the honest mistake he made about the position of the moon, I foresaw that when I showed he was mistaken in that particular, his testimony would be questioned in all other particulars."

"Nelson Watkins said he did not want to testify because he saw something that would not help your client, and that you promised he would never have to testify about it," said Dietrich.

"I hope Watkins is a good farmer because he has very poor prospects as an attorney. I did not promise him anything, albeit I advised him strongly that questions he did not want to answer had a low likelihood of being asked. He did not appear to quite grasp it. Cross-examination is limited by the scope of direct examination just as questions on re-direct are limited by the scope of cross-examination. I intended to ask questions only about the slungshot. That is one reason why I did not ask about whatever it was that concerned him. I guessed it to be the assault and I reckoned that he would say that he thought Duff had some sort of weapon, not a slungshot. Had the prosecution ever been able to ask if he discussed seeing the assault with me, I wanted the answer to the question to be no. Of course, I could not tell him that directly lest that discussion be revealed by prosecution questioning. I desired that if the prosecution asked about my questions to him, he could say I asked only about the slungshot. I desired if the prosecution asked him whether I had given him advice, he could say the sole advice I gave him was to answer all questions fully and honestly. Now, that I did tell him."

"He said he talked to the sheriff. Did that concern you?" asked Chapel.

"Not at all. It made the chance of him being asked about the assault even less. The prosecution had a theory of the crime. All of the witnesses they chose to call backed up the version of events the prosecution was using. Nelson would doubtlessly give a different account. Imagine, gentlemen, that you are jurors and the prosecution tells you that Uncle Jim assaulted Uncle Bob using a slungshot, or else a barrel stave. Is that more convincing than if they chose the one or the other weapon?"

"Did you in any way suggest that he make up testimony about how the slungshot came to be moved from under the wagon to the scuffle ground?" asked Chapel.

"Not at all," answered Lincoln. "If I thought he was inventing testimony, I would never have put him on the stand. The testimony would be fraudulent."

"Watkins also said that the moonlight was sufficient for him to see clearly," said Dietrich.

"That was another reason for limiting Watkins's testimony. I did not want Mr. Allen to focus on the brightness or position of the moon in his thinking until I handed him the almanac."

"Is that altogether honest?" asked Chapel.

Lincoln paused.

"I truly believe that it is. Remember that I advised Watkins and all other witnesses, too, to be wholly honest. The law is a struggle between champions of the accused and the accuser. Each side has pledged to tell only the truth and each side is pledged to advocate firmly for its client. Watkins' testimony was different from the other witnesses. He would have weakened the prosecutor's description of the events.

"I do not take lightly the death of Press Metzker," said Lincoln firmly. "Although I never met the man in life, from the testimony of his family and friends I believe that he was a man of good judgment and a man to admire. I have come to believe that Mr. Metzker, had he been on the jury, would have voted to acquit."

"You advised everyone connected with the trial to speak to us and answer honestly every question we asked," said Dietrich. "Did you consider that we could have reported the slander and rumors, which we have also heard?"

"The Savior tells us 'the truth cannot be hidden.' I believe that. I trusted that eventually you would learn the truth — that I did nothing wrong. It is far easier, I believe, to tell the truth and to engage in right behavior so that when the truth comes out it will be in my favor. As I told you, I read your articles and I judged you to be honest men. Therefore, the very best that I could do for myself was to ask all involved to be wholly honest with you."

"On another matter entirely, do you fear that your loss in the election will encourage those who support slavery?" asked Dietrich.

"Not at all. The Republican Party did well. It is time that the issue of slavery is dragged to the fore of the public mind. Such wrongs dwell safely only in the dark. Slavery should be debated. I own I was wrong to leave it alone for some time. You know that, more than the shotgun, what the skunk fears is publicity." Lincoln shifted in his seat. "Can I ask you a few questions of my own? My own future is unclear. What do you gentlemen have in mind?"

Dietrich posed a thoughtful response: "I thought that I might do a series to present the Southern point of view about slavery. It occurs to me that my paper's readers have had too much preaching and not enough thinking about what slaveholders have to say. I hasten to add that I believe there is no defense of slavery and that it must be ended. However, I wonder if it might not be done in a peaceable way if the desires of the slaveholders could somehow be respected."

"I myself am thinking that I might return home to visit my father," said Chapel. "I came to the canvass with a personal interest in Abolitionism versus slavery. My family has slaves in our care, and has had for generations. Not long ago, my father had a religious conversion experience and decided that upon his death he will free his slaves. Our plantation is small but I cannot run it without them. He told me that I would have to find another means to earn my bread."

Chapel sighed. "I became a reporter because I thought that would shake his resolve, since no gentleman would ever write for a newspaper. Since then, however, I have come to believe that there can be a positive good by exposing the public mind to the important issues of the day.

"I do not agree with my father's wish to free his slaves, but it is his decision to make, and he made it freely. I am concerned about what will happen to the slaves once free, but I may be able to teach some of them skills they can put into practice once they have been freed. I will continue to write for the newspaper, of course."

"I thought you sounded too much like a gentleman to be a reporter," said Dietrich. "Don't worry, though, I shall never reveal your upbringing to another journalist. My own editor prefers to assign former bookkeepers to review opera. He says their total lack of experience makes them completely even-handed. He sends reporters to cover high finance who have the largest opportunities for knowing nothing about it. I was dispatched here only when the chosen man, a failed shoemaker, became ill. Our temperance reporter will surely draw his next sober breath in the grave."

Chapel and Dietrich put the newspapers they had carried into the office on Lincoln's desk.

"You told us that you liked to read newspapers from around the country. Thaddeus and I have found and marked some articles in these that you might find of interest. You are thought to be a man of some importance."

"Yes," said Chapel. "One editorial even names you as the best Republican candidate for president."

The reporters left.

"What do you think, Billy?" asked Lincoln. "I must show these to Mary."

"I think what I have always thought," answered Herndon. "I think that you will be a major player on the national scene. The Douglas-Lincoln debates have only called you to the attention of the nation."

"This makes me wonder. If I could obtain copies of all the debates, fairly showing how Douglas's friends reported his words and how my friends reported mine, do you think there might be interest such a thing?"

"I do," Herndon said, nodding. "I also warrant Mrs. Lincoln will snap up those articles that support you as a candidate for president in 1860."

"I've heard that there is a man named Lincoln who is a respected politician in Massachusetts," said Lincoln, scooping up the papers. "I imagine that is who the papers actually have in mind."

End

HISTORICAL NOTES

After the election, the Democrats ended up with fifty-four state legislators and the Republicans ended up with forty-six. In January of 1859, the legislators in joint session voted to elect the United States Senator from Illinois. They voted along party lines as expected, and Douglas was reelected.

In March of 1860, Follett, Foster and Company of Columbus, Ohio, published a book with early campaign speeches of Lincoln and Douglas, as well as the seven debates based upon Lincoln's scrapbook. The original scrapbook is now in the Library of Congress. The book became an immediate best seller and has been reprinted dozens of times since then.

Douglas's support for the idea that, despite the Supreme Court ruling in the Dred Scott case, people in a territory could choose to exclude slavery by territorial legislation came to be known as the "Freeport Doctrine." It was a major reason the Southern Democratic leaders chose to nominate John C. Breckenridge as their own candidate for president in 1860. They split the Democratic Party and insured the election of the Republican candidate, Abraham Lincoln. At his inauguration, Lincoln stood to speak and looked in vain for a safe place to put his stovepipe hat. Stephen Douglas noted his concern and reached out a hand. Lincoln handed Douglas his hat. Douglas held Lincoln's hat throughout Lincoln's inauguration speech.

Once Lincoln was elected and threats of succession became serious, Stephen A. Douglas gave his full support to Lincoln's efforts at holding the Union together. Douglas traveled extensively in the border states and made many speeches backing preservation of the Union. When the Civil War started, Douglas became a staunch supporter of the northern war effort. He died of typhoid in June of 1861, two months after South Carolina forces fired upon Fort Sumter.

If you enjoyed this, please check out my other novels: *Abraham Lincoln for the Defense* and *Heartland,* as well as my short story collections *Murder Manhattan Style* and *No Happy Endings.*

Made in the USA
San Bernardino, CA
20 January 2017